Nothing Left Unsaid

Janey Godley

Nothing Left Unsaid

HODDER &
STOUGHTON

First published in Great Britain in 2022 by Hodder & Stoughton
An Hachette UK company

2

Copyright © Janey Godley 2022

The right of Janey Godley to be identified as the Author of the Work has been asserted by her in accordance with the Copyright, Designs and Patents Act 1988.

A CIP catalogue record for this title is available from the British Library

Hardback ISBN 978 1 529 35712 7
eBook ISBN 978 1 529 35713 4

Typeset in Sabon MT by Manipal Technologies Limited.

Printed and bound in Great Britain by Clays Ltd, Elcograf S.p.A.

Hodder & Stoughton policy is to use papers that are natural, renewable and recyclable products and made from wood grown in sustainable forests. The logging and manufacturing processes are expected to conform to the environmental regulations of the country of origin.

Hodder & Stoughton Ltd
Carmelite House
50 Victoria Embankment
London EC4Y 0DZ

www.hodder.co.uk

This book is dedicated to a lot of people, who convinced me I could write a book whilst panicking about the pandemic of 2020.

Firstly to my agent Chris Davis, who stupidly thinks am good at stuff – I am glad he does. Rowena Webb at Hodder and Stoughton, who told me to do what I wanted and I did. My editor, Jo Dickinson, who made this an easy process, had great faith in me. Also to my amazing researcher Caitlin Mellon, whom I randomly met working in a bar one day. When I asked her what she wanted to do (because I'm nosy), she told me 'work in publishing', so, I offered her the job as she served me lunch because I believe in impulsive decisions. She said yes and has been my writing rock ever since. I will always be grateful to Caitlin for her amazing insight and help as in the final editing of the book, I was given a cancer diagnosis and my brain went into free fall.

I am genuinely grateful to my daughter, Ashley Storrie, and my husband, Mr Storrie, who helped me plot this book and made me physically sit down and write it. Mostly this whole story is a love letter to my mammy, Annie Currie, from Shettleston; she was killed by her boyfriend, left to float down the River Clyde and never got to see Ipanema, despite singing about that beach and endlessly dreaming of it. Her name will live on.

It's also to all the strong women who have given me the ability to shout back when told to shut up. I hope you enjoy it! Thanks.

Janey

PROLOGUE

The cold night breeze bites at their faces as snow drifts through the shattered glass of the back door. The group stand in silence, in shock. Everything is quiet apart from a dog barking in the distance and the gasping, ragged breaths of the women. The big plastic clock on the wall ticks loudly against the garish yellow floral wallpaper.

One set of brown wedge shoes begins to pace the kitchen and the crackle of broken glass pierces the air. The woman looks round the small kitchen, the matching yellow appliances all so incongruous with the blood slowly seeping across the floor.

'What the fuck do we do now?' she whispers.

'Let's get the hell out of here and stay quiet in case anyone sees us; grab your bag,' someone says with authority.

They go single file down the hallway, though one of them stops to straighten the wedding photo on the wall that got knocked sideways in the fight and finger the plastic palm fronds in the big ornamental vase at the door. The woman in the fake fur coat carries a small blood-spattered cast-iron skillet, her knuckles white with tension.

The front door opens, the street is silent, the thick snow muffles their footsteps.

'Don't make a fucking sound,' the one with brown wedges whispers.

Nobody makes a sound. A neighbour, watching from the windows, closes her curtains quickly.

They creep beyond the high hedges and leave. Shoes squeaking quietly in the deep snow.

Nobody speaks. They never go back.

CHAPTER I

My mother, Senga, was the knot that kept the fragile rope of our scattered family together.

Sitting in that gloomy hospital room, watching the Glasgow skyline form shadows on the curtains as the hours passed from morning to afternoon, I waited as all the daughters have waited before me, for the doctor to tell me if we were approaching the end of her life.

I stared at her. It had been a few months since I'd last seen her and so much had changed. I'd come back to Glasgow from Bristol this morning, as she'd deteriorated quickly from her initial diagnosis of cancer, but now she seemed stable. I had left a mess behind me and, to be truthful, I wasn't in a hurry to go home. My husband had left me after a fucking typical mid-life crisis, my daughter had a new baby to focus on and Mum needed me. Of all her children, I was always the closest geographically and the first to come back and see her when a crisis hit. My brother John was in Spain; my younger sister Janet lived in London, but was incredibly focused on her theatre job in the West End. My PR work could be done remotely from anywhere.

So, back I'd come, I didn't know how long for. I didn't know what the future held. But I knew Mum needed me.

Mum and I were both very alike in a sense, though not physically – I was the tall one with the lanky athletic figure and blonde hair; she was small, dark, curvy, with brilliant dimples that made her face almost cartoonish when she smiled. She still had the most amazing crystal-clear blue eyes, but now she looked as though someone had created an inflatable version of her but not quite inflated it.

Mum and I had always had a good relationship growing up. It was different times back then; as the eldest, at thirteen years old I'd had a wee Saturday job in the local fruit shop, which was normal back in the seventies. We'd kind of grown up together, as she'd had me so young. But, as always, time and life take you apart. I'd moved to England, got married and, well, you know how it goes. But she was always my rock if I ever needed anything. Now, she needed me.

In a small, pale green side room in the big Victorian hospital in Glasgow, the doctor sat me down and confirmed my fears. She was dying; he didn't know how long she had left but all they could do was keep her comfortable. He said that I should stay in Glasgow and contact my siblings as well and prepare for the hard news. Then he showed me out of the room and rushed off towards the lifts, his white coat flapping behind him.

I didn't know what to say, and he rushed off so quickly that I was momentarily stunned, left adrift in the high-ceilinged hallway, staring at a faded painting of a pale orchid, clutching my handbag to my chest as porters pushed sickly old people past me in giant wheeled beds.

Back at her bedside, the beeping of machines broke the silence; and the smell of disinfectant and lingering aroma of boiled food hung in the air as I stared at her. Long gone was her thick hair, loud laugh and big smile. Here lay a selection of fragile bones covered in pale, yellowish skin, breathing quietly and intermittently. I watched and waited; I tried to match her breathing but it made me feel dizzy.

Then she stirred and her eyes opened and she looked at me. We hadn't spoken since I'd arrived in Glasgow – her neighbours had phoned to tell me she'd collapsed at home and they'd called an ambulance.

'Mum, it's me, Sharon,' I whispered. I just wanted to hear her voice.

She was working her mouth but nothing was coming out; her lips were dry and she was struggling to swallow. I held up the beaker of water and let her sip through the straw.

She took another breath and locked eyes with me.

Her first words weren't what I expected. Not 'Sharon, I love you' or 'It's good to see you' or 'Thanks for coming'. She sat up, grabbed the side of the bed and rasped, 'Sharon, I wrote it all down in the big red book, it's in my house. You must stay there and read it.' She lay back gently and I was sure she gave a weak smile. She patted my hand and added, 'I'd like to see the old gang again before I die.' Then her eyes closed.

I stared at her, confused. Could she be gibbering from the morphine, and half believe that that bloke from *This Is Your Life*, the old TV show, was about to meet her at the gates of heaven with his Big Red Book and present her whole life in one episode?

I sat in the quiet room just watching her, waiting for more information, but it was clear she was asleep; her breathing was weak but steady.

What the hell was that about? A book?

Then, somewhere in my memory, I saw a young Senga sitting in a tank top and shorts, writing in a red book as she chain-smoked at the big open tenement window. She was singing along to the radio – 'You to me are everything' – as the airless bedroom flooded with sunlight, and I suddenly knew what she was talking about. I remembered that book. She used to pop it on top of the old wooden wardrobe when she heard anyone come into the room.

That big red book.

I left the hospital at seven o'clock, after a hunt for my car in the massive car park, and parked on the road outside her building. The streetlights illuminated a neat row of flats and mature trees lining the pavements, so different from the loud, imposing tenements where we'd grown up. I knew Senga was close to her new neighbours so nothing had changed there; I would pop in and thank Betty, who had called me and let her know the news.

I unpacked my car, grabbed my small case, laptop and coat, and crunched through the autumn leaves, which were ankle-deep as I walked to her white-painted door. It had marbled glass panels at the top in the shape of a sunrise, and a big gold horseshoe door knocker.

There were three locks to negotiate. I got everything into the ground floor flat and switched on the lights.

Her place was small, tidy and smelled of her favourite scent, Tweed. Everything was floral; every time I visited, she'd added more floral chintz.

I closed the curtains and unpacked the food I'd bought in the city centre supermarket on the way back from the Royal Infirmary. I had a wander round the flat to check all was OK; there was some unopened mail on her hall mat, and a single slice of stale bread in the toaster. There was no sign of where she'd fallen, other than an undrunk cup of tea on a side table. My chest tightened with guilt: she must have been terrified lying in here, so weak, dependent on a neighbour coming by to help. Why hadn't she told me she was so bloody ill? I'd spoken to her last week and she'd assured me she was fine and I didn't need to 'come up the road' as she called it.

I felt like a shitty daughter.

I opened a few cupboards and drawers and checked all the obvious places, but no sign of the red book. But Mum was right: it was here, just as she said. Still on top of her big brown freestanding wardrobe, of course, along with her floral folder of important documents. Not such a secret hiding place, if you knew where to look.

Senga's big red book.

She did write everything down. She must have wanted it to be read. Why else would she write it?

I clutched it. I could smell the old cracked leather on the cover and I tentatively opened it. A stained, brown official-looking envelope slid out the back, and I could see through the transparent window on the front that it had some photos in it. I couldn't wait to look at them, but right now I just wanted to start reading, so I put them to one side.

Suddenly I could hear the clacking sound of Scholl's wooden sandals on the concrete and the voices from the tenements, feel the catch in my throat from cheap cigarettes. These were the scents and sounds of my mother as I remembered her – the feisty, gobby woman who sat in her bra out in the back garden in the summer and let me count the freckles on her chest as she stared into the wide, open sky. Her voice shouted off the pages as I started to read.

I settled down and got stuck in.

1976
June, Monday

So, I have decided to write my diary again. The last one got burned in the great caravan fire of 1975 in Anstruther, when the gas bottle exploded and my auntie, wee Bridie McBride, who used to come on holiday with us, near had a heart attack. She lives up in Springburn now where she runs a shop. So, I am starting my diary again, because I like writing.

Well, I say it's a diary – it's just me putting everything down. It helps me think better when I can get all this out. Keeps my head clearer and gives me something just for me. I want to write about my pals, the strongest women I know. They've seen me through thick and thin.

Anyway, Sharon has given the whole street nits AGAIN. I can do without the neighbours shouting at me, like it's my fault all the kids huddle together on a blanket out the back court.

Just heard a radio programme about Sid James. He died a couple of months ago. I liked his *Carry On* films; Davie Dunsmore, our coalman, is his spitting image when his face is washed. Davie lives near to me and looks out for me, as do my neighbours, especially Frank downstairs.

My husband Billy left me two years ago and is now living with a woman called Donna who lives up at the bus terminus, so he better not be bothering me again. He's a bastard and I never should have married him. I was too young – we were all too young, getting married as teenagers. Who the fuck lets kids get married? Anyway, Dirty Donna can keep him, I don't want him back. Apparently she makes good soup and is awfully energetic in bed, according to Frank downstairs. The stupid lassie is nineteen and loves the Bay City Rollers, so now at thirty years of age, Billy is head to foot in tartan, the daft eejit. Well, they can Shang-a-Lang together for all I care. Good riddance. He couldn't wire a plug, change a baby or keep a job. I hope she can get the shit stains out of his underpants, because his mammy never showed him how to wipe his own arse.

Need to go, the provy man is here and I don't have the money this week so I am going to let our dog Laddie chase him down the close.

Thursday

Am sweating. Apparently, it's the hottest summer since the sun was invented.

Woke up, smoked three fags, made tea and pulled on my good American Tan tights and Scholl's sandals with my new floral smock from Chelsea Girl. I look OK for a twenty-nine-year-old woman who's had three kids, with one boob bigger than the other and soaked in sweat.

It's the kids' school trip today. Who knew they needed suntan cream for the bus run? I don't know anyone who has any. So there's me hanging out the back window screaming, 'Does anyone have suntan cream for the weans?' I startled Mrs Wilson, who was out beating her big rug over the washing line. Apparently it's the carpet's fault her son Derek still hasn't got married. She never stops going on about it, even tried to pair me up with him, no chance!

Anyway, nobody had any sun cream, coz it's Glasgow and when would we need it! So I just sent the kids on the school trip and hoped for the best, and no doubt they'll come back like wee grilled tomatoes. Won't do them any harm, some calamine lotion will sort them out. No lasting damage. I love my weans, they keep me going.

Sharon sorted the packed lunches for everyone. She's thirteen and always helps me out – she's a doer and doesn't moan the face off me. She'll be a great mother.

Her younger sister Janet is only ten but already scares me shitless – she can't play skipping with her rope after she near-choked the Catholic twins up the next block. We're sticking with 'it was an accident' but she scares us all with her Boris Karloff eyes and her weird dreams that she keeps writing down at school in her story jotter.

My John, my angel, my sunshine boy, is eight years old and he is going to play football for Rangers when he's old enough, according to his da. John might actually love dancing more than football but he's got fast feet and, unlike our Janet, he's great at skipping. He's the quietest of them all, a thinker.

Anyway, I got the kids out the door, told them not to eat all their lunch on the bus to the beach and let Laddie out at the same time, and then I poured myself some orange squash. Fuck, I was thirsty.

It's exhausting getting them all out in the morning and they only have to walk half a mile to school. When I was a kid, we had to walk three miles rain, hail or shine, and that was after I had helped my mammy at her job cleaning the bingo hall at seven a.m.

Kids nowadays have it so easy.

Friday

Woke up, smoked two fags and had an instant coffee with dry milk as we don't have a fridge and every pint turns to cheese in this heat.

Still really hot. Mrs Galbraith fainted in the steamie. She was folding her clothes one minute, lying on top of them the next. At least they were clean.

Me, Bunty, Isa, Sandra and Philomena Fitzgerald have started a menage. We've known each other since we were wee, and we're always reminiscing about the stuff we've got up to over the years. There's five of us in all and we all pay £3 a week, and every Friday one of us gets the £15 kitty. Menage is also a French word and someone asked me if it meant three people having sex, but that's big Lorna over the way for you, the weirdo. They've been my pals for years; we all met as school lassies at the youth Co-op dance hall and some of us go as far back as the Brownies. We lived in each other's houses growing up. Since Billy left, we've seen each other every other day, when we can. I wouldn't have got through the past year without them.

It was my turn this week for the menage, so I bought the kids summer clothes and treated myself to a demi-wave with the money. I felt like Princess Margaret with a full purse.

Went down to the phone box to call my cousin Bella, who now lives in Leeds with her husband, Carl. She moved there after she got hitched because Carl's from Jamaica and people round our way didn't take well to mixed marriages. Personally I don't care – he laughs loud and cooks good food and, unlike my daft bastard of a husband, he doesn't punch his wife's face into blue tattoos, so he's all right by me.

My other cousin Monica has moved to Canada – I'm the one who got stuck here.

Picked up the *Daily Record* and some fags and headed back home, then I put on the radio and listened in to Tony Blackburn and danced about to the music. Gary Glitter is brilliant and, yes, I would love to be in his gang!

We watched *Top of the Pops* last night. I like to imagine I could be one of those dancers like Pan's People or whatever they're called now. I have hot pants at the ready. Sharon tells me I am so embarrassing but I don't mind, at least I can still squeeze into them, and am still young-ish.

CHAPTER 2

What a night. I fell asleep dreaming about the seventies. I got up and made myself a coffee as the morning light poured through the stiff, white net curtains in Mum's wee ground floor flat. So much floral going on. Why did everything she own have to be covered in flowers? It was enough to give you a migraine. But then again, I'm not surprised: our childhood home had been a mishmash of second-hand sofas and clashing wooden tables (my uncle Alex had even painted our Artex-coated walls in an array of garish colours over the years before he died in the late eighties). Maybe all the floral was Senga's own style finally coming out, now that she could afford it.

I picked up the book from the duvet and took it to the living room to get back into it. It was wonderful to hear Mum's voice again, through the red book.

It was utterly compelling, but not a diary in the sense of what I imagined a diary to be: no short mentions of appointments, as in my work diary, or middle-class mutterings of weddings and happy records of births; no recipes, or polite descriptions of local events with some interesting pressings of local flora. It was a full-on stream of consciousness about everything she experienced in the seventies.

So, Mum was a secret writer, a bloody good, interesting writer, my forgotten childhood documented in biro, written at pace, full of sweary language. You wouldn't get that on Mumsnet.

The memories felt so present, so real, almost as though I was right there with her; she certainly had a way with words. Her beautiful handwriting was neat and clear and she described all those people with such vivid clarity, I could see them all. Davie Dunsmore and his big daft face, Laddie, our old black and white mongrel dog, Mrs Wilson in her floral pinny and Janet with her deadly skipping rope!

Mum was right, she had looked good in hot pants, though it had made me so furious back then: why couldn't she dress like my schoolteacher and be like a normal mum? I forgot she was only twenty-nine years old when I was thirteen.

The old woman lying in that hospital bed was so far removed from the woman who'd had a fist-fight with a big Alsatian dog outside the grocer's when it tried to bite our John and drag him on to the main road. This was the woman who'd called Maggie Thatcher a cow at the top of her voice. It seemed unbelievable that such a vibrant life force could fade.

When did she go from that vivacious, young woman, dancing to Gary Glitter, to the frumpy, middle-aged curtain-twitcher who'd hated swearing and sex scenes on the telly? Never mind that . . . my dad and Dirty Donna dressed in Bay City Rollers tartan? That's a horrible flashback!

Yet here it was. In her own blue pen in her big red book.

My mum had never told me exactly what happened between her and my dad. I do have memories of the fighting and anguish he caused her, but the details were forgotten. Maybe she felt it wasn't something you discussed with your kids.

But her pals, she had so many pals, they shared everything. I haven't heard her mention Isa and the gang in years; what the hell happened to this merry band of women?

I wanted to find out more, but there was so much to do.

I took a quick peek out of the curtains. Autumn was in full flow in Govan: the trees were golden and heavy with crisp leaves and there was a fine frost on my car window. Thank God, I'd brought my good boots and heavy coat.

I pulled a pair of jeans and a warm jumper out of my suitcase, got changed, tried to check my phone for work emails but the signal was bad and Mum didn't have an internet connection. So I grabbed her keys and my laptop bag and headed out to find a local café to get on to their Wi-Fi.

Mum's neighbours, old Maggie and wee Betty, were waiting outside. They had brought me a bag of 'messages', Glasgow-speak for bread, milk and teabags. 'Just to get you by, hen,' Maggie said as she peered into the flat to see what I'd been up to and then patted my hand. Both of them like sentinels, not letting me wriggle away.

'We haven't seen you in a few months, hen – are your brother and sister coming back too?' Betty asked.

'Betty, I don't know everything yet. Thanks for this, so kind of you. I've just got here so I'm taking it all in,' I said as I held up the bag and opened the door to pop it back onto the kitchen table. I really didn't need this right now.

'Your mammy got a new hall carpet – it's lovely, isn't it?' Maggie shouted up the hall as they made their way in, wee women in wide-fitting shoes, with the stealth of Cold War spies.

'Yes, it's lovely, full of flowers,' I said as I hustled them back out. If they cornered me in that living room, I would never get to leave. I managed to get past them and the cold wind whipped my hair into my face. I wished I had brought a woolly hat; I always forgot how freezing Glasgow could get. 'I'll give you both a full update when I come back from the hospital,' I shouted over my shoulder as I reached the car. They both stood with arms folded, watching me.

Here I was, back in Glasgow, the daughter who'd run away first, now back to see her mum die, and suddenly I couldn't face the future. All I could do was read about the past.

Glasgow had changed so much since I left for Bristol University thirty-eight years ago. Gone were the black tenements that stood like giant battlements in every scheme – they'd either been demolished, or sandblasted to a sultry shade of blush pink in an effort to clean up the city, back in the early eighties. My sporadic visits home had been like a slow-motion time-shift.

The wee ice-cream cafés from my childhood were all gone. I recalled the old, fancy glass-fronted doors with a giant plastic knickerbocker glory in the window, the Formica booths and the big jukebox, all demolished or revamped as more of the city continued to be gentrified. Sure enough, the local Govan café was a funky hip coffee shop called 'Raw Coffee and Cake'. Who ate 'raw cakes'? But I needed to log on to emails so it would have to do.

The Farrow and Ball pale grey frontage with big windows and hanging bare light bulbs were like every other café on the upmarket wharfside in Bristol. I walked in and a huge bell clanged above my head and frightened a baby that was strapped to a man in a strange wraparound papoose. I ordered a coffee from the chalkboard menu. I looked around the place – no Formica to be seen: it was all squashy tan leather sofas and reclaimed wooden tables with an array of potted plants. People were working on laptops, prams were parked around tables and Fleetwood Mac was playing softly over the noise of steaming soya milk.

The man behind the counter was chatting easily with everyone; they obviously had lots of regulars here. He laughed a lot, and smiled broadly at me as he took my order. He was taller than me and had one of those faces that looked as if it had grown into itself with age, with thick, sandy-silver hair and hazel eyes, and big dimples when he grinned.

'Hey, how are you?' he asked.

I looked around to see who he was speaking to, but it was definitely me.

'Oh, fine, thanks,' I replied, not used to this level of intimacy with a barista.

'I haven't seen you in here before?' he said as he banged the steamer jug on the counter. 'I have a good memory for faces.'

'I live in Bristol – just visiting my mum,' I replied, not wanting to get into the details. 'I'm Sharon Parker; it's nice to meet you. Can I use your Wi-Fi?'

He gave me the card with the password on. 'I'm Clyde, like the river,' he said. 'It's nice to meet you too.'

Clyde looked as if he might have played rugby in his youth. He looked incongruous in his cornflower-blue sweater, with big shoulders, standing there holding a tiny cup of espresso as though he were playing at a dolls' tea party.

I took my coffee and settled at one of the big tables near the grandfather clock at the back of the room.

'Self-employed marketing consultant' doesn't sound like a real job, but that was how I made a living. I'd worked hard to get to this point in my life and I was proud of my achievements. I'd stumbled into PR after a brief stint in journalism and discovered I could write snappy copy and keep calm in a crisis. I spent my life telling companies what was best for their product or which of the latest Instagram influencers they should avoid because of their sexually deviant tendencies, and how to source ethical accreditation to avoid bad press. The good news was, I could do a lot of my work remotely. So I answered the few work emails that had come in overnight, told the clients I would be working in Glasgow for the foreseeable and got down to the family stuff.

I needed to let Janet and John know just how critical Mum's condition was. Yes, she'd had health scares before, but this time the urgency was real, the doctor had been clear about that.

What wasn't clear was the urgency behind the red book. She was adamant I needed to read it, but why? Maybe Janet and John would shed some light on it. Did they even know about it? I sat quietly staring at my coffee, wishing I could make some sense of the past twenty-four hours.

The baby in the papoose started crying and it brought me back to the present. I would call Janet and John later back at Mum's flat and find out what they knew.

Doing this alone was hard. I wished my daughter, Louise, were here, but she was down in Lincoln with a new baby and her own life. Thinking of her made me remember Mum's comment in the book, that she thought I would be a good mum. For the first time,

I felt tearful. Louise and her husband, Simon, meant the world to me and I just adored my new granddaughter, Poppy. She looked so like our John as a baby – those huge blue eyes and a very quiet way of watching everyone around her. I FaceTimed Louise whenever I could and insisted she point the camera at Poppy so I could stare at her. My heart would be just full to see her tiny wee fingers and those eyes staring back. Family was everything.

I could feel tears welling up in my eyes, and I went into my bag for a paper hankie.

'You OK there? Need a top-up?' Clyde was stood over the table.

'I'm fine, thanks,' I said, as I sat crying in a café that sold raw cakes and worried that my mum would die and I would be here alone to deal with it all.

Clyde smiled down at me and said, 'I'll bring you some water,' and walked off.

I felt so alone.

Until recently, the first person I would have shared my pain with was my husband, Steven. Well, I say husband, but we are on a 'trial separation' and we both know this isn't a break, it is broken. I didn't know what he was to me anymore. We'd met at university many years ago and he'd been everything to me, but this past year I had felt him pulling away and constantly criticising everything I did. Of course, he'd denied it all and called me hysterical and a nag. I wasn't wrong.

He left me for a young, hot yoga teacher; no doubt had Mum been aware, she would have said history was repeating itself. I didn't know if the woman was hot or the yoga was done in a sweaty room, but how clichéd was that? Hit middle age, start a paleo diet, try skateboarding and pretend you like Coldplay . . . he was such a twat. I should have seen it coming: our John said years ago that he was a self-important idiot who liked to spout Latin verses at dinner parties. He'd impressed me with his knowledge when we'd first met: he had been so different from everyone else I knew. His confidence had really attracted me to him. It took me long enough to realise that that confidence was arrogance. He was basically a prick who couldn't play golf, using well-worn statements like 'I need to find myself'.

Suddenly I heard Senga's voice ringing in my ears: 'He's trying to find himself by shagging other women? Typical.'

When Clyde brought over my glass of water, I ordered a panini.

'You feeling better?' he asked me.

'Yeah. I just realised my husband's a prick and pretended he could play golf,' I blurted out.

What was wrong with me?

'Cool. Want some salad with your panini?' he batted back without missing a beat.

Suddenly I felt better, and for the first time since arriving in Glasgow, I laughed out loud.

I got out my phone to call my pal Elaine in Bristol to give her my news. She got a brief outline about my mum and the book. I stuffed the burning hot panini into my mouth, happy at least that it wasn't raw.

'Wow, that's not a "Dear Diary" at all, is it? I never knew your mum was a Glasgow Samuel Pepys. Are there any dirty bits?' Elaine laughed.

It was a relief to hear a friendly voice.

'God, I hope not. I'm only at the beginning. Why do you think she told me about it after all these years?' I asked.

'Because you're her daughter and she knows she doesn't have much time left. She might want to share her stories with you and see her old pals, God love her. Do they still live local, could you find them?' Elaine shouted as her wee dog barked in the background.

'I'm not sure – I haven't a clue if they're even still alive. The book is from way back in the seventies, from the time when Gary Glitter was a good guy and Prince Charles was a single man. I wouldn't know where to start. But I'll give it a go,' I answered.

'Try Facebook,' Elaine said. 'Everyone is on that. Let me know how you get on, speak later.' And she went back to shouting at her dog.

Calling John later was a different situation. He was so emotional; as expected, he took the news badly. 'I didn't realise the cancer was back so aggressively – she said nothing when we spoke ten days ago. She just said she was waiting on blood tests.' He descended into huge gulping tears. 'Oh, Sharon, I just want my mammy,' he said.

'I know, darling,' I said.

'Oh God, I dreamt about her last night. She was at the big bedroom window, screaming at Laddie and wearing her pink, shiny nylon housecoat.' His voice broke again down the line from Spain.

He was still the baby of the family and he now ran a very successful dance academy in Spain with his boyfriend, Carlos; I loved going to visit them when I could, but I hadn't seen him in at least six months. Poor John had been bullied from a young age, called a 'sissy' and a 'poof'. He had loved all things glittery, dancing and ponies. He was the boy who'd wanted to join a ballroom dancing class after seeing *Come Dancing* on the telly. And now he'd made it his living – he'd never given up on his dreams or settled for boring middle-class mock-Tudor mundanity as I had. I was so proud of him.

When I told him he needed to come home as soon as possible, he was silent apart from a lot of sniffing. He finally said, 'My passport has run out and I'm waiting to get the new one. I asked the airline if they would let me fly and they won't and I just cannae cope . . . Sharon, I'm so sorry I can't fly home tomorrow.'

He was sobbing; I could hear Carlos comforting him in the background.

'She's stable at the moment, please don't panic, she won't go without seeing her sunshine boy,' I said.

I felt him smile and heard him say, 'Aw bless.'

'She's asked to see everyone, and the doctor just thinks we should get ready.' I paused as he blew his nose. 'She also wants me to read her diary, the red book she used to write in. John, do you know anything about that?'

'A diary?' He stopped sniffing for a moment.

'Yes, she asked me to read it – ring any bells?' I added.

'I remember her writing in a book! She used to say it was personal, that we couldn't look at it. I haven't seen her write a diary for years, though. What's in it?' He sounded calmer.

'Memories really, that's all so far. I'll show you when you get here. I'll call Janet and I'll set us all up in a WhatsApp group as well so we can stay in contact. We can all be together with Mum soon,' I said, and paused. 'We all should have come back more often, John. I think Mum's been wanting to tell us something.'

'Well, we can do that now,' he said. 'Are you OK, Sharon? How are you coping?'

I gave him a brief update of the state of my marriage. 'Look, all that's going to be what it's going to be. I just want to focus on Mum just now, John. See you soon, darling.' And we rang off.

Janet was in London, where she worked as a theatre director; we'd all scattered far and wide from the tall tenement. She lived with her writer husband, Anthony, and his son, Josh, her stepson. I tried to call but it went straight to voicemail, so I left a message. I hadn't seen Janet for almost a year, what with work commitments and her busy life, although we spoke every week and I got to see her theatre clips online.

I needed to hear her voice; I needed to connect with my sister.

But we would all be together again soon, reunited in Glasgow for the first time in years.

1976
July, Sunday

Let Laddie out, and asked Sharon to keep an eye on the weans and put them to bed early for school. She heated up a big tin of macaroni cheese and made toast for their tea. I don't know what I would do without her.

Me and the lassies were having a wee bingo night at the social club. I was there first, as always, to secure a table. I had on my new Chelsea Girl top and patchwork jeans and for the first time in ages my hair was sitting nice. Isa breezed in next, smoking one of her roll-ups, her dark curls all pinned up in a neat bun, her long legs in a new pale blue crimplene dress. She always looks like she's a hostess on *The Generation Game* on the telly. 'Watch my bag,' she said as she threw down her leather patchwork tote, grabbed her purse and made her way to the bar. Fag hanging out of her mouth, she shouted back, 'Vodka and lemonade, Senga?' I nodded.

The doors banged open and Sandra, Philomena and Bunty came in together.

All the old guys at the bar watched Sandra walk by like they were on the beach at Ipanema. She's like a young Glaswegian Brigitte Bardot. Her long blonde hair was hanging over her face, making me worried she had another black eye, but then she smiled at me and I could see she didn't.

I hope that bastard Jim she's married to gets run over by a bus. She doesn't make the most of her gorgeous figure as Jealous Jim hates anyone looking at her, so she dresses like one of those dowdy Christian women that stand behind her man as they try to sell bibles at your door. Tonight she had on a loose smock dress that hid her amazing Dolly Parton boobs, and a pair of jeans beneath it.

Bunty had her long red hair in a fabulous curly perm; she does amazing home demi-waves. She is as petite as Sandra but a wee bit curvier round the belly and hips and hasn't quite outgrown her baby face. She is a bit of a rocker, the Suzi Quatro to Sandra's Brigitte, and is always dressed in the best of gear. She's a complete catalogue addict and her cousins always know someone who can get 'something cheap'. They probably helped her get the fancy denim flares she's wearing now.

Philomena is the most focused of all of us: she works at the factory, has a sideline selling football cards, looks after her family, especially her brother who's running with a wild crowd, and always looks unflustered by life. She even keeps chickens in her garden. She's like a swan – serene on top but paddling hard underneath. We sometimes call her Wonder Woman and she looks like her too – but with better curves, sturdy legs and the longest, thickest, blackest hair you ever saw. I'm always finding hairs in my house when she's been for a visit and I'm still surprised at how long and black they are when I lift them off the sofa cushions.

'The witches have arrived!' Old Jack the barman shouted over to us.

'Fuck off, Jack,' Bunty shouted back, and threw a beer mat at him. 'When does the bingo start?' She came and sat down. 'I can't stay out late, my niece is babysitting the twins and they're up early for a school trip,' she added.

When Sandra went to the toilet, Isa told us she saw Sandra's man Jim get into a fancy big white Mercedes outside the Drummonds' scrapyard, driven by one of the Devlins. 'You know what a bad lot they are – he'll fit right in with that bunch of violent bastards,' Philomena hissed as we spotted Sandra coming back. We are all scared of the Devlins – the whole family is dangerous, there are so many of them and they have a reputation for taking revenge on anyone who gets in their way.

Bunty told me her brother has broken up with his girlfriend, that lassie from Cyprus whose name I can never remember – they all called her Nana Mouskouri. Sandra was very quiet as usual and kept watching the door to see if Jim had arrived, as he likes to keep an eye on her. He called the bar phone twice to check she was still there. I saw Jack nod over at her and loudly say, 'Aye, Jim, she's still here,' then slam the old green phone down and shake his head, a look on his face that was a mixture of disgust and pity.

It's as if she can never fully relax or breathe out, he's always on her back.

Sandra took me aside when we went to the bar and said, 'Can I come up and see you tomorrow night, just us, Senga?'

I said, 'Aye, no bother, pal.' I've been close to Sandra since school. It's been hard to see her as much since she got married – Jim isn't keen on her having other people in her life.

I hope she's OK.

We had a good night! Isa won £4 with a full house and we headed down to the chip shop first, then got some fags and headed home.

My Sharon had the kids in bed and was still up doing her homework when I got in, so we shared the hot greasy chips and let Laddie lick the paper.

Got the washing looked out for tomorrow and let the dog out for a last pee.

Monday

Woke up with a dry, dusty mouth. I think I drank more vodkas than expected – really shouldn't have shoved all those greasy chips down my throat either. Great night last night, though I am worried about Sandra, she was like a coiled spring.

Been a busy day. Got the two bedrooms and the kitchen floor cleaned. The living room has a wee brown tweed sofa that pulls down into a bed and two mismatched velveteen green squashy armchairs, and I gave them a good beating with the carpet beater and washed all the windows. The hall, with its missing and broken lino tiles, was driving me mad, so I ripped up the whole lot and scrubbed at the wooden floor. I might save up for some lino, as I won't need much and Bunty's brother gets it cheap. I need to think about getting my Sharon her own room as she is growing up and needs her own space. Maybe I could use the living room sofa and let her have my room? Or try and find another council house with three bedrooms?

Or maybe go the whole hog and try and find Omar Sharif and see if he wants to marry me.

I'm lucky we have two bedrooms, to be honest. Many of these old tenements round here only have one, but the ceilings are so high you could easily build an upstairs inside your own flat. The Victorians really did overestimate the amount of height us wee Glaswegians would need in our life. We all need more floor room and less headroom!

Washed the shared close and wiped down the metal stair railings as it was my turn and let Laddie out for a piss again.

I shoved on the twin tub and got a load of washing done, then hung it round the back and sat down for a smoke with Old Wullie, the candy apple guy. He makes candied apples in his house and then walks round all the back courts and sells them for five pence each. The weans go mad for them but they pull out half their teeth! Turns out apples aren't that good for you after all.

A quick whizz round with the carpet sweeper and that was the housework done. I made sure I had a 50p to pop in the back of the telly meter to watch some Fanny Cradock. I have a screwdriver thingy that opens the money slot on the meter so I just keep putting in the same coin. When the Radio Rentals guy comes round to collect the takings I tell him the reason it's empty is that I don't have time to watch telly, and then get one of the kids to pretend to choke and faint on the floor and he runs out, petrified.

He must think none of my kids can swallow properly.

I do love Fanny Cradock though, she wears a lovely chiffon dress and makes the kind of food that Princess Margaret or anybody who owns a horse would eat. I mean, who round our way would eat brandy butter and devilled kidneys with cucumber in an aspic jelly? You couldn't get that off the van. I usually cook stuff like braised liver, turnip, carrots, butter beans and potatoes. I know it sounds like plain food and you wouldn't see Bianca Jagger cook that for her pals, but it fills up the kids and it is cheap and it's what my mammy fed me.

They get apples for pudding, and for choking on when the telly man comes round.

Talking about food, I saw an advert on telly for the new Vesta Indian range. Apparently, you boil the bag of dusty dry powder and it makes an authentic Indian curry with things that taste like woodchip and are just as hard to chew. I'm not so sure about full dinners in a cardboard box yet.

I did buy some of them new frozen crispy pancakes. I fried them but near shit myself with fear after dropping the frozen half-discs into hot, spattering fat. The noise and splashback were petrifying. The insides were like molten lava, but the kids loved them, wolfed them down.

There is a new supermarket just open down the main street, beside Eusebi's café. You just wander about touching stuff and picking it up yourself, then take it to the till and pay. The kids fucking run riot and grab everything that I can't afford. Convenience my arse! I spotted wee Les the shoplifter in the canned meat aisle too, filling up his big coat. Don't think they have sussed him out yet.

We're all shopping there as it's cheaper with lots of choices, but I miss seeing wee Megan in Healy's Dairy every day – she knows exactly how to cut the butter and pack your message bag. Soon we'll have robots telling us what to buy and taking our money off us. I saw that on *Tomorrow's World* on the telly, but you can't get gossip and an extra cake off a robot, can you? And I bet you they all smell of tin.

Better get a move on, the weans will be home soon.

Sandra was coming up to see me tonight, but now she says she needs to stay at home with Jim – she told my Sharon outside the fruit shop to tell me. She looks like a goddess but her life's more like hell. Maybe she will get out the house and come to the beach with us this week, if Jim lets her.

Got some cans of sardines and made the kids a picnic dinner – it's too hot to eat.

I put the candy apples in some waxed paper in the back of the cupboard for the weans and gave Laddie a slice of cold meat as a treat.

CHAPTER 3

2019
Day two
Sharon

Well, those candy apples! I remembered them, and realised they were the reason half my teeth were now expensive dental implants. I found it hard to believe I was one generation away from supermarkets being a 'brand new thing'. Senga still did her own shopping even now – having her shop delivered to her door would have blown her mind. God, I had forgotten about Vesta dried curries, Fanny Cradock and crispy pancakes. Those fried things took the roof off your mouth!

I had a walk around Govan after today's hospital visit. Mum was stable and much the same, so I got on the new WhatsApp group and updated everyone. I took a wander around Elder Park, which was stunningly beautiful in the autumnal sunshine: the swans on the pond were all huddled into the reeds on the bankside and the unusual jagged architecture of the Riverside Transport Museum looked absolutely spectacular on the far banks of the Clyde. Govan had changed a lot in the past few decades and the regeneration had been ongoing since the Glasgow Garden Festival of 1988. I could see why Mum liked it here.

Back at her flat, I waved at Betty, who was across the road waiting for a bus.

Mum's place was starting to feel like home.

I drew the curtains and lay on the bed with her book. It was as though I was being hugged by her through this diary. She'd spent so long being so poor that it was good to see she'd had some comfort in her old age. This flat was very different from the tenement we'd grown up in. Still very floral, but a lovely wee haven for her.

Looking back, she'd clearly had a lot on her plate, but she sounded happy, despite the hardships. I wished I had her here to talk about all these things. It was as though my past was being slowly coloured in and becoming fully formed again, not just vague sketches of memories I'd relied on before.

The only thing that was puzzling me about her diary was the back, where there was a page and a bit ripped out. Actually, ripped out with such force that the spine now bulged and the other pages were warped at the back. What was missing? I would have to ask Senga about it, if she woke up for long enough to be quizzed.

I picked up my phone and gave Janet another call. I wasn't expecting her to pick up, she was always busy with rehearsals, but she answered. I heard the empty echo of the theatre in the background, and some loud voices. I could picture her striding about, waving her arms, her short grey hair sticking out wildly. She whispered, 'Hang on,' and then I heard the familiar sound of seats clacking back into position as she clambered into the aisle and out of the auditorium and shut the door behind her.

'Hiya, I got your message last night. How's Mum today?' she said, sounding anxious and exhausted. There had been a period in her youth where Janet had gone off the rails and we hadn't been close, but, when she'd settled in her career and found happiness in it, she'd come back to us all and made peace with her past, and it was as though she'd never been away. Blood was always thicker than water.

'Hanging on, Janet. You need to come up the road, though.'

'I'm days from press night, but I'm getting cover. I'll come as soon as I can,' she replied. I knew the show had been getting good feedback from its previews. Janet was a real star director now. Her plays were pretty dark and twisted – her mind hadn't changed much since her childhood days – but they were clever too. She used her macabre creative brain to her advantage.

'Aw, Janet, it will be great to have you here. I miss you. Mum's like a wee shadow of herself, it's breaking my heart to see her like that,' I said.

'Oh, fuck, that's scary, sorry. I'll be there soon as I can, Sharon,' she said, and went very quiet.

I didn't want her feeling so guilty – there was nothing worse than being so far away and having that helpless feeling – so I changed the subject. 'Govan's looking posh: they have vegetarians and poodles,' I added.

She snorted. 'How are you coping?'

'It's strange being back but I'm finding my way. Listen, do you recall anything about Mum's big red book, like a diary?' I asked her.

'A red book?'

'Yeah, she used to write in it when we were small, do you remember? When I got to the hospital she told me to find it and read it. I've had a look – there's a wee bit in it about you pretending to choke on apples when the Radio Rentals man turned up looking for his money. Ring any bells?'

'I vaguely recall choking on demand, but why was she writing a book?' Janet replied, her voice rising a few octaves.

'Well, it *is* her diary, but it reads like a novel from the seventies. She absolutely insisted we read it. I'll show you when you get here.'

'I don't remember it, sounds bizarre, but I'll see you soon and we can talk,' Janet said, after a pause. I heard someone call her name in the background. 'Sharon, I need to go or I'll be here all night, sorry. Love you, sis.' And she hung up.

I lay back on the floral frilly pillows and wondered how Mum could sleep in this acrylic rose garden without an eye mask. I opened the diary again.

1976
July

Woke up at the crack of dawn and the city was already heating up; even that early you could feel it. The smell of melting tarmac filled my nostrils when I went out for some fresh milk. These big stone tenements hold the heat – the bricks suck up every bit of sun and dry out the dampness that torments us all winter.

I shouted to Sharon to let the dog out as I packed spam sandwiches, two apples, a big bottle of Kia-Ora orange and half-bottle of vodka into a plastic bag. We were going to the beach for the day! And Sandra was coming with us, she was allowed out.

I let Laddie out to wander about the streets till we came home as I didn't want him shitting in the house during this hot weather. He usually gets himself out and walks up to Springburn to visit Bridie McBride who always gives him treats; he spends the day fighting with her two cats. It's a wee day out for him as well and he knows the journey like the pads on his paws. Someone would give him a drink of water on the way, I was sure, or he would paddle through the Shettleston burn to cool down and frighten the shit out the water rats. He knows his way around, like all dogs; you just leave them to it and they get on with it.

Sharon dragged the pink candlewick bedspread off my bed and rolled it into a big bag to use on the beach. The weans have pulled out lots of the woven threads and it's half baldy, like my old grandad.

Three kids, two pals, three big bags, two wee bags, some mugs and a half-bottle of vodka and we were off on the bus to Glasgow Central. No Bunty or Philomena as they were at work, but Sandra and Isa were there with me. The kids started fighting before I could light a ciggie on the top deck of the 62. I pulled off my Scholl's sandal and threatened to smack three pairs of legs, shouting that if they didn't behave I would leave the lot of them with one-eyed Harry, who hangs about outside the Co-op and tells everyone that aliens are invading Shettleston (good luck to them).

I was glad Sandra could make it after her no-show on Monday – she still hasn't explained what that was about.

Everyone laughed at me threatening the weans and they soon stopped their nonsense – honest to God, my mammy would have beaten me to death for annoying her on a bus. Just as well I'm good-tempered. Kids don't know how easy they have it nowadays. My cousin Monica, who lives in Canada, doesn't hit her kids, and she was horrified when she was over last year and saw me threaten to take a hand to Janet for playing with the coal fire. Monica says she's a feminist and I didn't even know they had them in Canada. We need more of them in Glasgow, that's for sure.

Anyway, it was hot as hell when we got on the train, the kids were tired and had eaten all the spam sandwiches and started crying because they didn't want the apples. All except Janet, who was refusing to eat at all. They didn't know I had saved some money from the menage to buy them a fish supper and some rides at the fairground. I am not a bad mammy. I know how to pull out the treats when they least expect them.

Me and the girls cracked open the vodka and had a few drinks (Sandra doesn't drink, though, Jim doesn't like it). It felt like ages since the three of us got together. Isa has been looking after her mammy since she got the hysterectomy – apparently her insides were sliding out of her. I sometimes wish Isa wasn't so descriptive and loud, but she's such a laugh. She even stood up and did the actions of her mammy pulling up her girdle to 'haud my bits in'. I near peed myself. The men sitting near us were appalled, I could see, but I couldn't persuade her to speak more quietly. Sandra said nothing, she seemed a bit out of it.

When we arrived at Saltcoats I sent Sharon to buy some more fags as we'd smoked my ten-pack on the train. I told her to get some ice lollies for her and the wee ones.

We spread the candlewick cover on the sand and sent the kids away to play so we could have some peace; they were overjoyed to get on the fairground rides. Out came more vodka and Kia-Ora orange juice and off came my cardigan. Isa stripped down to her swimming costume – a bright green swirly design with bows at the hips and boobs. She stood up and hoisted her boobs up in it, opening her legs to 'fix herself'.

'I got it out of Bunty's catalogue,' she said as she snapped the elasticated crotch, much to the horror of a family sitting near us. We laughed, rolling on our backs holding our drinks aloft as we squealed at her antics.

There were two young guys near us on the beach with their portable radio on loud, and soon me and Isa were up on the bed-spread dancing to 'Silly Love Songs' by Wings, and they came over to try to chat us up. The lanky one with a big feathered haircut and high-waisted jeans tried to sit on our blanket.

Isa has had a few dates with a soldier from the American army base, but she still says she's single, and with a drink in her she's up for a laugh with guys. I'm not ready to repeat that mistake. It's been two years since me and Billy separated, and I am enjoying my freedom and the fact I don't have to explain my every move to a man.

Sandra didn't even look in their direction, as her man would go mad if he found out she'd spoken to another guy on the beach. Sometimes he stands outside her work at the fruit shop and watches her bag up the turnips and cabbages as she serves people. She says that he even inspects her handbag and bus tickets to check she's been where she says every day. She doesn't seem to find it weird, even though it is. If he's anything like my ex, Billy, she should borrow one of the cleaver knives from the butchers next door, because that clingy behaviour is not right. She says he's just looking out for her. But I worry.

She isn't allowed to wear a bikini either. He picked out what she was wearing, so she was sitting there in a crimplene trouser suit sweating like a sausage. It's a shame, because she's the kind of woman Rod Stewart would run away with. If I had tits up that high, I would be showing them off to the entire street.

Sandra's parents were so happy when she married Jim two years ago – we all were. We went to her wedding and her wee daddy was bursting with pride, and what a vision in white she was. My Sharon was a very proud flower girl. I still have the photos in my display cabinet.

'Are you OK?' I asked Sandra eventually.

'Just remembering the last time I was here,' she said quietly, looking at a couple holding hands as they splashed in the sea.

Jim was an absolute gentleman when she first met him at the pub. The perfect boyfriend – he really couldn't do enough for her, we all thought she'd done so well. But according to Sandra it wasn't long into the honeymoon, at a wee hotel in Saltcoats, that he first punched her as they walked along the beach. She was so shocked she said she ran to a phone box and called her mammy. Her mammy told her to stop making him angry and learn to please her man more. Women just accepting shite from generation to generation – it's always our fault. She said she sat in the bandstand on the promenade crying as Jim pulled her hair at the back, smiling as onlookers thought they were hugging.

'He can go months without hurting me, then suddenly he turns on me,' she told me once.

My mammy knew his family and she said they were all work-shy bullies, even the women. His Aunty Bella even frightened the men with her nasty mouth and attitude.

I've since discovered Jim has always been a smarmy, sneaky bas-tard, on the fringes of danger, trying to ingratiate himself with the Devlins but presenting a clean-cut image of a hardworking lad with the lovely wife. On the occasions when I am not arguing with Billy and we chat like normal people, Billy tells me what Jim's up to. I am so happy she isn't pregnant – that would slow down any plans to escape that monster.

I watched her nibble sandwiches and stare out to sea.

'You said you wanted to talk, in the pub the other night?' I asked when Isa was out of earshot.

'I can't, not now. Maybe another time. Let's get our fish supper.'

After a while we rounded up the kids, grabbed our bags and staggered out to the train platform. The kids were exhausted but happy, the fish and chips were delicious. Time to head back to our scheme.

When the bus pulled into our main street at eleven, Jim was there at the bus stop with his angry face, waiting for Sandra. It was so hard to leave her.

Got the kids washed down with a wet flannel in the bath and covered them in calamine lotion to cool the sunburn and got them all to bed. Many of the old brown tenements round here still have the one communal lavatory on each landing, to be shared by three families on each floor. Most people in those flats piss in a pot in their lobby and tip it out the next day. We are lucky to have an inside toilet with a bath.

Tonight, I am sleeping with the windows open – it brings in the moths but Laddie eats them after chasing them round the house. He was waiting at the close for us, and he had a note tucked in his collar from Bridie saying that she'll be up next Friday to get her hair done. I am going to do a wee demi-wave on her with my new foam rollers.

I thought I would open my Jackie Collins book in bed. I love a good story about a woman who dresses in gold and rides horses and fucks rich doctors on a cruise to Egypt. Am too pissed, I can't see the words.

Goodnight.

CHAPTER 4

2019
Day two
Sharon

The wind and rain were battering Mum's bedroom window; you could hardly see out there. I slipped under her duvet, pulled over the bedside lamp and opened up the book again.

The memories of that beach day have come flooding back. This diary had grabbed all my emotions and my eyes were smarting with tears, thinking about how my mum had saved for months to get us that day out. She really was on her own, struggling to keep us all clothed, fed and happy, and trying to have a wee bit of sunshine for herself.

That heatwave of 1976 – it was recorded as one of the hottest summers for decades and it lasted so long. It felt as if the world was burning, and Glasgow isn't a city known for its air-conditioning.

Senga had clearly loved spending time with Isa and Sandra and her pals. They were such a strong circle of women, facing poverty daily and laughing like cackling hens one minute and crying over someone's domestic drama the next. It made me realise that even in these days of networking and communication, I didn't have that kind of strength from pals. My mates were few and close but we didn't have that sense of a day-to-day update on our lives. There were plenty of modern memes of 'Queens Fix Each Other's Crowns' and 'Sisters Help Sisters' but, in reality, we were all too bloody busy, and maybe I was just too closed off or too focused on my work to share my feelings as I should. Suddenly I was really envious of these women and their collective strength.

Isa's face came back to me now, and Sandra's too. Sandra was always so patient with all us kids; she once gave me her new cardigan to wear for my school photo. She was a kind soul. I think she and Jim left Glasgow years ago, moved away – that was what Mum said, anyway. I didn't recall seeing them around the house when I went off to university. My mum never mentioned Sandra to me again.

I went into the kitchen to make a coffee and there was a wee photo magnet on the fridge of Mum and baby John at the beach. That reminded me of the envelope I'd found inside the red book and so I went to get it off the windowsill. I put down the coffee and opened the crackled brown paper, spreading all the photographs out on the bed.

The pictures I was looking for were at the top.

We were all small and slightly out of focus, but it was us on that candlewick bedspread, all sun-scorched and smiling. The other picture was of my mum with her thick dark hair and a smile that split her face in two, Isa in a David Bowie T-shirt, with her untameable home perm taking up most of the photo, laughing with her head thrown back, and Sandra staring off into the distance.

The scene brought back so many memories. The emotions bubbled up and I felt my throat tighten, looking at those young women full of hope and gallus swagger. 'Where are you, Isa and Sandra?' I said as I held the image under the lamp.

I decided there and then to make it my mission to find them. What was Isa's maiden name? I flipped the photo and scrawled on the back in bingo pen was: *Isa Harrington, Miss World. 1976.*

'Thank you, Isa,' I laughed, and launched Facebook and started the search.

And suddenly there was Isa on screen, with her dark perm now shiny and silver framing her face. She was listed under her maiden name on Facebook. She had aged well, softer around the jawline but unmistakably Isa across the eyes. There were very few personal details but I could see she was married and now lived in Stow-on-the-Wold, all pale sofas in the background with tasteful cushions as she sat in her conservatory, holding up a glass of wine to whoever had taken the photo. She looked fabulous and happy. There were some other photos of her near a pool in some foreign country, and some images of a wee white terrier dog in a bath.

So, I sent her a private message.

Isa
Stow-on-the-Wold

I sit down at the kitchen island, pick up my glass of red wine, put my wee dog on my knee and open Facebook. There's a friend request from Sharon Parker. Who the hell is she? Do I know a Sharon Parker?

Hang on, she's sent a private message.

Dear Isa, I hope this finds you well. You may not remember me but I am Senga Gray's daughter Sharon (the eldest one). You and Senga were best pals back in the '70s and Mum is presently gravely ill in the Royal Infirmary. Mum has made it clear to me that she is desperate to see her pals one last time. I know the timing is urgent and probably inconvenient, but I thought I would try my best to find you all. Also, she left a brilliant diary from the '70s and I veer between laughing and crying at the many adventures of her gang from Shettleston. If you want to call me or email me and reach out, you can do so on the number and email address below.

My heart pounds loud in my ears, my mouth goes dry.

I blurt out, 'Fuck's sake, poor Senga.' My wee terrier barks at me as I grip his ears too tight.

William looks up sharply from his newspaper. 'Language, Isabel, please. Who is Senga?' he asks, disapprovingly. I met him twenty years ago on a cruise and moved down here; he doesn't know that much about my old life in Glasgow.

'Sorry, William, just had a message from an old friend back home. She's very ill; I might to have head up the road soon.'

He replies, 'OK, do you want me to come?'

'No, darling, but thanks. I'll look at some trains tonight and get it organised.'

William goes back to his paper and I go back to staring at the message.

I gulp the wine and look out into the dark night through the patio doors, top up my glass, and type a message back to Sharon:

Dear Sharon, I'm very sorry to hear the news about Senga. I hate typing; I'll give you a call.

Jesus, Senga wrote a diary? What about? I'd better get up the road, my wee pal needs me. I'll need to call Bunty and Philomena too.
What exactly does Sharon mean by 'adventures'?

CHAPTER 5

2019
Day three
Sharon

The next morning, I got up and headed back to the hospital. The traffic was horrendous beside the Clyde after the heavy floods and rain. I got into the massive car park – the first few times I'd done this I'd got lost but I was getting better at finding my way around. My heart beat just a little bit faster every time I opened the door to her room, that tiny single moment of fear and anticipation. It was good to be back at Mum's bedside; every moment apart was a worry.

The room was too warm and suddenly I was very hot. I pulled off my jumper and stripped down to my T-shirt. Mum was still asleep. I opened my bag to get my phone out and the red book was the first thing my hand touched. I pulled it out, sat down on Mum's bed and lifted her hand on to it.

'Mum, I brought your book,' I whispered. 'Remember that day at the beach?'

Mum stirred slightly and turned her head towards the big window and I was sure I saw a smile trace across her face.

I wished she would wake up and be lucid enough to chat. I had so many questions for her. Her diary was full of so many memories, so much to take in. I couldn't wait for Janet and John to arrive; there would be so much to go over.

Then she stirred again and opened her eyes.

'You OK, hen?' she whispered.

'I'm here, Mum,' I said.

I held her hand and told her about Louise and Poppy.

'Send them my love,' she rasped, and before I could get into any real conversation she closed her eyes again. I stroked her hair as I watched her take short, shallow breaths.

The silence was broken by the loud ping of an email notification on my phone. Shit, I thought as I read the subject, it was from one of my biggest clients. I hated leaving Mum on her own like this, but I needed to go, so I kissed her goodbye and headed to the café to do some work.

The coffee shop was having a lull – the mummy and pram gang were nowhere to be seen – and it was nice to have some peace and quiet. I was surprised and happy to see that Clyde remembered me. He told me quietly, doing a theatrical 'hand cupping the mouth' action and pointing below the till, that they had reserved cooked scones for select customers. I was officially a regular, getting 'under-the-counter' goods. I grinned happily at him, sat down at my usual table, logged on and sorted my inbox, sending replies to the office and to my client.

But I was distracted: my head was still full of Mum's diary. I got out my glasses ready to do a Miss Marple and find Bunty and Sandra, but the phone rang and startled me. I didn't know why my phone ringing always gave me a wee fright.

'Well, Sharon, it's been years, hen, how are you? This is Isa.'

The Scottish women I grew up with didn't do preambles and polite introductions, they dived straight in and got to the point.

Her raspy voice took me right back to her sitting with me at my mum's fireside, braiding my long hair into plaits with a ciggie hanging out the side of her mouth.

'Isa, how are you?' I said, excitedly. It was lovely to hear her voice after seeing her face online yesterday. She sounded just the same – direct, but gentle.

'Fine, hen. Listen, so much to say and not over the phone, but I'm coming up the road as soon as I can. Tell your mammy to hold on for me – I want to see her. I'll call when I arrive and we can go to the hospital together. I have Bunty's number for you too, she'll want to know what's going on.' She rattled off a number. I scribbled it on a napkin.

'Oh, that's great; listen—' I said, but she spoke over the top of me.

'Right, so we'll speak soon, I have to go, hen.' And she ended the call. She clearly didn't want to say much more; she'd seemed to want to hang up as quickly as possible. But she was coming! And now I had contact details for Bunty. Just Sandra and Philomena to go now.

I sat, staring at the phone in my hand and with a flutter in my chest. Isa was coming back. Mum, you will soon see your pals.

Clyde came over with a mug of coffee and a wee fruit scone on a plate. 'Well, something's made you happy. Good to see you smiling,' he said, and winked. My stomach gave a little jump; that hadn't happened in a while.

I'd just been winked at, secured a warm scone and found Isa. What a day! Time to get back to the diary.

1976
August, Monday

Woke up, smoked three fags and opened a window. Let Laddie out. Gently shoved the X-ray paper into the front of the electric meter to stop the wheel going too fast. Fair cuts down the bills, and easily whipped out when the meter-reader man comes round. All these wee bits help cut down the cost of living.

Sent my Sharon down to the shops with 550 Embassy coupons to get ten Capstan Full Strength ciggies. I was up all night counting the coupons and wrapping them in elastic bands. You can also go into town and exchange them for stuff like a toaster and exercise bike, if you want to keep fit in between smoking your lungs sore to get the right number of coupons. Crazy world.

She popped into McKay's, the bakers, to get a bag of yesterday's buns (no cream ones obviously) for the weans' breakfast. A big bun dipped in tea is a good way to start the day.

Took my Ayds, a new slimming sweetie I saw in the *Reader's Digest* in the doctor's waiting room. It's a chewy chocolate jelly that you eat before meals and it expands in your stomach to make you feel full. Apparently it's wallpaper-paste-like cellulose or something, but it stops me eating a whole loaf before twelve o'clock. It would be easier and cheaper to just eat half a damp bath sponge, and it would taste better and not come out the other end like slimy eels.

I saw Karen Carpenter on the telly over the weekend and she's skinny and beautiful and all the men love her, so I want to be that thin and wear long floaty Laura Ashley dresses, but right now they make me look like a panicked walrus in a nightgown.

I managed to shave my legs, and plucked out all my eyebrow hairs so I could draw them back in higher up like sexy mistress Joan Collins. She is so classy and fabulously fashionable.

I am thinking of getting myself a man. But who will take a woman with three kids on? And where would I meet anyone new? I never go anywhere and I don't fancy any of the men I already know but Billy has moved on quicker than Warren Beatty so it's my time to do the same. I don't want a man like Sandra's Jim – that bastard gave her a right sore face last week because she spoke to the rent man out the back court when she was hanging up washing. Clearly a clandestine meeting of lovers . . . if you're an idiot. We all know the rent man, Andy, lives with a man called Gary and they breed angelfish. I wish she would do something about Jim, but there's no telling her. Once when I pulled him up for slapping Sandra he told me I was 'too cheeky' and I 'answer back' and that's why I can't keep a man. My ex, Billy, punched me in the stomach when I was pregnant with my Sharon, and my brother Alex near beat him to a pulp in the bookies. It's punch or be punched. You don't see that on *Coronation Street* or on the cover of *Woman's Own* magazine.

So, I don't want a wife-beater or an angelfish breeder. I just want a guy who will bring me chocolates in the dead of night like the Black Magic man off the adverts. On second thoughts that's terrifying and Laddie would bite the fuck out of him and it would traumatise the weans. Nobody needs a creepy burglar who delivers chocolates.

I think I'll stay single just now, unless someone can knit me a man. That's a joke my mammy always says.

Made a quick egg salad and drank a gallon of water today. Spent the night doing the ironing, pissing like a racehorse and catching up with the telly.

Watched *Coronation Street* – Ken and Rita get together at Deidre's party and she invites him back for a nightcap. Deidre tells Ray she's pregnant. He announces it during the party.

Tuesday

It's still sweltering and I am sick of lettuce. There are no tomatoes to be had anywhere, the country is tomato-less, as everyone is living off salad.

I went to see Bunty – she has some nice new electric rollers her dodgy cousin got off a van. Her cousin was there too, he always looks scared when there's a knock on the door. I can use the rollers on the lassies when I'm doing my wee hair jobs for extra cash around my cleaning job. I don't do that many hair jobs, just for friends and family really, but I enjoy them. Wee Carol, another one of my many cousins, is coming up this week and I am going to do a home perm on her. She has just been told she is diabetic and needs cheering up. These rollers are expensive in the big shop in town, and do make a great Farrah Fawcett Majors flick on the hair. I am so excited to try them. I took two sets off Bunty as they come at a bargain price. I asked no questions about where they'd come from. We have to keep quiet about them as it has been all over the local news about a factory getting burgled. Bunty says the police raided her mum's house but found nothing, thank the baby Jesus and his wee donkey. Her cousin is too wide to get caught and Bunty makes a few quid selling the stuff on. The Devlins have been involved, no doubt, but everyone round here just keeps their mouths shut. Bunty says one of her twins has an ear infection again, poor wean, nothing worse in this heat.

My kids keep themselves busy. Sharon went down the street and took out Mrs Kelly's newborn twins in the pram, down to the big park. It was really hot but she knows to keep them in the shade when she is playing on the swings. Wee John runs errands for the pensioner up the stairs – he gets bags of coal for her and sometimes cleans out her budgie's cage. Janet does the rounds of the closes, offering to wash the stairs for people who can't manage. Ten years old and she has her own wee cleaning business and a bucket and mop. 'Get your stairs done for ten pence,' she shouts up the back courts.

I saw the news on the telly and people were fainting in the heat. The weans watched people frying an egg on the pavement and cracked a whole box on the street. I was so annoyed at them. 'Mammy, we made you an egg,' they said as they brought up the dirty dribbling mess. I wanted an omelette, but not one that contained gravel off the tarmac. Laddie ate it.

Thursday

I got the big green bus with the kids all the way up through the scheme to Easterhouse, to visit my pal Janine. They built the new houses up there but forgot to add some decent shops and somewhere for the kids to play. Just rows upon rows of blocks of houses, not old, dirty black tenements like we have but white blocks of six with inside toilets. I met Janine in my first job in the betting shop, before I knew Billy. I left my job when I married him but I kept in touch with Janine because she is just such a wise woman. She's a bit older than me, and she's the manager of the shop now.

And my pal Janine has one thing nobody else has – a veranda.

I yearn for a veranda . . . a word I had to practise saying as it was so foreign to me.

The kids love a visit to the veranda up in Easterhouse, we can all cram out there in the blasting sunshine. Me, Janine, all our weans and her big dog Prince who takes up most of the room when he stretches out. She lives alone with her two lassies Brenda and Shona, who both are medallists at Scottish country dancing, and she makes all the outfits herself on her Singer sewing machine. She never really mentions her ex-man and I don't like to pry; I think he's in the Army though because she used to live in Germany and there's photos of the kids on a military base.

Me and Janine like to slip off our bras, roll up our shorts and sit on the veranda cushions and watch the world go by. She has gorgeous natural blonde hair and really fine features. I always think she's Scandinavian and my John says she looks like the woman out of Abba. Janine says she comes from Vikings and I believe her. I have seen her swing an axe in the garden. She loves her wee flat in Easterhouse, calls it her 'sanctuary', so a lot of shit must have gone down before she got here.

There aren't a lot of men up here in Easterhouse, they call it 'single mother city' and we love it. We get comfy on the pillows and get our vodka and orange in picnic cups and bake in the sun. We are no longer two fed-up women sitting on sponge squares.

This is not Easterhouse on the farmlands near Gartloch Mental Asylum. We are ladies on the Riviera, we are 'tall and tan and young and lovely', we are barefoot on the beach in Ipanema. We stare out to an azure sea and wave to Sophia Loren who is passing by on her yacht with Frank Sinatra at the helm. The world is full of sunshine and beauty.

That is, until Prince saw a cat in the street below and started barking and pissing everywhere, then we were back to our own real life with a bump. The kids were downstairs getting an ice-cream cone off the van and singing songs.

Me and Janine put the world to rights on that veranda and sometimes, like today, I do her hair too. I put it up into a very posh chignon and she looked like she could be a presenter on *Sale of the Century* on the telly. She has wonderful thick hair, so it takes about thirty kirby grips to hold it in place.

We talked about Jim and Sandra. Janine said some women don't want to admit they've picked a bad man as it makes them feel ashamed. I reminded her that I threw that bastard Billy out because of his handy fists, and she reminded me that he left me and I accepted the punches.

I don't like it when Janine is like that – sometimes she can be too honest and it hurts. But deep down I know she is right so I can't argue back. I want a man like Tom from *The Good Life* on the telly. He's kind and you can't imagine him screaming with a hangover or punching Felicity Kendal in the head if his football team got beat.

We sat in silence a while and then I gathered the weans and we walked to get the big green bus back down to our tenements, just as Alan the delivery man arrived. He is always keen to speak to Janine and runs up the stairs two at a time, carrying two crates of lemonade and orangeade. I think he likes her.

When will this weather break?

Got home and forgot Laddie was locked in and he'd pissed the floor and Mrs Wilson was shouting at Derek.

This is not Ipanema.

CHAPTER 6

2019
Day three
Sharon

By lunchtime when I went back to the flat the sky was overcast and the leaves were falling everywhere. I nearly slipped on them taking the rubbish out, but managed to right myself and grab on to the railings.

Betty was watching me from her bedroom and, seeing me slip, threw open her window and shouted, 'Watch yerself, hen, thon wet leaves will kill you!'

'Thanks, Betty.' She missed nothing.

I got back into the flat and, after an age of fiddling with buttons, I managed to put on a small wash in Mum's front-loader. I was suddenly reminded of the old twin tub she used to haul out and hook over the sink, spending a whole day getting all the laundry done.

I stuck on the radio and listened to BBC Scotland, then ran a hoover around her living room and did a wee bit of housework. There was a phone-in debate about whether Catholic schools should exist and a man called in and shouted about the Orange Walk parades and I said, 'Nothing changes, Glasgow,' to the kettle as I wiped around the units. I couldn't wait to get back to Mum.

The excitement of contacting Isa had kept me buoyed; wait till Mum heard that.

I drove to the hospital again and sipped my coffee in the recyclable cup that Clyde had given me as I climbed the stairs, walked through the myriad corridors to the backdrop of low voices and beds being pushed about on squeaky wheels, and got to her ward.

She was propped up on several white pillows with her hands on her chest. I thought for a horrible moment she was dead. Then she gently turned her head towards me.

'Hi, Mum,' I said. 'It's beautiful out there, I know it's your favourite time of year but I nearly slipped on my arse on the leaves today.'

She smiled.

Seeing her so reduced and small made my chest hurt. I just couldn't get used to her being so frail and meek. Especially now I was immersed in her diary and her young voice was so fresh in my mind. I kept expecting her to sit up, push her hair behind her ears and launch into a conversation about the price of mince, or laugh at something her neighbours had said.

I put my bag on the floor, took off my coat and dragged the plastic chair towards her bedside. Then I chatted away, the way you do to someone who isn't really listening, just small talk about Janet and John. I am sure I even rambled on about Steven and the shite he's been up to.

The nurses came in and fussed around her bed. I pulled out my iPhone, pressed play and put the phone beside her bed. The sound of 'Hotel California' drifted through the sunlit room and Mum smiled and actually tapped her fingers. I desperately wished she could just talk me through all these emotions and memories. I knew that wouldn't happen. But I was hoping that in her morphine-soaked dreams she was dancing around the room with Laddie jumping at her feet to the beat.

The nurse leaned over the bed, tucked in the sheet and said to me, 'Maybe she would like some music that the elderly enjoy, like Bing Crosby or some big band tunes?'

'She hated that stuff, it's too old for her. My mum loved Meatloaf and The Eagles,' I explained.

The nurse raised an eyebrow as if I was kidding myself; she checked Senga's intravenous drip and had a look at her temperature.

'Mum is younger than Mick Jagger, she was born the same day as David Bowie – she was a young woman once, who loved music,' I told her. Mum faintly jigged her feet to the music as if to back me up. She was still in there somewhere, and I wished she could talk to me about the book.

I still had strong memories of the veranda and that summer. Janine had been funny and full of life; I wondered where she was now.

Reading about how Mum suffered so much at the hands of my dad, and how other women just accepted their lot back then, had really shaken me. I hadn't known my dad had treated her like that. But weak men attacking women still happens to this day; not much has changed, has it?

I tried hard to think of the times I'd seen her and Dad together, but every time I strained to grasp the images the memories were like grainy home videos, out of focus with no dialogue. I wondered if I had deliberately forgotten the arguments and violence. I must have been witness to it; there were tiny snatches of images of Mum crying in the toilet and one strong memory of Dad shouting outside in the street, but they were so out of context I couldn't make sense of it. Was that what trauma did? Your mind just blanked it out to protect you?

I knew he'd left her for a much younger woman; that was something none of us could avoid as we grew up, it was rubbed in our faces as kids, him believing he could recapture his youth and get away from too many kids and too much responsibility. But he'd ended up alone, washing his pants in the bathroom sink of a bedsit near Paisley. What a waste, a life unlived.

He'd died of liver problems when I was twenty-one years old. The drink finally got him. I often wondered if they played the Bay City Rollers at his funeral. None of us went; we didn't want to.

When Mum told me he was ill, I'd once called him from my halls of residence in Bristol. John had got me his number. He'd sounded so broken and sad, but ultimately, he was a stranger to me. He knew nothing about my life. Senga had been everything to us: she'd worked hard and helped me save for the course and books, Dad used to walk past us in the street holding hands with Donna and not even acknowledge us.

John missed him the most, I think, but I don't know why; he was the youngest and had the least time with him. Sometimes there's no working out why things happen.

Lifting my bag from the floor, I pulled out the red book and the brown envelope. I carried them everywhere with me now, as though I couldn't let them out of my sight.

I sat beneath the hospital anglepoise lamp and flicked through some of the photos. There was a wee snap of me standing at our tenement close in a pale pink short dress. I must have been about ten years old. My face was sunburned and I had bare feet in sandals, my dark hair cut in a home-made 'bob' which was squint at one side. Laddie was standing behind me; I had forgotten how big he was. His tongue was lolling out and he was staring straight down the lens. I was sure my mum had taken this photo. I took out my phone and snapped photos of a few of the images and sent them to our family WhatsApp group, so we could all check them out later.

I held each image up and described them to Mum, and then tucked them back into the envelope. She lay there still but with a shadow of a smile on her face again. The late afternoon sun bounced off the city skyscrapers and flooded into the room, one big shaft of light shone right across her bed.

'So, you found the book,' she whispered and then added, 'I love the music.'

We sat until the tea trolley made its way round. Mum sipped some water and I scoffed a damp Jammie Dodger washed down with weak NHS tea.

When she fell asleep again, I walked outside the room and down to the car park and called Janet and John on our WhatsApp. I read them a bit of the diary and brought up the subject of Dad. It was shocking to realise how little Janet and John remembered of him.

'Dad was a prick,' Janet said in her usual off-hand way. 'How is Mum doing?'

'Yeah, Janet is right, fuck Dad, how is Mum?' added John.

'You know, John, it's not great. She's weak but she had a wee sip of water today, plus she said a few words, which was amazing. She's hanging on,' I replied. 'Janet, can you remember Dad much in your life when you were wee?'

I couldn't get Dad out of my head. I wanted to know what they remembered.

She went quiet and I could hear her breathing, then she just let rip. 'He was worse than useless as a father. He was only a few months older than her and yet *he* couldn't handle the responsibility of kids; he was never really there. I have patchy memories of him and Mum fighting, and one good memory of him swinging me about down the park, but other than that he always seemed to be some vague shadow that annoyed us all. Do you remember him much?'

'Yes, I recall the mad outfits he wore and him being drunk at parties or shouting at us round the back court,' I said.

'Yes, the Bay City Rollers tartan, I remember that,' John added with a laugh, and we all went quiet.

John said, 'I remember him trying to show me how to bounce on a space hopper and the times he tried to make me play football. It's a shame really – as much as I get upset about him, he never really seemed to get his life together, and Mum had to be strong because he kept messing her about.'

'I know – looking back, you wonder how we all made it out of there,' I said. 'Look, I'll call you with any more news tomorrow, speak soon.'

'Give her a kiss from us both,' said Janet, and John chimed in with,

'And a wee hug.'

We did have lovely memories as well as the dark ones that the book was throwing up. Mum had been so good with us. God knows how she had the patience: she cuddled us in bed, read stories to us and sometimes, when the wee ones were asleep, she would let me sit up late at the window on hot summer nights and chat to me about stuff that was happening in my life. She was so interested in my world, and in making it bigger than hers. She'd wanted me to have all the opportunities she hadn't had. She would look up to the horizon, as the sun streaked orange over the sky, and say things like, 'You should get a passport and travel, Sharon, go and see all the big oceans, find yourself out there, walk down the streets in New York.' She'd wave her hand at the window, indicating 'out there'. All I could remember seeing was Barlinnie prison and the water towers up in Cranhill. At that age I could only vaguely imagine the ocean, and America beyond that.

The radio would be playing softly in the background as she smoked a ciggie and blew the smoke out the window, watching the neighbours walking home from the chip shop or the pub. I missed that love and affection now. I realised I hadn't thought of Steven nearly as much. My heart was being filled up with real love from people who cared about me and wanted more for me.

I needed to find the rest of Mum's pals and get through the book, to find out why it was so important to Mum. I started the car, got out of the car park and drove to a mini-supermarket in town. There was a dark-haired woman about my age in a two-piece velour tracksuit in front of me in the queue at the till and I was sure I recognised her. My brain began flicking through a guessing game.

She turned round and made full eye-contact and said, 'Sharon, is that you?' She had on a full face of make-up and a bright butterfly clip in her hair, and there were two wee toddlers trying to get her attention. 'Granny, I want one too,' one of them cried as he grabbed her trouser leg, holding a bag of sweets.

'Yeah, sorry, do we know—?' I started to say.

She interrupted me, smiled, and leaned into my space. 'It's me, Gillian Breen; well, I was Breen, I've been Mrs Dunn for years now. We were at school together? I married Tommy Dunn, mind him that used to sell the jumpers and night gowns down the Barras with his maw?'

I was struggling to remember her. 'No, sorry . . . oh, hi, Gillian . . . ' Her grandchild cried louder, and before I could get a full sentence out she spoke again, and she sounded annoyed that I couldn't remember her husband Tommy.

'YOU DO,' she repeated, louder now, and held my arm. 'He used to have asthma and his sister ran away with the guy that looked after the parrots in Calderpark Zoo, remember?'

I had forgotten how determined Glasgow women could be at making you remember their back stories. I fiddled with the quiche I'd chosen and started spacing out my items on the conveyor belt just to distract her.

Her hand gripped my arm more tightly. 'YOU DO! Mind, his granny Mrs Foy lived beside your maw's pal Sandra in Glenfadden Street years ago?'

This stopped me in my tracks. 'Sandra? Do you remember Sandra? Is she still there?'

She finally let go of her vice-like grip on my arm. 'Aye, I remember Sandra, she was the most beautiful woman I ever saw. She's moved away now, though, don't know where. So, do you remember my Tommy now? He lived near your old house up the back road.'

I had a good think as she stared at me without blinking. I could picture him now. And I could remember her more clearly too.

'Did he have a birthmark on his face?' I asked.

She brightened at this, her face becoming even more animated. 'Aye, it was a red mark the shape of a boomerang.'

Exhausted, I nodded my head. 'Yes, I do remember him: he had black hair and a Chopper bike?'

We both let out a big laugh, breaking the tension. 'Yes, that was him,' she said. Finally, we could move this on.

'How is he?' I asked as I started to push my shopping down the conveyor belt.

'Dead. I hear your mammy is in the hospital – how is she?'

I was temporarily stumped once more at the sudden change this conversation had taken. 'I'm so sorry for your loss, Gillian,' I said.

'Och, it's OK, it was years ago. Listen, say hello to your mammy for me and any time you want a natter, let me know. Is that you back up the road in your mammy's flat? How many grand-weans do you have? I have six. Find me on Facebook, I'm there under Gillian Dunn, you'll see a picture of me and my Alsatian, Rex,' she said as she stuffed her purse into her bag.

Before I could answer any of her questions, she turned away, took the arms of both the kids and headed out of the shop.

Gillian Breen – what a throwback. I'd wanted to ask her more about Sandra; maybe I would look her up on Facebook and see what I could find out. I remembered I'd had a fight with Gillian once at school.

When I finally got back to the flat, I ate my quiche, had a cup of tea, and settled down to read again.

1976
September

The kids are back at school, the weather is cooling down and my Sharon got them all up and out and dressed in time. She's a great lassie. She used her birthday money to buy me cigarettes last night. Not a word from her useless father on the actual day – poor kid was watching for the postman and didn't think anyone noticed. I couldn't give her a proper party but I let her choose her tea in the supermarket and I did her hair for her. And Janine came down with her girls to see us – said she wanted to get out of the house for a while, don't know why.

Laddie has been missing for two days but there's a bitch on heat across the back so he's probably out there waiting to jump her – he gets more action than me.

Lorna from across the street brought a bottle of BelAir hair lacquer over last night and I did big rollers in her hair, she looked like Barbra Streisand going to the bingo. She is finally off the Valium – knocked her half mad, it did. Am really happy for her – those Valium pills have half the women round our way walking about like zombies. It makes them forget how shit their lives are, but the kids are left with half-dead mothers who can't cope with reality. Isa tried the 'goofy pills' for about six months when she felt depressed and they definitely turned her brain – and it took her a year to come off them. She got sweats and dizzy spells when she stopped and spent a whole fair fortnight on her knees crying. They should stop giving them out and just fucking listen to women for a change.

I got Sharon some birthday clothes from Bunty's catalogue, as well as some leather trousers for me, very Suzi Quatro but they baked my legs and the smell made Laddie horny and he tried to pump me in front of the priest who was visiting Frank downstairs. Our Sharon is very sensitive, she's missing her dad, I think. She spotted him at the Co-op with his new girlfriend and he ignored her. What a prick of a man. He now has a Rod Stewart haircut and giant flares, I think Donna just wanted a Ken doll to dress up and bagged herself a fat unemployed alcoholic. Can't wait to see what happens when she finds out he drinks all the food money and likes to punch you in the face because he got sacked from work.

Wee John has taken up tap dancing at the community centre. He's the only boy there but he loves it, so who cares. Janet has been thrown out the Brownies for swearing at Brown Owl. I've met Brown Owl and I'm sure she deserved it.

CHAPTER 7

2019
Day three
Sharon

Dad was such an embarrassment. Like John, I remembered seeing him around the housing scheme dressed in big tartan flares, hobbling about on platforms holding Donna's hand. She was a blonde, skinny young woman with really thick make-up, that's all I could recall. Her dad owned the ice-cream van and she always looked very well dressed in the latest fashions. Mammy used to say she was a spoiled only child and got everything she wanted.

Mum never really slagged Dad off to us, or, if she did, I didn't recall it. I think she tried to keep the options open for him to have a decent relationship with us. She really lived in the hope that he would one day be a dad to us. It must have been so embarrassing for her to have him around her social circle with a teenage girl on his arm. She took it well, though, and reading the diary has shown me she had a lucky escape. We all did.

Imagine wanting my dad and dressing him up as your favourite pop star! He really was a sad case. In terms of useless men, it seemed I had more in common with my mum than I wanted to admit. According to his Facebook page, Steven had started wearing cargo pants and sporting a soul patch, and he was holding the hand of a slim blonde woman. His new profile picture looked strained, as if he was holding in his stomach. He had weird sports sunglasses wrapped around his head. Trial separation my arse; we all knew what was happening here, and I needed to face up to it and lawyer up.

57

I decided to call him. I'd set off in a hurry three days ago to get to Glasgow. I'd left him a message on the way up the M6 for him to check on the house – he'd moved out a few months ago to 'give us some space' and discreetly moved in with his bendy new yoga woman, but he still had a key.

'Hello, Sharon, how are you?' he opened, like a professional game show host. He sounded out of breath.

'Why are you puffed out, Steven? Are you jogging off your quinoa flatbread?'

'No need to be sarcastic, Sharon; I was actually running up the stairs. What do you want?' he replied. I could picture him running his hands through his sweaty hair and grimaced slightly.

'I just wanted to let you know I'm staying in Glasgow for a while; Mum is very poorly. I'll be working remotely. Give your daughter a call and see how your granddaughter is doing, and make sure you water the garden if you go round to the house, will you?'

'I'm sorry to hear about your mum,' he said.

'Don't lie, you never liked her.'

'Actually, I admire Senga's strength. *She* didn't like *me* – remember after our wedding she said I had more faces than Big Ben?' he replied.

'She wasn't fucking wrong, was she? Look, I don't want to hold you back from your ten thousand steps a day, you boring flan, I just wanted to let you know what I was doing,' I said. And I hung up.

I suddenly felt so . . . free. Finally, I didn't have to step around his myriad insecurities and let him control every conversation. Fuck him. He had clearly moved on, and it was time for me to do the same. I suspected this meant we were now definitely heading for divorce . . . but that was a thought for another day. I would have to talk to Louise first.

Before I went to bed, I uploaded a new photo of me in the coffee shop, with Clyde standing in the background holding up my coffee. I didn't need to hold in my abs: I still had a pretty athletic figure and my mum's good bone structure.

I wished she would come around and let me speak to her. I called her ward to check up before I went to sleep and the nurse called Shirley said Senga was 'surprising everyone with her tenacity'. They had stabilised her drugs and they had begun feeding her a little bit. Shirley said that after I left today, Senga had woken up and asked for me. I felt so upset: guilt swept over me. I would stay for longer tomorrow.

Outside, I could hear a fox screaming as I turned on the floral bedside lamp in the bedroom.

1976
September

Bunty took her gold ring to the pawn shop and got four pounds. Her kids need new school shoes, they seem to grow an inch a week.

She came up to mine after the kids went to school. She's got twin boys who run around with my Janet and when the three of them are together it's like living in the seventh circle of hell. They got sent home from school the other week for passing the class hamster round like a football and some poor wee girl got hit in the face with it and apparently her mammy says she's so traumatised she hasn't slept in four days. Bunty says boys will be boys and leaves them to it but if they were my kids I think I'd be chasing big Lorna for some of her Valium – can you imagine having two kids at the same time? No wonder Bunty likes a drink.

I had just finished the cleaning job in the Calvary pub behind the bingo hall. You'd think ashtrays hadn't been invented – the floor was covered in fag ends and don't even start me on men who just piss the floor of the toilet. So, stinking of bleach and smoke, we sat down and ate rolls and square sausage with mugs of tea. Bunty was telling me that she has ditched her latest boyfriend, big Frankie – turns out he's been seen up the Masonic club with another lassie and, as Bunty says, she's 'not playing second fiddle to a woman who wears orange culottes'.

I don't know how she knows what the other lassie wears but Bunty is like the Blackhill Transmitter – that's her nickname as she knows everything about everyone. A dog can't piss round here without Bunty getting wind of it. Her knowledge of the entire community is encyclopaedic. That's how we first met, when we were seven years old – she moved into our street from Govan, marched through the back courts, climbed over our fence, came up to Sandra and me, pointed a finger at my chest and said, 'I heard your big brother had a twisted testicle.' I didn't know how she knew this but I soon discovered Bunty's mum was the cleaner in the doctor's surgery and Bunty knew EVERYTHING about everyone. Me, Bunty, Sandra, and then Philomena and Isa (who joined the gang later when they moved into the next close) became firm friends. Bunty has wee twin boys to big Jackie MacNamara and he ran away to Spain when she told him she was pregnant. Apparently, he does a brilliant Shirley Bassey tribute act. When Bunty found that out she said, 'That explains everything,' as he took her good strappy sandals.

We worry her big mouth will get her into trouble one day, along with her shady dealing. She's treading dangerous ground spending time with the Devlins too.

Isa is the real bold one of our group; she can sing brilliant as well and her home perms are legendary. She still has this on/off relationship with an American soldier from Tallahassee, down in the port at Dunoon where they have a naval base. It's a big draw for all the Glasgow lassies sick of men with potato faces and no teeth – they head down on the ferry to the coast and meet big handsome Yanks who talk like movie stars and buy them drinks. Isa says Dunoon is like being in California but with sideways rain and no palm trees. She keeps trying to drag me down on the train with her, but I'm not sure. I'd like to have someone to talk to, but I'm also not ready to let the kids meet a new man, they can do without that stress. Unless he has his own place and trust me that won't happen – this isn't a Jackie Collins book, it's my life, and this is Shettleston in Glasgow. I can talk to my diary instead!

Made sausage casserole and after dinner Laddie came home and choked on a bone and caused a huge screaming session with the kids. We managed to get it out of his throat. He needs to stop digging old carcasses out of the bins. I will keep an eye on him. What a night.

Watched *Coronation Street*. Annie and Alf have had a car crash, and Albert comes to Glasgow when Hilda threatens to sue him over a dog incident.

CHAPTER 8

2019
Day four
Sharon

I sat for hours at the hospital today, Mum was drifting in and out of consciousness, not quite as settled as she had been. I ate lunch at her bedside and read out some crossword questions, probably bored her rigid, but I wanted to be here if she woke up. The doctor came in, checked her vitals and said, 'Senga is a fighter, go and get some rest, nothing will change tonight.' I didn't want to go, but he seemed sure and I needed a shower. Getting my bag off the floor, I patted the side to check I had the diary in there.

As I left, I switched on the radio so she could hear some music, as she'd seemed to enjoy that yesterday. She was never one for silence.

I had really wanted to talk to her about all the memories her diary had thrown up. I had looked up Dunoon online and read all about how the US Navy stationed there had been like 'America in Scotland'. They'd imported their fancy big cars and had American shops at the base selling Twinkies, US newspapers and many of their favourite foods.

So many of the American guys had married local women and taken them back home when the naval base had closed. Clearly this hadn't happened to Isa; what had gone wrong?

I could have grown up in California if Mum had bagged herself a big, handsome American, but I supposed things didn't always work out like that. As far as I could tell Mum hadn't gone near the naval base, she'd stayed in Shettleston and got on with her lot.

63

Sitting in the car, I checked my emails and scrolled through Facebook and my socials. I'd found Gillian Dunn and Rex, and I'd seen that she was linked to other people I remembered from school.

I'd also seen the latest picture on Instagram of Steven's new girlfriend sitting on a mountain in a yoga pose, with 'LIVE, LOVE, BREATH' written in pink italics over the image. If only she could spell as well as she could bend. I really wasn't stalking them, honestly, but after speaking to him on the phone I couldn't stop myself checking up on her. I couldn't wait to see him dressed in some ridiculous Lycra outfit next. I now planned to nickname his yoga girlfriend 'Donna'.

As I was driving back to Mum's, a text pinged into my phone. It was from Bunty, she'd *heard the news from Isa. Lots to talk about, hen.*

I texted back to ask if she knew how I could contact Philomena and Sandra, but she didn't reply. I supposed I would just have to wait until she got back to me.

1976
November

Woke up with Laddie on the bed, barking. That bastard Billy was at the door, wanting back in. Pleading with me – seems Dirty Donna has got bored with his lazy work-shy arse and his mammy Margaret won't let him stay, she's so upset he's been hanging about with the Devlins and that's something she will not tolerate. Messing women and kids about? Carry right on, Billy boy. Hanging about with Irish Catholic two-bit gangsters? NO! 'He's your man, Senga, you need to look after him,' was all she could say when we discussed her stupid son. Honestly, if my John grew up and messed a woman about, I would kick his arse. Why don't mothers raise their sons to be good to other women?

I hate him upsetting the kids, and I wanted him gone so I went to the front door to try and calm him down.

'Let me in, Senga,' he shouted.

I pushed my back against the door with all my might.

'I still have a key, you know – I could come in at night, you mad cow,' he shouted through the letterbox.

My heart sank – he probably does have a key. I will get Davie Dunsmore to change my locks later. He's the man for that job.

'Billy, get back from the door or one of the neighbours will call the police and you don't want that.' My throat was dry – he can still frighten me when he starts his madness. Old memories of that wee teenage lassie I used to be when he dominated my life and made me scared of my own shadow.

Then Sharon appeared behind me, told me to leave and then she went out and sent him down the stairs. I heard her shouting, 'First cut is the deepest, Da,' as she slammed the door. He's been parading around in his Rod Stewart outfit again. My Sharon can be right sarcastic for a teenager. Good on her.

Got the kids sat down in front of *The Tomorrow People*. It's all science fiction stuff, but they love it. I wish I had a 'jolt belt' that took me to other places, I would go straight to America and hang

out with Rocky – Sylvester Stallone. I bet you he wouldn't sleep
with a lassie that dressed him up in glitter. Money was tight this
week so the kids are eating mainly soup. Janine came down to see
us, she said there's some man pushing notes through her door,
saying he loves her and wants to look after her, and she is sure she
heard someone climb up her veranda at three in the morning but
she couldn't see anyone when she got up. I am worried sick for
her, being way up beside the old Gartloch Asylum, but I never mentioned that to her, don't want her petrified. She lent me her big
soup pot and I had a ham hock on the go, so at least the kids are
warm and fed. That big pot has done the rounds in this scheme,
big enough to boil a blanket in and wide enough to use as a baby
bath! We all get a turn of it when it's needed.

Sandra was up last night and we smoked through half a packet
of cigs. She was nursing another sore face, and she looks so thin
and tired. I hate that bastard of a man, but his mum says as soon
as Sandra gets pregnant he will calm down. Can you imagine
putting up with this shit with a belly the size of a small couch
and puffy ankles, though? 'I can't have kids to him, Senga,' she
pleaded as she sat wringing her hands in my living room. So, we
came up with a plan. She is now secretly taking my birth control
pills as her doctor knows the priest and isn't up for that, and my
doctor doesn't care so her secret is safe with me. The last thing
she needs is a baby, and it's not as if there's sex on the horizon for
me! My clamshell is out of action!

Even Sandra's mum is starting the see the light, but Catholics
don't get divorced round here. I wish Sandra could leave and start
again somewhere else. We've talked about starting a wee savings
club for her but she always says she couldn't do it. She told me she
tried before. The last time she put some cash aside she managed
to save nearly a hundred pounds. She hid it in her big Lladro vase
and that bastard Jim found it – apparently, he owed the Devlins
some money and he took the lot. When she went to find her stash
there was just a scrawled note from Jim saying, 'You hide money
again and I will sort you out, bitch.' She managed to calm him

down by explaining that she was saving for a layette for the baby they might soon have. That shut him up for a while.

But you never know if she might need our help at some point, so we need to get planning and start putting away a few quid, a wee 'runaway fund', so to speak.

Off to the steamie tomorrow. I've got the old pram and all the kids' clothes and bedsheets bundled and ready to go. One big wash day and that's the whole house done for the week. Sharon is good at rinsing the weans' underwear at the sink for me and the twin tub is good for wee washings in the summer and getting it out the back to dry off.

In the winter the steamie is the place to be and I love it. If you miss any episodes of *Coronation Street* you can catch up on it over the big sinks, as the women talk about nothing else. It's the one place where you don't see any men, and the smell of the steaming hot soapy water is good for the soul.

I have another cleaning job coming up too, a big house in the West End, as living on social security money with three kids is just too fucking tough. But trying to make a wage, pay the bills and feed four people and a scabby dog is a hard show, and that bastard Billy hasn't put a hand in his pocket to pay a penny for the kids.

I suppose dressing up as Rod Stewart must cost a fortune.

Doing secret cleaning jobs and claiming on the social is scary as fuck – you can get the jail if you get caught and there's always some old nosy bastard that'll grass you up. Bunty keeps her ear to the ground for me. I take a different route every time I head out for the jobs, like a sexy French Résistance member heading out to beat the Nazis, except with a chamois cloth and some bleach. Bunty knows everything – she would tell me if anyone has sussed what I am doing.

Bought the kids new shoes this week out of the Co-op. All three of them keep growing like weeds. I can put lino in my own shoes to make them last the winter and I have some boots I got from the second-hand shop.

Went to see *All the President's Men* with Janine at the Odeon cinema – she took me out for a treat. Saw big Alan from the Alpine van there on his own. He was wearing a sheepskin coat and sunglasses, swaggering about beside the ice-cream counter. He wanted to sit with us but we said no. Me and Janine laughed about it later.

It was all about the Watergate scandal in America, I didn't quite grasp all the politics but by fuck Robert Redford is one hot man. Bet you he doesn't sit about the local club arguing about Catholics and picking his nose.

CHAPTER 9

2019
Day four
Sharon

After a few hours of work online, a quick shower and a fish supper, I'd come back to sit with Mum. Dusk was falling over Glasgow and the lights were coming on all over the city. You could see the traffic from the hospital window, moving along the M8, all the red lights heading out to the suburbs, taking people back to their homes and into the comfort of their families.

I sat with the book on my knee as Mum lay breathing and the machines softly beeped, nurses moved about on squeaking soles, visitors arrived for the other patients in the busy ward. Adults looking strained, kids staring into each room as they held on to their parents.

I got up and shut the curtain on her window and stared at Mum, just lying there.

This diary was breaking my heart at times. It was making me look at my own life and see how trivial my issues were, but also how I tended to bury my feelings.

That couldn't be good for me, could it? OK, my husband had pissed off with a young yoga vegan, but, if the marriage ended, my real problems would be just legal and administrative. I'd known we were drifting apart for a long time; I'd started to find myself disagreeing with Steven so much more, about everything. If we split for good, I could support myself. I had a job and we would sell the house. And Louise had a family of her own now.

We'd given her the best upbringing we could, had never worn our pain on our skin the way my mum and her pals had. We'd internalised and got therapy. They'd got drunk and shouted and still fed their families through every single drama. Louise had been a much wilder teenager than I had been, but she had stayed closer to me too.

Senga had worked miracles with so little money. I didn't remember ever being hungry or poor. We never had the latest fashions or toys, but nobody we knew did. I found it shocking that Dad used to harass her regularly, despite not paying a penny for any of us.

I'd found a photo stuck in the front inside cover of the book, a picture of my mum and dad before the babies, and they actually looked good together. They were so young, though, barely sixteen. Mum had her dark hair short and teased out like Jackie Kennedy, and was wearing a dress that was plain but nipped in to show off a tiny waist. Dad's hair was swept back, and he wore a polo neck as he stood with his arm around her shoulders. She was laughing as he grinned and pointed at the camera. They looked genuinely happy, but somehow that black brick of the Gorbals and the sooty skyline behind them made everything else look so grim.

Three babies in, he was gone, and she was ducking and diving to keep her head above water. I wished I could go back in time and do more for her.

The machines round her bed were still flashing and beeping softly as I brushed her hair and washed her face with a flannel. I looked out of the big Victorian hospital window and watched the sky darken over the rooftops of Glasgow. Church steeples spiking the deep blue sky, the deepening roar of the motorway as rush hour steadily built up. I had thought about reading some of the diary out to her, but I was worried it might upset her. She had smiled a few times in her sleep while I'd been there. I hoped she was dreaming of dancing on *Top of the Pops* (but not the episodes with Jimmy Savile). I told her that Bunty and Isa had contacted me and she stirred and opened her eyes, her face growing serious. 'It's about time we were all together again,' she said, quietly, and stared at the ceiling.

'Yes,' I replied, 'it is.'

1976
November

Got a letter from my cousin Monica in Canada. She sent some nice photos of the family and their house. We've always got on well – I was so sad when my uncle got a job as an engineer in Vancouver and they all moved away. She's never been as gobby as me; she thinks before she opens her mouth. I should be more like that. Her house looks like something out of *Gone with the Wind* but with heavy snow and fewer women in big frilly frocks carrying satin parasols. She's always very busy, gets involved in committees and causes. Monica is kind and I write her long letters back, all the news about the family and what's happening in my life. She says I am a good writer and she can actually 'see' the people and situations I am writing about. She said I should write for a magazine and send in some short stories. Can you imagine? I think she's just being nice, boosting my confidence because she knows I am on my own and my man left me.

We had a menage meeting, everyone except Sandra who was at her mum's, and we smoked a full packet of fags and Isa brought up a bottle of Blue Nun wine she stole off the priest when she was cleaning his house. We felt dead posh drinking it. I was being Margo Leadbetter from *The Good Life* and she was being Joanna Lumley. Philomena brought up a home-cooked quiche and Bunty had a bag of kids' corduroy dungarees that she got from her pal who works on the delivery vans. They were in beautiful colours; my John got a pair in bright purple and Janet picked the navy ones. Bunty is selling the rest down the club on Sunday.

'That's me sold all the football cards at the factory, Bunty,' Philomena said. 'Can you pick me up some more at the club this weekend? That Isobel McGuire won three cards in one week. We should take her to the bingo with us one night and see if her lucky streak rubs off.'

Isa laughed. 'She's not that lucky – have you seen her husband?'

Bunty and Isa made us howl with laughter as they both took turns with my washing board, rattling bottle tops off it as they sang 'Blanket on the Ground'.

It was good seeing all my pals. Everyone is just getting on with life and I am feeling more secure since Davie changed my locks and I have new keys to the door. That idiot Billy has a lot to answer for.

Wee John was crying for his daddy last night. You know, it's hard trying to explain to the kids that their dad is a bastard and at the same time accept they might still love the idea of him. You spend more time biting back the words you really want to say, but my mammy said if I spend my time running their daddy down I will only make them disrespectful and it will come back to haunt me. I suppose she's right but by fuck it's hard not to. He doesn't deserve their love or loyalty, he needs a right kick up the arse. But at the end of the day I picked that man, so I have to make the best of a bad job.

John has been getting bullied at school by Gordon Wilson's big fat son Stuart. I went round to his door and threatened to kick his head in if he didn't sort his son out.

'Your boy is a fucking monster,' I shouted at him as he stood at his door, the smell of boiled mince and lager floating past his big bloated body.

'He can't help it,' Gordon said. 'He has anger issues, the teacher said.'

Stuart was stood in the hall staring, smirking, sticking two fingers up at me behind his dad's back. I wanted to punch the wee fucker.

'If my John comes home with one more bruise I am going to batter you, because I have anger issues too,' I shouted and walked down his close. A neighbour across from him came out, a thin woman with a thick Irish accent, and said, 'He's a wee bastard, he tried to tie a firework to my cat's tail. The whole family needs putting in the madhouse.'

She's right. Well, his dad's been told and I am not going to let this go. I will get Billy involved if I have to. I mean he's no hard man but he can use his fists when he needs to, I'm testimony to that. He could always shout on the Devlins if he needs to put the frighteners on someone.

John is scared to walk to school and my Sharon is at the big school now so she can't protect him. Our Janet, even though she's only ten, has offered to help but she can go a bit overboard with her temper. The teacher says she has a 'very dark' sense of humour and writes ghost stories for her school essays that frighten everyone. She told a wee lassie in her class who lives up in Sandyhills that dead people float in the windows at night and suck the breath out of the babies in the house. What would possess her to say that?

I think Janet likes to shock, she's just funny and loves scary stories. But I'm worried that she will strangle Stuart with her skipping rope outside the tuck shop, as that seems to be her weapon of choice. She is teaching Bunty's twins how to climb up the drainpipes. She said it was for fire safety but I am already terrified I will see her running along the rooftops and climbing in people's windows. She is fucking fearless, is our Janet. She's either going to be a mad creative genius, or a cat burglar.

I want John to be happy and to do the things he loves, but he needs to toughen up a bit too. I told him to join the local football team but he says he hates it. It's a shame, he's so good on his feet as well. He keeps saying his daddy would stick up for him if he was here. Maybe that's the one thing Billy would do. I try my best. I can be scary as hell when I need to.

The kids came home from school and made bread pieces on sugar and I let them watch *Blue Peter* till the dinner was made. We got four bottles of ginger on tick off Alan on the Alpine van – I told him I would pay him next week. He said, 'No problem, Senga, I might catch you if you're up at Janine's next week, eh?' I was about to go back inside when I wondered how would he know when I am up at Janine's?

'Alan, are you a spy for the social security or the Russians? Are you watching my movements?' I laughed, but I was half-serious. What the fuck was that about?

'No, no.' He grinned and leaned against his door. 'It's just, I've noticed you up there sometimes! How is she, by the way? I haven't seen her much . . . '

'She's fine, Alan. I'll be seeing you,' I said as I shut the door. The kids were wanting their lemonade. I need to speak to Janine about him.

The weans saw a programme on TV about Disneyland in America, and it just looked so magical with all the Mickey Mouse characters. My wee John was mesmerised. 'Mammy can we go there?' he squealed.

'If my name was Carnegie you could,' I replied.

Carnegie is the famous rich Scottish man who went to America and made his billions. Every Scottish kid I knew frequently got told if only they were called 'Carnegie', they could have everything they ever wanted. I've never once met anyone called Carnegie in my life so far. Even a week at Butlin's in Ayr is out of my reach right now, with the debt I'm dealing with. Bunty goes every year with the twins to the holiday camp. She says they have a flashing electric volcano in the tropical bar that goes off every night and everyone cheers when it happens. I wish I could take the kids for a decent holiday away from all of this, but it looks unlikely.

Watched *Coronation Street*; Gail has started working at the Rover's and Stan has left Hilda.

Bunty let me tape her new Stevie Wonder LP on to my portable cassette deck (I didn't ask how she'd got it). I am making a mix tape for Janine to cheer her up as she is still getting weird notes through her door. I'll go and deliver it and check up on her.

CHAPTER 10

2019
Day five
Sharon

After a fitful night's sleep full of dreams of old buildings and drunk men shouting at women, I put in a few hours working on press releases and calls to clients, got some breakfast and took a long, hot shower.

As I got dressed, I wondered why we had all moved away from Glasgow. Had we been reacting to our childhood? My own plans to travel the world had been thwarted by my husband's career coming first and by being a very busy working mother. Things hadn't changed much at all, had they?

My mum hadn't always understood the reality of our lives back then: she hadn't fully realised for ages why John was bullied so badly. I found that astounding given her absolutely candid take on life. Maybe she hadn't wanted to face the fact of John being gay back in the seventies; it was a different time.

I remembered Janet's scary stories being truly horrifying; she'd often turn up at random funerals in the housing scheme to chat about the dead to their relatives. It was funny to think back to her odd sense of humour but no surprise that, after a very rocky time with drugs in her early twenties, her creativity had blossomed and made her so successful in the theatre. I supposed we'd all inherited our mother's creative gift for writing and expression, one way or another. We had all, in our own way, made it out of there. I knew she was proud of the three of us; she certainly told us often enough when we spoke to her.

I was accosted again by Betty and Maggie, Mum's neighbours, as I was leaving the flat. They were the only people I spoke to in Glasgow, outside of the hospital staff and Clyde, and they were hardly sparkling company. They grilled me as I fumbled for my keys; I gave them a quick update on Senga's condition and then the conversation moved on to my marriage.

'What's happening with your man, then?' Maggie demanded as she sucked on a sweetie that clattered around her false teeth.

Both stood in pale blue poplin coats and wide-fitting shoes with handbags over their arms, on their way to the shopping centre. Their faces clearly demanded answers. Betty asked, 'What is your actual job?' as she offered me a barley sugar, which I politely refused and she promptly just put it in my pocket 'for later'.

Trying to explain what I did to two women who didn't understand 'branding and market influences' and who really just wanted to know why my man wasn't with me any more, was really awkward and painful.

Betty asked me if my menopause was bothering me because she thought I looked flushed. I had forgotten how forthright old Glasgow women could be. 'My pee started to smell like sugar puffs when I hit the change,' Maggie offered, out of nowhere. I gave them a run-down on my hormonal status and that seemed to appease them. I showed them photos of my granddaughter on my iPhone and they finally released me from questioning. Till the next time, and I knew without a doubt there would be a next time.

I really missed my daughter and the baby; it felt like ages since we'd spoken. I would FaceTime them tonight to catch up.

I headed along to the coffee shop before the hospital and it was almost empty. Clyde was working, and because he wasn't run off his feet we had a longer chat. He leaned on the counter and drank an espresso.

'How you coping, Sharon?' he asked. I'd told him I was visiting Mum.

'I'm fine, thanks, just dodged Mum's neighbours. I had forgotten how nosy wee Glasgow women are,' I said, laughing.

'Yep, welcome to Glasgow, where everyone knows your name.'
He smiled. It was easy to chat to Clyde; he had a nice comfortable
way about him.

'Have you always lived here?' I asked.

He told me he was forty-eight and worked with a local rock
band as well as running a few other coffee shops. He was such
good company and I suddenly realised I was lonely; it had been
ages since I had spoken about myself and my life to a stranger.

I sat on a stool at the counter and drank my latte. Clyde asked
me how things were panning out at Mum's, and whether I was
staying in Glasgow for long, so I ended up pouring out the whole
story of Mum's illness, the family dynamics and the big red book.
He was really intrigued.

'That sounds like a time capsule; you're lucky to have the memories,' he said, wiping the counter. 'My mum left a pile of debt
and a parakeet.'

The doorbell clanged and some office workers streamed in. I
slid off the metal stool and made my way to a table at the window
to let him get on with his job.

Talking to him made me even more determined to find Philomena and Sandra for Mum. As he served a customer, I pulled out my
phone and texted Isa to ask if she knew how I could contact them.

She texted back: *Yes, will be in touch.* I wondered if I should look
for Janine or any of the others too. *Let me know if you hear anything,* I replied, and waited for an answer, but nothing came back.

I noticed Clyde had a big circle of friends who popped into the
café and chatted away as he worked. There was a girl with sharp
bobbed hair and eyeliner so precise I presumed she got it tattooed
on. Was she his girlfriend?

I felt very old among these vibrant people who seemed to chat
easily and laugh loudly and spend hours lounging over big leather
chairs. In the old days, you were turfed out of places if you took
up the seats longer than necessary.

I watched Clyde move about, picking up cups, making coffee,
turning up the music, helping mothers move high chairs for

babies, bending down to make a fuss of wee woolly dogs, and I realised with a jolt that I liked Clyde and his leather sofas.

Thanking him for the coffee, I left the café and headed for the Royal Infirmary. 'See you later, Sharon,' he shouted as the door pinged behind me.

My favourite nurse, Shirley, was at Mum's bedside when I arrived at the hospital. 'Is she OK?' I asked, panicked, as I moved quickly to her bedside.

'She's fine, she was singing "Devil Gate Drive" with me earlier on, weren't you, Senga?' Shirley said as she changed Mum's water beaker.

Mum smiled and held Shirley's hand.

'Aye, she loved Suzi Quatro,' I said.

'Wonder what she's doing now?' Shirley said. 'Probably wearing leather trousers in an old folks' home.'

Today might be a better day.

Isa: Bunty, what do we do about Senga? Her Sharon contacted me again, she has a lot of questions about back then. She wants to contact Philomena and Sandra.

> *Bunty: I'm messaging Sharon too. Say nothing until we can all meet in Glasgow. When can you get here?*

Isa: I can't leave straight away. I'll let you know when I'm on my way and where I'm staying, then let's meet up. Lots to discuss.

> *Bunty: We all need to have the same story – and we need to know what's in that diary. Will call Philomena too, so she knows what's going on. She's the closest to the hospital so maybe she can try and see Senga and Sharon now? Say nothing about Sandra.*

1976
December

I had the lassies over to plan for the Christmas Day dinner and have a wee get-together. Sandra couldn't make it; I hope she's OK.

I have saved up some Green Shield stamps, the menage money, the Kensitas cigarette coupons and the Co-op dividend card to be able to get the kids some Christmas presents. Billy's mum gave me £20 to get the weans some toys as her useless son couldn't put his hand in his own pocket.

Janet wants a 'Stretch Armstrong' doll, which makes perfect sense: she would literally tear the limbs off anyone if she got the chance. Wee John wants a bike, and Sharon asked for some nice platform sandals from Chelsea Girl. It's hard trying to give them everything they want; but I have finally started that new job, cash-in-hand cleaning Mrs Bradshaw's big house up the West End of Glasgow. Six bedrooms and a conservatory. She has three older kids who have fucking EVERYTHING – one even has a portable telly in her bedroom. Can you imagine that? A wee telly you can watch lying in your bed.

Mrs Bradshaw is a good-hearted woman and already has given me some dresses her daughters have grown out of for my Sharon. Sharon loves it – she got a Biba frock in blue and wee John said she looked like Lulu in it. Sharon sent a thank-you letter to Mrs Bradshaw. My kids might be skint but they have good manners.

My mammy scrubbed stairs and cleaned the big houses in the Southside and my dad did back shifts in the shipyards to keep everyone fed. You do what you have to.

This year, Isa, her mum Cathy, Bunty and her twins, Philomena and her kids and my cousin Bridie are coming around for Christmas dinner. Sandra will be with Jim at his mum's. It will be a full house so we'll need to get the big pasting table out and borrow folding chairs from the church hall. Janet stole the baby Jesus from the class Nativity and he's sat beside the fireplace. I need to get him back before he melts or the dog chews him.

Christmas Day

Went food shopping the other day and the supermarket is now full of Brussels sprouts, frozen quiche and duck pâté. Am not that experimental, but I saw a recipe for a gelatine fish salad in Mrs Bradshaw's recipe cards and thought I would give it a go. Honest to God, it was so bad the kids were crying and even Laddie the dog refused to eat it.

So, no more fancy food. We stuck to the classic chicken, roast potatoes, wee sausages and gravy for the dinner. Afterwards we had Arctic roll and raspberry jelly. The kids loved it.

Wee Bridie, like Isa's mum Cathy, has womb problems after having eleven kids. Listening to her and Cathy compare prolapse stories in between downing sherry and singing 'White Christmas' was hysterical. Bridie keeps talking about her 'bits' falling out, which makes me feel ill, and watching her hoist up the big forty-eight-hour girdle to hold her in is a sight to behold. Bridie looks great for her age, she tells everyone that people mistake her for Meg Mortimer from the TV series *Crossroads*. My Janet says she looks like the man that dresses as a woman from that American TV show *M.A.S.H.* I laughed myself into a kink at that.

Billy came around drunk and shouted abuse up at the window. I went down round the back and he tried to grab me by the hair near Davie's coal bunker, but he was too slow and I pushed him on to the back stairs.

'Watch yourself, Senga, I know people that could hurt you,' he mumbled.

I shouted, 'I know people who could hurt me and it's fucking you! Stop coming around here Billy, you're scaring the weans.' I went back upstairs but I was shaking. What a carry-on. I don't need this.

Isa showed us some photos of her American boyfriend and went on about him taking her back to the USA. She was all misty-eyed and giggly – it must be more serious than I thought. Bunty said to me in the kitchen that she's heard he's a big Yankee liar and has a wife back home. I said it was just nice to see Isa happy and to keep that quiet, she'll soon find out if she needs to.

Billy was still round the back court, shouting up at the window. We just put the telly up louder and watched *Morecambe and Wise* singing and dancing with newsreader Angela Rippon. Bunty cleared back the chairs and did the high kicks, nearly booted baby Jesus right into the fire, so we screamed with laughter and we let the kids stay up late. It was good but we all wished Sandra could have been with us. We haven't seen her in a wee while. Last time I saw her she took a new pack of birth control pills. Maybe she is starting to see what we can see and is ready to make an escape? I hope so.

CHAPTER 11

2019
Day six
Sharon

Last night I lay in my mum's bed in her flat and thought about how dramatically her life had changed. Or did people just get older and we didn't really notice?

The floral bedspread, curtains and carpet were still pretty overwhelming – when had Senga gone from the woman who wanted to be Suzi Quatro in leathers to a collector of frilly rose-covered cushions?

Had *I* changed that much? Or was I always pretty reliable and predictable in my style and life? The solid, steady route was easiest for me, I was never the Cindy Lauper/Madonna girl, all lace and chains dancing on tables. I could easily have passed for one of Princess Diana's Sloane Rangers in modest frocks and court shoes, studying hard and saving for a pension, even at twenty-seven years old. I was dull, wasn't I?

But Mum had fundamentally changed. Why, and when?

We had never lived in each other's pockets after I'd left, but we were close in our own way. She was always my Mum and always there. Admittedly, when I'd had a child, she had been much more focused on Louise; she'd loved the role of grandmother, and now great-grandmother. Finding out from her red book about the situations she had come through that she had managed to hide from us kids was pretty alarming, yet she'd still managed to have fun.

That Christmas sounded tough for these women – Mum and her pals fighting the system, and the men in their life just making

85

it harder. She'd come home from her cleaning job shattered but still had time for us. I didn't know if I could have that strength. I'd thought my life was falling apart when my NutriBullet stopped working and I couldn't have a smoothie for breakfast. Fucking hell, how life had changed. Could I find that strength in myself?

My daughter Louise had FaceTimed me for a quick chat and it was so good to see her and Poppy, although seeing my own face had been a bit of a shock. My hair looked dull, my roots needed touching up, my otherwise slim face looked puffy and tired. My personalised, bespoke skincare regime had gone to the wall. I had been using Mum's Astral face cream; the smell warmed me with memories and it actually didn't seem to be doing that bad a job on my face. My legs needed waxing but, to be honest, nobody was getting to see them, so I planned to let my winter pelt grow in.

Steven had sent me an email. He wanted us to speak about selling our house: he wants to travel the globe with Hot Yoga Girl, as he felt he had missed out on enjoying his life. The irony wasn't lost on me; maybe when we'd split the cash I could finally go and do what I wanted with my life too. Maybe an *Eat Pray Love* trip to Spain to see John and discover a swarthy Spanish man who would finally find my G-spot. Knowing my luck, he'd be married and big on Tinder.

I had finally spoken to Bunty on the phone. She was anxious about Senga but seemed to calm down when I said she was stable and speaking a little. Bunty still lived in Glasgow, now up near the Campsie Hills, a granny and retired. She'd asked about my life and I had given her the short summary – and when I'd explained that Steven was soon to be my ex-husband it had felt less shocking than I'd expected. 'Plenty more fish in the sea for a smart girl like you,' Bunty had said calmly.

'Did you know Mum wrote a diary, all those years ago?' I'd asked her. 'She was insistent that I read it now.'

Silence, then Bunty had blurted out in a rush, 'No, hen, I had no idea. Is it like a scrapbook? What's in it?'

'Oh, just lots of stuff about her life back in the tenement, written about two years after she and Dad split up. Lots about us as kids, you know – and can I ask you, what the hell ever happened to Sandra and Philomena, and Janine and Bridie? According to my mum and her red book, you lot were forever caught up in Sandra's drama. She sounded a poor soul, Bunty,' I replied.

'Sandra?' she said, as if she had never spoken the name before in her life. 'Oh, God. No, I haven't heard of her in donkey's years. Sandra? God, hen, that's taking me back, I don't think I know, did she not move to Oban, or was that Katie Lee van Longhorn?'

'Who the hell is Katie Lee van Longhorn?'

'She was that big lassie that lived near the Co-op and started dressing as a cowboy woman, changed her name and played the harmonica in a country band.'

'Mum never mentioned her! Now I wish she had. You really don't remember anything about Sandra at all?' I insisted.

Bunty let out a slow breath. 'I will give my brain a shake and try, but I don't think I know much; we weren't that close to thon Sandra, to be honest.'

I knew that wasn't true. 'What about the others, then?'

'Philomena is still in Glasgow; I can put you in touch. Janine, I think she's in a care home last I heard, but the others might know more. And I'm afraid Bridie died a few years back, did your mum not mention?'

And she'd hung up before I could ask anything else.

I took Mum up a fresh nightie and her own housecoat to the hospital. I knew it was probably daft but I was sick of seeing her in those white starchy NHS gowns, and it made her look more comfortable. I thought I managed to hide the shock on my face as Shirley and I stripped her down to change her – her body looked so thin, white and bony. But Shirley nodded to me to sit down and I gulped back the tears. She brought me some tea. 'She's still fighting in there and she needs you to be strong for her,' she said as she offered me the biscuit tin.

Mum drank some water, and I told her what Bunty had said. She tried to speak but was too weak, and she looked upset so I changed the subject and showed her some photos of Poppy on my iPhone. She might need her glasses next time I come up, but she smiled – to please me, I think – and lay quiet for the rest of my visit.

Rain was slashing sideways on the big window and you could hardly see out into the world. The trees on the streets below were bent sideways in the wind and I didn't look forward to driving back to Govan in that storm.

1977
2 January

Sandra has been staying with me for a few days. She came up to mine for the bells at Hogmanay to get away from Jim as he was out cold, full of booze. She was clutching her chest and she had a suitcase with her. She said that was it. But Jim woke up and ended up banging on my door at four in the morning, swearing and shouting. Frank downstairs heard it all through the ceiling and called the police. The whole street was turned out and I was terrified and set Laddie on Jim. He was like a man possessed.

He got dragged away and put in the local cells. Sandra just froze, watching him. She must be used to this shit. His mum got him out the next day, no charges of course – it's a drunk New Year domestic.

Sandra told me everything he's been doing to her – the broken ribs, the hair-pulling, the threats, the absolute terror he's been putting her through. Janine was right, some women just can't acknowledge they have picked a bad man. But here she was, telling me everything – could she leave him now? All her cuts and bruises . . . I felt sick that I hadn't asked her more about what was going on. Even Billy seems like a saint in comparison. I can't look the other way now, though, I'm right in the middle of this mess with her.

I sent my Sharon out to get the rest of the lassies round while Sandra was in my room sleeping. Philomena, Isa and Bunty were here within the hour. We had a wee emergency meeting. We need to get her out of here.

'I know people in London, we can get down there by bus and then she can move on from there,' Philomena said.

'Aye, but the Devlins have connections down there, don't forget,' Bunty added.

I said, 'London's a big fucking place, they won't find her. She could stay with her cousin Bernie to begin with and move on if need be?'

'Look, if we just get her out of Glasgow we can work on the next step. As long as she is out of his reach that's a good enough start,' Isa added. We all agreed.

Jim's lying low, for now. That arsehole comes near my door again, I am heating up a frying pan and scalding him. No doubt I would get sent to jail but he has broken that lassie's nose twice, she said, and they let him walk. Seems he's been punching her for a while, and he won't stop now.

I feel for Sandra. Her beautiful blonde hair is falling out with the stress and she's as thin as a rake. We tried to cheer her up by doing a wee demi-wave on her and we all went through the catalogue picking out outfits we can't afford but would wear if we were ever invited to a garden party at Buckingham Palace.

Me and Bunty are scared Jim is going to kill her one day, but we said this quietly in the kitchen. Bunty has heard he's running about with the Devlins and their gang. He's been spotted at Drummond's scrapyard and everyone knows dodgy dealings go on there. She needs to get out, and we tried to tell her this but she didn't say much. We need to keep her away from Jim so she can breathe a bit and start to see sense.

I had a weird sex dream about Richard Nixon. Why is it never a Kennedy?

Mid-January

Sandra is back with Jim. After everything she's been through and everything we have done. He wore her down like dirty sandpaper to her soul. He followed her up the close from the shops, on his knees, crying and begging her to come back. She said he mentioned her mammy – 'You don't want me up at her door in this state, do you?' – which is a fucking horrible thing to put in her head. Jim came up to my house with Sandra to collect her stuff. She just hung her head as she threw clothes in her wee vanity case.

He came up behind me in the kitchen when Sandra was out of earshot, grabbed my hair and hissed in my ear, 'You and your wee gang better stay out of my business. She belongs with me. Unless you want your fucking jaw broke, bitch, don't any of you come near our house.'

I took a fork from the sink, turned around and jabbed it in his hand, and said, 'You don't scare me, you shitty wee woman-beater, your day will come.' He yelped in pain and raised his hand to hit me, until Laddie stood up and growled at him; even the dog knows he's a prick.

So, things have got worse rather than better. We're seeing even less of Sandra than before as she's embarrassed about it all, so it's harder to keep an eye on her. Luckily I had hidden another packet of pills in her things to keep her going.

I hate January. It's my birthday and I've been feeling a bit down. Not only is the sky dark but everything seems a bit bleak. I really thought Sandra might be OK. And I met a fella called Graeme at the social club last week and he seemed so nice. Tall, dark-haired and good-mannered and loves Queen, Fleetwood Mac and Joan Baez. He brought up his selection of LPs last week and we sat in the living room listening to music. Even Laddie didn't bite him, which was a good sign.

The kids were over at Isa's and we had a bit of a kiss and ended up in bed. He was very modern about sex – who knew men could do that with their mouth? The thing is, he hasn't come back to the club or seen me since. I think he might be married or he's got a girlfriend – Bunty has definitely seen him with another woman. He was very evasive about his life and background. It's like I get one wee bit of good luck then a full run of crap.

I need to put in extra cleaning shifts to clear off the Christmas debt. Got the bus up the West End to Mrs Bradshaw's mansion and read in the newspaper that Prince Charles has met a new girl. I can guarantee you that she doesn't collect Embassy cigarette coupons or scrub posh toilets to buy tinned meat for the family. She looked so demure and horsey. I think Charles needs a woman who likes to ride. All those toffee-nosed 'English rose' girls are made to cook soufflés, ski downhill and dress in frills as they stroke a horse's mane. Girls like me were made to have babies, learn to decorate a single-end and be thankful we don't have an outside toilet. Such is life.

Bunty, Philomena and Isa told me in the pub last night that they spotted Sandra arm in arm with Jim, heading to the chapel last Sunday. Wonder if the bastard goes to confession and tells Jesus he hits women. Sandra was limping. She won't come and see any of us at the moment.

Philomena said Billy and Jim had a fight in the street. The usual Catholic/Protestant crap, no doubt, but she said Billy also shouted at Jim to 'stay away from my Senga and weans', so Billy must have heard about him coming up to mine to get Sandra back. Well, that only made Jim angrier. 'I can clear these streets of you and your cow of an ex-wife, don't think I can't. I know people, you weak bastard. At least I can keep a wife.'

Billy shouted back, 'Yeah, but you cannae have weans, can you?' and then the fists flew. One of the Devlins appeared and pulled them apart. Philomena said she saw Billy running away in his platform shoes as the Devlins' car mounted the pavement to get him. The whole street was talking about it.

Fuck-all stays private here. All these men fighting and shouting and still the women are not safe. Bunch of arseholes, the lot of them.

I watched *Crossroads* today and am starting to think big Benny would make a better husband than the men round our way.

Top of the Pops was amazing this week. Noel Edmonds presented it and they had on Thin Lizzy and Leo Sayer. Janet fancies Leo and I think Phil Lynott looks sexy as fuck; I bet you he knows his way around a double divan.

It's the Queen's jubilee year and I am taking the kids to London by bus in celebration to do the sights. Isa has promised to look out for Laddie and the kids are really excited.

CHAPTER 12

2019
Day seven
Sharon

The storm abated overnight but the wheelie bins were all strewn over the back court this morning, so I went out with a big brush and cleared up the place. Mum would never forgive me for letting her bin shelter look a mess.

I was getting into the thrum of life here in Glasgow: I had a bag for life and a Tesco Clubcard.

Reading Senga's diary often made me snort with laughter. Mum matchmaking for Prince Charles was hysterically funny – if only she had known! She'd loved *Crossroads* and I can still see her sitting round the one-bar electric fire, arms folded, chinwagging about Miss Diane and Benny with a fag and a mug of tea. Mum worked so hard that year to pay for Christmas and get us to London, God love her.

Today was a work day. I had meetings to attend and a campaign pitch to write. But the most interesting development was a message from Philomena.

Hello, hen, I got ur number from Bunty. Hope U R OK. Would love to visit ur mammy up the hospital. I'll stop by the house 2 pick up some bits 2 take to her. See u soon. Philomena x

It looked as though Bunty the Blackhill Transmitter had struck again, but it was great that Philomena still lived in Glasgow.

93

I thought about trying to explain that there wouldn't be much point in her taking anything to Mum given her current state, but I knew that once a wee old Glasgow woman had her mind set on something there was no changing it.

I'd tried very hard to dodge Mum's neighbours, but Betty cornered me this afternoon for her daily update on Mum's situation and to ask again if I wanted to come to the bingo with her. Betty would make a great procurator fiscal: she needed full, detailed statements and physical descriptions of my mother's 'pallor' and what medicine she was on. These wee women could easily be pharmacists. 'Oh, aye, that will be to thin her blood,' she interjected as I was giving evidence at the main door to the flats.

The day did not end well. At the hospital Mum looked weaker, and Shirley came through to see how I was coping and said the doctor needed a word. My stomach soured immediately. What now?

Mum had got her blood tests back. The cancer had spread further.

I had expected this. Of course it was getting worse; what had I thought was going to happen? But it was still so hard to hear it confirmed. I sat with Mum as she slept and just chatted away to her sunken face and tried hard to stay positive. I wanted to be strong for her but my heart was breaking.

I updated the family WhatsApp and had a wee cry on the phone with Janet in the hospital toilets. Then I FaceTimed Louise and Poppy, I needed to see new life. Steven was with her, presenting as the perfect grandfather, and he'd dyed his thinning hair jet-black. He seemed to have forgotten I was sitting at my mum's deathbed, as he offered to send me a recipe for a healing organic guava tea. I told him what hole to shove it up, and they both looked quite shocked.

1977
February
Weather is fucking freezing, snow is knee-deep.

Woke up late for the kids, with a tiny bit of a hangover – me and Isa and Bunty had a wee drinking session last night. Sandra was banned and Philomena was working. Frank downstairs came up and asked us to keep the noise down – his daughter was over from Ireland and her new baby was trying to sleep.

Isa was worried her American man was going off her so Bunty brought a new catalogue delivery and we had a fashion show, all trying on the new clothes. I got a lovely tight striped tank top and a new pair of high-heeled boots; I looked like the dark-haired one from Abba. We didn't ask how Bunty had got hold of these outfits or who they were meant to have gone to. She will get herself into big trouble one day.

Saw *Charlie's Angels* on the telly and I've decided that I want to look like Jaclyn Smith, if only I could lose three stone, grow my legs by three inches and get a new face! Life in America on the telly looks amazing, just people walking about all tanned and drinking champagne and fighting baddies. You don't get that on Scottish TV. Basically, all the women on our TV look like they've never scaled a fence in a bikini – other than Purdey from *The New Avengers*. She is so amazing and sexy, you won't see a woman like her standing in the queue at Fine Fare, headscarf under the chin, waiting on a quarter pound of chopped pork with three kids screaming at her knee.

I tried to cut my Sharon's hair into a Purdey, everyone is doing it and it's basically a bowl cut, but I fucked it up. She looked like an angry Mormon, and she threw away her school photos when she saw it.

There's been a big scandal in the scheme – seems the local doctor, Mr Rafferty, has been taking Polaroid photos of women's vaginas. He said it was for special research, but his surgery got burgled and all the pictures have been stolen. The photos have been passed round the whole area. Davie Dunsmore said he saw Bunty's fanny in the betting shop. Bunty spoke to her contacts about it and turns out the doctor is a perverted liar and now everyone wants their photos back but the problem is, he never named them and we don't know whose fanny is whose. What a creepy bastard! He's been charged by the police, struck off the medical register and everyone round our way needs to find a new doctor, one without a polaroid camera.

Wee John has won a cup at tap dancing in the community hall and Janet found a woman's purse there too. It had a bingo card in it and Janet caught two buses to Gartocher to give it back. I'm so proud of them, I have good kids.

Big Davie Dunsmore gave me some bags of coal on tick. I will pay him next week. He spent an hour telling me how he got his ears syringed at the doctors, and now all the coal dust is out he 'can hear a fly fart'.

He told me he saw my Sharon fighting with two lassies outside the school last week when he was doing his rounds on the coal van. He said he had to jump down and separate them. She never said a word about this and am worried sick she is being bullied. My Sharon is strong and a good lassie but she is right into her school studies and that can mark you out as a victim or a swot. I will have a word with her.

We heard Alan arrive in the close as Davie was saying goodbye. Alan called out and waved at me. 'You need to watch out for that one,' Davie said darkly.

Laddie's got worms again.

CHAPTER 13

2019
Day eight
Sharon

Mum was looking a bit better today: some colour in her cheeks. I took a photo of her face to show wee Betty next door so she can give a firm diagnosis and tell the bingo gang what's what.

The doctor asked me if we've got all Mum's affairs in order, as though she were the head of a global conglomerate and needed the legal team in to sort out who was taking over as CEO. I knew he was trying to be nice and put me in the picture, but it did sound very formal.

'Did your mother have any thoughts with regard to her plans and wishes?' he said, obviously meaning her funeral and her will.

I wanted to tell him, *Well, with regard to her plans, I am reading her diary if that helps and she wanted to have sex with Phil Lynott and push my dad out of a window*, but I knew that would be facetious; he was only doing his job.

'We have everything in order, thanks; my brother and sister are arriving soon.'

Her 'affairs' were simple. Mum owned her wee flat (she'd bought it when Thatcher gave the right to buy, despite hating 'That Fucking Woman') and she'd got herself a bit more financially on her feet by the time John had left home. She'd managed to scrape a wee mortgage together and of course we'd all helped her. My husband had complained, of course he had, but I'd reminded Steven that it was my money and I didn't always need a consultation on how to manage my own fucking finances.

97

Basically, everything she had would get split three ways, and I knew she had a funeral plan that she'd paid for years ago. It was all in the floral folder that contained all her important papers. Senga was always very organised, in her own way – she knew where every last penny was.

'What happens now?' I ran my hand through my hair and stared at the pale flower mural painted on the hallway wall. 'Can she come home?'

'It will be best for her to stay here. You know, it's not like on the telly when you get a definite date – the condition of some people stays stable, and some people can rapidly diminish and pass away quickly,' the doctor explained.

I thanked him, shoved my bag up my shoulder, got back into her room, hugged Mum then left, crying. I walked down the big circular staircase, past the wee shop and café and right out into the cold air.

I headed back to Govan, straight to the coffee shop; I needed an under-the-counter cooked scone and some strong Java.

Clyde was getting a delivery of milk in when I arrived. A toddler was crying on the street, a dog was tied to a lamppost outside, barking loudly, the mummies were trying to push prams through the glass-fronted doors, Betty and Maggie were coming out of the butchers . . . life was continuing.

Steven had called, clearly hurt by my outburst yesterday, but I didn't listen to his voicemail; I could do without his shit right now. I turned off my phone and buried my head in the red book again. How funny to have seen Gillian in the supermarket so recently. I clearly remembered fighting with her at school now, but I couldn't for the life of me remember who the other girl was, or what we'd been fighting about.

1977
June

Trip to London!

Spent the week cleaning the house before we went on our holiday. Washed all the windows, had a big washing load done at the steamie, did my cleaning shifts and came home to pack the bags. I got all the kids nightwear from Philomena's Pippa Dee party – she had all sorts of things for sale there and makes a wee profit on the commission. I got the girls full long nighties with frilly bibs and bows at the front. John got proper boy's pyjamas with button-down collar and long trousers, and he loves them. Sharon said she felt like she was being suffocated by a gingham tea cosy but she's at that teenage phase where she thinks she's ready for a full-cup bra and a cheesecloth shirt. She has nothing to fill it, her chest is like two wee kittens' noses poking out her ribs, and Janet doesn't care what she wears as long as she can climb a fence and run about in it.

My John shouted out the window to the neighbours out the back, 'We're off to London to see the Queen!' He's very dramatic, he loves making announcements.

Well, we won't see the Queen personally, it's not as if she's going to throw open her big gold door and welcome in a rag-taggle bunch of Glaswegians who are dragging a tartan shopping trolley full of Irn-Bru and corned beef sandwiches. Can you imagine Prince Charles, all handsome at the door of a sitting room, waiting to ring a bell to get us our tea? Well, I can dream!

The kids were beside themselves on the way to Buchanan Street bus station with all our luggage and food for the trip. We are staying out in East London with Bernie, who is a cousin of Sandra's – she has a wee flat with outside space and we all know how much I love a veranda. Bernie told me not to get too excited as it looks over the high flats in Poplar with trains rattling past constantly. She says the place isn't as posh as I think it is. But it's LONDON! The bus couldn't go fast enough.

The driver was Robert McGuire, who used to work alongside Philomena, and he helped pack all our stuff in the big space under the bus. He even let wee John sit up on the driver's seat before we left, and John was so excited.

But, to be honest, the bus trip was fucking hell. I have tried to remember everything to write it all down – there was good and bad bits.

The heat on that bus, the sheer number of people pressed into one vehicle and the smell of everyone's feet almost knocked me for six. Who sits on a bus with their shoes off and shoves their big honking feet up on the back of a seat?

My John vomited all the way to Carlisle and ended up sitting in his pants with a plastic bag at his face. Sharon was affronted. Janet had on her Abba T-shirt and her school shorts and picked at her knee scabs as she sang loudly to a woman behind her. Poor woman pretended to sleep.

The bus stopped lots of times to give people a break and it gave me a chance to empty my wee ashtray. We had a flask filled with tea and two big bottles of Alpine American Cream Soda. I got chatting to a woman called Yvonne; she was alone and the guy beside her kept trying to chat her up and twice felt her knee. She leaned over and started speaking to me to distract him but he carried on. I shouted right into his face, 'Leave her alone, you fat bastard,' and he sulked, called me an old cow and got off near the border.

Once the smell of vomiting eased off, things got better.

The view out of the window was brilliant, I have never seen so many green fields and open spaces. This was the first time me and the kids had been so far away from Glasgow. The big black tenements, factories and housing schemes vanished behind us and we stared at the wide-open sky as the stunning views of the borders flashed before us. Someone had turned on a radio and 'Chanson d'Amour' rang out and people on the bus joined in, singing the French words and swaying about. It was magical. I was starting to relax and John fell asleep on the seat beside me.

Then the trip went downhill again. Two guys up the back got drunk and started fighting, scared the kids and people were screaming. They got thrown off somewhere in England. They were raging as they were heading down to see Scotland versus England at Wembley and they begged the driver to be let back on the bus, but Robert was having none of it and they spat at the windows as the bus pulled away.

Finally, we arrived at Victoria coach station and all I could see was hundreds of Scottish guys draped in tartan scarfs and football tops, people selling Wembley tickets, beggars, and one man in a kilt playing the bagpipes. Wee John was scanning the crowds. 'Maybe Daddy is here?' he said excitedly, but Sharon laughed and said, 'Not every man wearing tartan flares is your dad.' I actually met three guys who drank in my local social club. Was weird seeing big Davie and his pals in London, so out of place from Glasgow.

The place was everything I'd imagined: the big, beautiful buildings, the busy roads, the trundling red buses, the Union Jacks flying off tall poles, the big fancy shops and so many people. Janet pulled out a rope from her wee canvas bag and skipped through the busy crowds, clearing a path between a group of beautiful Indian women in colourful saris and two guys with big knotted hair like Bob Marley. They all looked a bit shocked. I don't think London was ready for my Janet.

The kids and I got on a bus to the East End and I felt exhausted. My feet were absolutely louping. It was stupid to wear my cork wedges and good tights on a long journey.

The bus conductor told me what stop to get off at. I couldn't really understand his accent, nor him mine, but he gave me a thumbs-up when I told him the street that Bernie had told me to get off at. We climbed the stairs to her flat, dragged up the big suitcase and the tartan trolley and finally slumped onto her couch. Her three cats just sat on her glass coffee table and stared at us. Janet tried to lasso them with her skipping rope.

I am already exhausted; holidays are just fights in another country as far I am concerned. A real holiday would be someone taking your kids to their house and you go and lie in a quiet room for two weeks on your own. I want to go on a cruise ship like Sophia Loren, I would buy all the gorgeous dresses from Goldberg's, and swan off to the Italian lakes and sip Cinzano Bianco as the sun sets. Me and that wee guy off the Cointreau advert. Wonder if he'd like a wee curvy woman with mad hair and her daddy's blue eyes?

Woke up, smoked two fags and drank some tea and watched the news on the telly. The Queen was back from the Commonwealth tour and was now in London. We were here to see the Queen and we were heading off to Buckingham Palace!

I had specially bought a big Union Jack from the boys at the Masonic club. Stevie Muir told me I had to make sure it was ironed nice and to wave it up the right way. It was folded into a tight square and fuck knows what the right way up was. He's obviously never travelled with three kids and a suitcase heavier than a big bag of coal.

I was so excited to see the place and the Londoners, but Trafalgar Square was full of Scottish men down for the big match at Wembley, jumping about drunk and lying in the fountain. Fuck's sake. I didn't come here to meet the people I left behind, yet there they were. We left and headed up past Piccadilly Circus – there was a lot of building work going on. We saw the West End theatres advertising their shows and Janet was fascinated. I wanted to wander round Soho but the big signs shouting 'SEX SHOP AND GIRLS' made me do a body-swerve. I grabbed the kids' hands and we crossed the road.

Walking through Covent Garden we saw the punks with dark rings round their eyes, ripped jeans, wearing dog collars on their necks, their pink hair crafted into giant stalagmites. Poor fuckers looked like they were held together with safety pins. This was definitely not Shettleston. Sharon was fascinated and took some photos of them with her wee Kodak Instamatic camera.

I took the kids into Leicester Square, which was all done up for the Jubilee, with lots of big Union Jacks flying high and

Queen Elizabeth banners. There were buskers and people playing music, the riot of colour and the sheer amount of people
was staggering. I had my purse tucked into my knickers under
my flares, as Bernie says everyone steals your money in London.
I think she forgets we are from a place where people would steal
the milk out of your tea.

Finally, we found a Wimpy bar and the kids were so excited
to get a burger and Coke. It was all very posh and bright. This
was their first time in a burger bar and they ate like kings. I have
to admit, though, Eusebi's café in Shettleston was so much better, Old Edmondo can make a great roll and sausage and his ice-
cream is the best I have ever tasted. But the kids loved it and it
was so good to see them happy. I sat and stared out the window,
watching all the massive flags blow about in the sunshine and the
big red buses trundle past, and I almost shed a wee tear, I was that
happy. I couldn't wait to tell Bunty all about this!

The crowds were gathering outside the palace and the sun
came out. We got a really good spot and eventually the Queen
and her family came out onto the balcony and the crowd soared
and swelled as we all chanted 'God Save the Queen'. I noticed
Sharon was on tiptoes taking photos and the people cheered and
waved. My kids were witnessing history! We stayed there for a
good while, chatting to people and sharing bottles of pop and
rolls with cheese. Soon it was time to head back to East London
and the street party near Bernie's flats. John vomited on the bus
again, a dog peed on Sharon's leg and Janet climbed a flagpole
like a wee monkey and ripped down an ER banner as a keepsake.
Was a brilliant day.

CHAPTER 14

2019
Day eight
Sharon

Sitting in the coffee shop, nursing a latte, I felt the tears run down my face. Just big, unabashed, fat, snotty tears dripping off my chin. My poor mammy, lying in that hospital bed, waiting on her pals, waiting on her kids and, ultimately, waiting to die.

A wee old man in an anorak and bunnet sitting at the near table leaned over. 'You OK, hen?' he asked.

I nodded and blew my nose. It felt as though a brick was lodged in my chest and I couldn't push it down. I wiped my eyes and stuck my face into the big coffee mug to hide myself.

Poor Senga, trying her best to give her kids a decent holiday. She had given us meat as she ate plates of potatoes; she had walked in lino-lined plastic shoes so we could have leather ones for school. She really had been a big kid herself at times, eager to see the world and treating a trip to London like a world tour.

That trip to London! Reading the diary had triggered such strong memories. Mum still loved the royal family; she had all the commemorative plates in a cabinet in the flat. Even now I couldn't see a big tour bus without those memories rushing back. I couldn't believe how she'd managed to take three kids on that journey on public transport and on such a tight budget. We used to call her Scrooge, but she had done her best to make each penny count.

As I walked back to her flat, I could remember her beaming face as she led us through Leicester Square, pointing out the big buildings, flags and tourist attractions. Fucking hell, the grief of a life unlived made me feel so broken. To think, last December I had almost had a nervous breakdown because we'd had a flood that damaged my reclaimed wooden floor in the dining room. And here was Senga, happy as Larry, walking through London with three kids, spam rolls and a ten-pound note in her purse.

My head was full of the past, memories flickering through my brain, as I rounded the corner to the flat and someone called out to me. I stopped.

'Sharon, is that you, hen?'

An older woman waited ahead of me, tucked up in a warm coat and scarf with a big soft leather handbag across her body, smiling broadly. Her face was vaguely familiar; my own face must have clearly shown my confusion. How did she know me? Was this another nosy neighbour coming around for a new briefing on Senga?

She smiled again and said, 'It's me, hen, Philomena, your mammy's pal. Remember me? I used to have chickens that terrified you?' she said as she tucked her scarf tighter around her neck.

So, there was Philomena, all smiles with her once dark hair now white and shorn close to her scalp like a Glasgow Judi Dench, but dressed in a thick coat, leggings and crocs.

'Philomena, how are you?' We hugged and I brought her into Mum's flat before the two sentry guards in support tights came out for a quick nosy. I knew Betty would want to interrogate us both.

Philomena took off her coat and set down her bag. 'I'm desperate for a cuppa,' she said. 'I know where everything is, I'll make it. I've been here a few times to see your mammy . . . She does like roses, doesn't she?' Philomena commented as she looked round at the floral assault.

We both laughed. 'I know,' I said. 'When did you rock chicks go from Suzi Quatro, Led Zeppelin and Rod Stewart to women who decided flowers and frills were your friends?'

'Age, hen: we get old and just want comfort,' Philomena said as she bustled about the kitchen and I followed her. 'How is Senga doing?' she asked. 'The last time I saw her, I could see she had lost weight. She didn't want to talk about it, though.'

I said nothing; Philomena had definitely seen her more recently than me. The last time I'd seen Mum was a few months ago, or was it more than six months? I hadn't noticed any big changes, but she had looked pretty exhausted. I clearly hadn't been paying enough attention, I had talked only about my marriage. I swallowed down the wave of guilt.

Philomena handed me a floral mug steaming with milky tea, then brought a packet of fig rolls out of her bag and placed them between us as we sat on the matching two-seater sofas.

'Tell me everything about yourself,' she invited, smiling, as the steaming mug misted her glasses.

We caught up with our lives. I told her about Steven and I showed her photos of my granddaughter, and she told me all about her kids and their lives. Philomena was talking nineteen to the dozen; she could summarise four decades and drink tea while also munching biscuits.

She wasn't making much eye-contact, and she suddenly ran out of steam and went quiet. The air was thick with expectation. I watched her fiddle with her watch strap and look about the room. She took a big breath and looked at the floor.

'What's all this about this book your mammy wrote?' she asked eventually.

'Well, she asked me to read it – she was very clear indeed about me doing that. It's a kind of diary about your lives back in the late seventies. Lots of memories, some good and some bad. It's been quite hard to be taken back there, if I'm being honest. She was . . . ' I paused and corrected myself. 'Sorry, *is* a very good writer, actually. She held nothing back,' I replied.

'Can I have a look at it?' Philomena finally stared me right in the eye and then her gaze flicked over the living room, as if she expected to see it lying on the display unit or on Mum's wee nest of tables.

Something was bothering her now. My spider sense tickled me – this wasn't a social visit. She *really* wanted to see Mum's book, and I needed to figure out why.

But I felt protective of Mum's thoughts and feelings. A diary was a collection of private writings and thoughts, it wasn't something someone could just ask to read. Besides, I hadn't read the whole book yet and Mum hadn't said, *Let everyone read it.* So, no, Philomena couldn't see it.

'I'm waiting to show Janet and John first,' I said, firmly. Then I pointed vaguely to the window. 'I've left it in the car. I'll show you another time, when I get the chance.'

Her face darkened. 'Oh, your mammy would love me to read it. Go and get it, I can wait?'

My eyebrows went up into my hairline. I am not a crisis management public relations expert for nothing. I smiled, put down my cup, and looked her square on.

'No, Philomena, I'd rather the family saw it first,' I said again and added, 'she hasn't said anything bad about you, if that's what's bothering you? You don't feature that much, but you were a rock to her as far as I can see. Now, do you want more tea?'

She opened her mouth and then closed it again. She wasn't going to push it.

I changed the topic and showed her a picture of Steven on Instagram, struggling with a canoe, and we laughed at his midlife crisis, the confrontation expertly avoided – or just delayed for another day, I suspected.

As she was leaving, I asked if she knew how I could contact Sandra and Janine. 'I would love to get them up to see Mum. We don't have much time.'

Philomena paused, her eyebrows knitted into a sharp V. Then she opened her leather bag, had a rummage through it and took out a small black book. She flipped to the page marked J.

'I don't know where Sandra is now,' she said as an aside as she ran a finger down the page. 'We all lost touch, you know how it is. But Janine is in a care home in Glasgow. Here's the phone number.'

She pulled on her coat as I typed the number into my phone, and then hugged me. 'So, Senga is still in the Royal Infirmary, Ward 23?' she asked. 'I'll go visit her.'

'How do you know that?' I asked, surprised.

'I've spoken to the ward sister.'

I nodded, momentarily lost for words. 'OK. She wants to see you all together, though, Philomena – Bunty and Isa are coming up soon. Just a heads-up, too – Mum is so tired and weak, she's sleeping most of the time and she does look very . . . diminished, just so you know.'

'I understand, but I'll try to see her anyway, just in case she wants some company. Stay in touch, hen.'

She patted my arm gently as she passed, wrapped her scarf around her neck and went down the hallway to open the front door, and I walked behind her to lock it.

I stood there for a few moments, my back against the door.

'That was intense,' I whispered to myself, letting out a sigh. Then I heard Philomena's voice. I peered through the marbled glass section of the door and could make out a mottled version of her standing near the main door alone. She must be on her phone.

'She says it's in her car,' was all I could make out. Then the sound of her crocs slapping down the path as her voice faded.

That was weird.

1977
June

My Sharon wanted to go see The Stranglers, a punk band, in the City Halls, but I put a stop to that. I don't understand the shouty music and if I see my Sharon with a safety pin in her nose she's getting a Scholl's sandal to the legs.

Couldn't sleep last night – heard about another wee lassie found dead in Leeds. The police still don't know who did it. Bet it was some fucking creep. Poor wee girl, only a few years older than our Sharon – it seems women just aren't safe anywhere. Lay in bed and listened to Radio Luxembourg and let Laddie up beside me; he's a better bed-mate than Billy and smells less.

Took the kids to the Orange Walk on Saturday, lots of Protestants on parade to celebrate King William of Orange. The biggest protesting was from my kids – they moaned and moaned about it. Sharon said to me, 'Religion divides people, look at what's happening in Northern Ireland.' But I was brought up following the Walk, and I enjoy the music and the marches. It's like a hike, a picnic and a singsong but with religion thrown in. Some people can be bitter about Catholics, though I am not. Some of my pals are Catholic so it doesn't really affect me that way. The walk can go on for miles and we always end up in some part of city we are unfamiliar with, but it's always a good day out. Sometimes there's trouble. I suppose religion, drinking and singing about the Queen is going to throw up some shite for people to fight about.

Saw Frank downstairs giving the two fingers from his window. He told me sectarianism is there to divide the working classes and keep the poor people fighting amongst themselves. He is right into politics, is Frank; he told us his dad fought Franco in Spain in the 1930s. I told him Bunty's brother Jack fought two guys in a bar in Benidorm. Frank said I should read more about the history of our working-class people, I told him I read romances by Jackie Collins. He just laughed at me.

I don't just read romances, but Frank doesn't need to know I am writing this all down. I think people would laugh at me if they knew I wrote this.

I saw Janine briefly and asked how she was. She told me that big Alan off the Alpine van came to her door last week at 11.30 at night – apparently every dog in the close was barking like mad because it was so late for someone to be wandering around. Alan said he just wanted to check she was OK, like he's suddenly the home guard for single women. Janine said she kept him at the door and her neighbour came out to see what the kerfuffle was all about. I'm glad someone is keeping an eye on her.

'He stood there, Senga, smiling and staring at me like I was a prize he won at a raffle. The weans were in their bed, and he said, 'You want to stick the kettle on?' and tried to walk into my flat. I pushed him back out. 'What the fuck was that about?' she asked me.

She said, when her neighbour appeared, Alan just made up something about 'keeping an eye on her' and bolted. It's really unsettled her; he keeps popping up in places. I remembered he was there at the cinema, and he appeared at the pub and a country dancing event at the community centre too. He's starting to be a big weirdo. I told her never to be on her own with him. I will keep away from him too.

You never get a man from a fizzy drink van stalking women in a Jackie Collins book. Big arsehole that he is.

CHAPTER 15

2019
Day nine
Sharon

It was a rare sunny autumn day in Glasgow.

The light was dappled through the leaves and making sunspots on the road as I drove up to the hospital. Glasgow really looked beautiful in the sunlight – I would open Mum's curtains wide and let her see the sky when I got to her room.

Betty was there when I arrived, sitting beside Mum.

'I'm just telling your mammy all about Mrs Callaghan dying last night,' she said cheerily as she clacked together knitting needles that held a giant swathe of pink fluffy wool.

'Is that really something she needs to hear right now, Betty?' Jesus fucking Christ, these wee women were something else.

'Oh aye, hen, me and your mammy always looked through the death notices when we were at the bingo,' Betty said as she put her knitting on Mum's bed and plumped up her breasts with her arms crossed.

Mum was lying peacefully and she smiled and waved a hand at me. Maybe she was enjoying it?

I opened the curtains wide and let the light flood the room. 'I'll come back later and let you have your visit,' I said as I backed out of the door. Mum seemed settled, so I left them to it and headed off for a cup of NHS tea and a read of the diary.

I took the tea outside and found a bench in the sun. As I read on, I was aware yet again that I didn't have neighbours and people in my life as Mum had. If I died suddenly on my front lawn,

I would be left there until the postman turned up one day and found my stiff body near the hydrangeas. I loved my house with its garden and period features, but I had always kept myself to myself. I wasn't part of the community.

I didn't know my own neighbours in Bristol. I now knew more about Betty and Margaret than I did about anyone back at home. These women had really stuck by each other, and community was very much part of the fabric of their daily life.

That last entry about religion, though, was something that I was glad I had left behind in Glasgow. I hated the Orange Walk: all those drunk and angry folk jostling and arguing. It had been embarrassing passing my Catholic pals in the street. Janet had loved it, as she always said it was the only time that she got to see other big parks in Glasgow. We saw amazing Victorian gardens, huge boating ponds and wonderful old museums on the south side of the city, and as the adults got drunk we would go exploring. The walk home at teatime wasn't as pleasant. I could recall several times when I'd had to pour my mum and her pals into a taxi that they could ill afford, but there was no way they were getting back to Shettleston otherwise. Wee John had hated all the noise and arguing and often opted to stay at our granny's house and clean her budgie cage and lie on her couch watching Saturday television, eating pieces of toast with jam.

When I got back to Mum's room, Betty had gone. Mum opened her eyes and smiled at me. 'It was easier to keep my eyes shut and hope she'd go home. She got the message eventually,' she said in a weak voice.

For the first time in days, I laughed out loud, and Mum did too. I hugged her close. I needed to treasure these moments of lucidity and closeness; I didn't think we'd have many more left.

I remembered that Isa had given me Janine's details, so I looked up the care home on Google maps. It wasn't far away, I could drive there one day soon.

Bunty: Philomena, we need to try again to get a look at this fucking diary thing Senga kept.

Philomena: I spoke to Sharon, just like we agreed. She's not letting me see it, made up some excuse about her family needing to see it first, but I think she only knows so much. I'll visit Senga as well to see if I can talk to her. She's in the Infirmary.

Bunty: I mean, why write a diary?

Philomena: Let's not worry for now, we don't know what she's written, if anything. We need to be sure before we say anything to anyone. Sharon's trying to find Sandra and Janine too. I've given her Janine's details but said I didn't have anything for Sandra. Tell Isa, in case Sharon asks her too. I could punch Senga for that diary if she wasn't already ill.

Bunty: God forgive you, lol.

1977
July

Woke up, smoked three fags, let Laddie out for a pee and put on Radio Clyde and danced around the kitchen to Donna Summer's 'I Feel Love'. The kids are still off school for summer but Janet is up early watching *Multi-Coloured Swap Shop* with Noel Edmonds. She said she wants to swap wee John for a bike and I told her I wanted to swap my life for Bianca Jagger's and head to a disco in New York on a fucking white horse, but we don't always get what we want and more often we get what we need.

Sandra came up and I sent the kids out to play. We watched *Little House on the Prairie*. All happy families and weans in floral dresses behaving well and patting horses as they sing Jesus songs. Sandra said to me, 'Where the fuck do you get those men that can chop down trees, tame a wild horse and love their wives as they look after the kids?'

I told her, 'They all came from the olden days in the Wild West apparently, they all died before they could come to Scotland, or shot each other in a saloon.'

We had a laugh, and I was so pleased to see her. She hasn't been around in a while because Jim doesn't trust me and won't let her talk to me. But she needs more birth control pills. It looks a lot like Sandra is recovering from another black eye but she won't speak about Jim's behaviour towards her at all. I tried and she said she would leave my house if I didn't change the subject. She's being so defensive and mentioned he's been making good money working with the Devlins in the car business. I don't trust Jim or the Devlins and I hope the bastard gets knocked down by his own fancy black Ford Capri that he roars up and down our street. Philomena swears he nearly knocked her down outside her work the other day. The man is a danger to us all.

Bunty came up in the evening and I did her hair and we got a Fray Bentos pie and three cans of lager and had a wee night to ourselves. I have the new *Rumours* album from Fleetwood Mac.

The kids sat in the bedroom and gave us some peace. Janet likes to tie John up with her skipping rope and tell him horror stories. It's no wonder that boy still wets the bed.

We chatted about Sandra and Jim. Bunty said Sandra told her Jim keeps nagging her to get pregnant. He will definitely kill me if he finds out I'm giving her my pills. Bunty looked alarmed at the mention of the Devlins as apparently the last batch of clothes we bought off her were supposed to have been for one of the Devlin wives. She doesn't know if they know she sold them on and kept the cash.

Isa is away down to Dunoon to see her American boy, Brock. I love his name, it's a mix of a brick and a rock and he's bought her a new dress – we laughed for hours saying Brock bought a frock. I hope Isa marries him and moves to Tallahassee and lives like someone from *Little House on the Prairie* or *The Waltons*. Mind you, Isa would shock those Yankees with her big loud swearing. She always brings back lots of American sweets and fancy playing cards from Dunoon. I would miss her if she left.

Janet has been in trouble again. She found a bag of kittens and kept them in the bedroom. Laddie went off his head barking and the poor wee things were too young to be away from their mammy. I had to take them up the police, and they just lifted them over the counter and said they would deal with them. I didn't know what that meant. You never see that on *The Sweeney*, two men driving about in a fast car with a bag of wee cats, do you?

Watched *Coronation Street*. Gail is upset that Roger is in love with a nun. Betty shouted at Hilda again.

August

Elvis has died.

Me, Isa, Philomena, Bunty, Sandra and Bridie McBride sat crying in the social club. Bridie was inconsolable. She once paid a whole week's wages to buy a scarf that Elvis had allegedly worn from a man in America who ran a fan club. Nobody had the heart to tell her she might have been conned.

Some people were screaming up our close, you could hear it through the open windows, it was awful. Davie Dunsmore told us he met Elvis when he landed in Prestwick years ago. We're not sure if that's true, because Davie also said he met Bryan Ferry in the whelk shop in Bridgeton.

Saw on the news that another woman has been attacked in Bradford. The cops think a madman is on the loose, like that terrifying Bible John who used to kill the lassies in Glasgow out at the dancing.

Sandra came up last night to tell me she and Jim are moving to a new house in Sandyhills. It's just a fifteen-minute walk from mine, up behind the Kingco supermarket and over near the old golf course. A lovely council house with a garden and Jim's been saving money to get it redecorated, like the good husband he is. I don't believe a word of it – it's all down to his dodgy dealing. It has a back and a front door and an upstairs and downstairs, and a garden. I am really jealous of her, I would love that. She says we can all go and sit in her garden during the summer. Like Jim would ever let that happen.

I finally went to the lawyers and got divorce papers organised. I can ill afford the paperwork but I hear that Dirty Donna has taken Billy back and is trying to get pregnant, so I want out of that whole mess. I think Billy will go fucking mental when he is faced with divorce papers. He likes to think he can just keep banging on my door to try to pick up the broken threads every time something goes wrong, like nothing has happened. He's been flying off the handle lately and he can still scare me at times.

Watched *Crossroads* today. Meg and Sandy had an argument. On *Coronation Street* Albert made a kite.

CHAPTER 16

2019
Day ten
Sharon

The weather had settled a bit. I woke up early and got some emails and press releases done, then I spent an hour with my accountant working out my and Steven's pension details and tax situation. I was just preparing for what might happen and I needed to know my financial situation. I had a lovely chat with Louise and Poppy and ordered some online shopping. I can't keep living on 'meals for one' and it was time to make some Senga Soup, as we called it. After a quick visit to the bin shelter to organise the recycling, I headed off to the café for my daily fix of caffeine – and Clyde.

As I arrived at the coffee shop, Clyde held out a small blue plastic box with clips on the side. 'I've been thinking how I can help, so here's a wee packed lunch for you,' he said. 'I don't want you to feel you're alone in this.'

What a nice man, how kind was that? I didn't know what to say.

'Thanks, Clyde, that's really kind of you. You shouldn't have, honestly,' I said, and I could feel a flush creep up my neck.

'Hey, we're neighbours now, we help each other. It's just some cold meat sandwiches and a scone,' he said.

'He's never made me a sandwich and I live next door,' an old man with a bunnet, sitting at the window, said loudly.

'Archie, do you want a sandwich?' Clyde shouted over to him.

'Naw, I'm just saying, you have to have nice legs to get treated well round here.' Archie laughed and started coughing loudly into a hankie.

Clyde shook his head, handed me my recyclable cup full of coffee and held the door open for me. 'See you later,' he said.

The hospital car park was so busy, it took ages to find a space.

Mum was sitting up and looking out of the window; for a woman who was dying she seemed to be outliving everyone else on her ward. She'd seen off two old men in the rooms either side of her and the old lady in the nightgown who shouted at everyone.

Shirley gave me a smile and brought me in a coffee refill. 'She was asking for you today,' she said as she tucked Mum's hair away from her face. Shirley was my hero she was always full of chat with Mum when she looked after her.

I gulped back tears, but sure enough Mum was gripping my hand with a degree of renewed strength. Shirley continued, 'Someone else came to visit last night – a lady called Philomena? Your mum was asleep so I sent her home again.'

I looked at Mum and stroked her hair. 'Mum, Philomena was here, remember her? She used to do the football cards and kept chickens? All your pals are like wee hens, Mum, they are all coming home to roost and rally round their pal.'

She opened her eyes and stared at me. 'Where are Bunty and Isa?' she asked. It was so good to hear her speak, I almost missed what she'd said and I just stared at her.

'What?' I replied.

She repeated it in her croaky voice. 'Where are Bunty and Isa?'

I quickly gathered my thoughts and said, 'They'll both be here soon. We'll all be with you, Mum, just as soon as we can.'

I wasn't sure if she was alarmed or happy, as she rolled her eyes and shook her head. 'What about Janet and John?' she whispered on a cracked breath.

'They're on their way too. I will bring them to see you as soon as they arrive.'

'My weans,' she smiled. 'I'm sorry I didn't do better for you.'

'You did everything you could, we know that,' I replied, taking her hand. 'You were amazing, I wish I had half your strength, Mum.'

'You're a good lassie, Sharon, you always were.'

'Mum, the diary is amazing, I have so much to ask you . . . '

She shook her head. 'Not just now, hen,' she said quietly and stroked my hand.

I played her some Elvis songs and she hummed along. When I went into the café on the way home, I used the Wi-Fi and sent a video on the family WhatsApp so we could all listen to Elvis together.

1977
August

There's a lookalike singing contest at the social club. Isa and I are doing Abba. We are playing the two women and Davie Dunsmore and Mrs Wilson's son Derek downstairs are going to dress as the guys in the group. Derek has a surprising number of wigs and spangly, sparkly tops, and I can't wait. We know all the words and have been practising the dance routine. Derek's mum is over the moon, she thinks he might finally get a girlfriend if he shows off his singing skills. I can't believe she really thinks that's going to happen. My Sharon said she heard her dad and Dirty Donna are going as Rod Stewart (of course) and Elkie Brooks. Bridie McBride is going as Dolly Parton and she has spent a fortune on account of her rhinestone boots, a big bouffant wig and huge fake boobs.

Bunty and all the girls from the menage are coming down to cheer us on. The prize is a £10 food hamper. Janet wanted to dress up as Lena Zavaroni and sing her heart out but we put a stop to that as her singing voice is horrendous. She sounds like a seagull being flung up a lum.

Got another letter from Monica in Canada. Her eldest son Bruce has gone to Los Angeles to work as a cameraman on the movies. It seems like another world. I can't really believe we are related. My Janet says she wants to work in films and might send him some of her horror stories. Her latest one is about dead cats coming back to life and stalking their owners. Who would want to watch that?

Sharon is doing well at school. Her school reports are saying that she might be top of her year. I don't know where she gets her brains from – certainly not me or her stupid dad. She has a boyfriend called Terry and he comes from Parkhead. I think he's a Catholic. She met him on her Saturday job in Mrs Mina's fruit shop. He's got bright red hair and that's all I know about him. I told her not to get 'up to anything' as she doesn't want to fall pregnant, and then explained about the birds and the bees.

She looked horrified and ran out of the house crying. My mammy never had that talk with me. I wish she had done but I would probably have ignored her and carried on being the Mrs Know It All that I am. I don't regret having kids young but, at the same time, I wish I had lived a wee bit first. I will never get a decent job or a long-term career, and if I had stuck at school I might have had a chance.

But I don't know anyone who went to university or did a fancy job. I come from a long line of factory workers, shop workers and cleaners. That's what we did in my family.

Paid the insurance man and the provy man and even managed to catch up with the electricity bill. Loads of hairdressing jobs came in alongside the cleaning, so it's been a good week. I also heard Father Gloan the local priest has run away with Mrs Coyle who cleans the chapel. What a scandal. Her man is called Holy Joe – he won't find another woman, will he? Poor Bastard.

It was a great night at the club. Our Abba group won the singing prize and a man from the local newspaper took some photos, I can't wait to see them. I felt like a star. I haven't laughed that much in ages and the group let me keep the hamper as I have the weans to feed.

Some awful news, Philomena's brother Michael has been stabbed to death in a gang fight down the Gallowgate. It's absolutely terrifying and she is distraught – she'd been trying to get him away from trouble for ages. These are just kids, running about stabbing each other, full of drink and pills. Imagine that! Young people selling tranquillisers and getting off their heads. I hope my Sharon is sensible enough to keep out of things like this, I worry more about Janet, and mind you, half the women round here are still on Valium – the doctors still give them out like sweeties. You don't see that on *Coronation Street*, do you? All the women swapping nerve tablets at the steamie.

I was up doing Philomena's hair for the funeral, along with her mammy and Sandra's mammy, when Sandra's mammy let slip that the Devlins are looking for Bunty's cousins to have a word about the goods that are disappearing. We all know what 'a word' means so I had to tell Bunty quick. I couldn't believe she hadn't heard already as she's the Blackhill Transmitter and should know everything.

So, I headed round to see her last night but seems I was too late, she had a black eye and a cracked rib. The cousins gave her a punching at her own door as a warning, poor Bunty. 'The fact we're related counts for fuck all when it comes to the Devlins,' they said. She says she's fine but I could see they had her rattled. 'Still made good money, though.' She tried to smile through the pain as she patted her purse.

Laddie went missing for two days again and the weans were crying for hours. Turns out he's been living with Mrs Jackson over the way for two days a week and she thought he was a stray. I spotted her walking him on a lead down Shettleston Road, and the animal just ignored me when I approached her and explained he was my dog and has been for seven years. She said, 'This is Bonnie and he's mine.'

Bonnie? Fucking Bonnie? I can't keep a man or a dog it seems. I ripped the collar off him and dragged him home.

CHAPTER 17

2019
Day eleven
Sharon

I went to see Mum early this morning as I have so much to do and I wanted to get the visit in first before I got too distracted with work. She was getting a bed bath from Shirley.

'She's had some water and a wee feed on the drip. She's looking stronger, isn't she?' Shirley said as she washed Mum's face and hands.

Mum did have a wee bit of colour in her cheeks. Maybe she was hanging on for the rest of her weans to arrive.

I spoke to Shirley outside Mum's room. 'My brother and sister are coming home soon; do you think she'll still be here?'

'Stranger things have happened, Sharon,' Shirley said as she headed off to the nurses' station. 'Your mum is one hell of a woman, and she seems pretty determined to stay for now.'

I'd planned to drive out and visit Janine, but instead I had to spend a lot of my day on Skype with a particularly fussy client who wasn't happy with a campaign I'd outlined for him. He was the type of person who, when I told him I was in Glasgow, said 'Oh, I've been to Aberdeen. Is that nearby?'

He talked loudly and said 'yah' a lot, so I was glad to have finally managed to connect to the internet with a dongle at Mum's flat. I didn't want to have to speak to him in full view of everyone in the coffee shop or hospital corridor.

Mum writing about my first boyfriend was such a throwback. I had forgotten about Terry, but I could see him now, skinny as a reed, big flared trousers and huge hair. We didn't have underage discos or family houses that welcomed teenage romances; if you wanted to get passionate you had to do it outside the dirty bin sheds and walk home from school together. Privacy was a luxury the poverty-stricken teenagers of the seventies couldn't afford.

We spent a lot of time heavy petting in bus shelters as women with shopping bags pushed us out the way to board the bus. 'Hen, make sure you get off at Paisley,' one wee lady with a big blue coat and head scarf once shouted at us, as her pals laughed loudly. We didn't live near Paisley, so we were confused. Years later I understood she was referring to the 'withdrawal method' of birth control. Glasgow women were full of good advice, even if it came in code.

I wondered what Terry was doing now. Probably living in Paisley with six kids.

Last night when I was in the café, Clyde asked me if I wanted to go see his local band play in a pub this weekend.

'They're brilliant, a bit like Counting Crows meets Del Amitri, all heavy acoustic sounds. Come along and have a wee night off?' he said with the ease of a man who often asks women to listen to local bands.

I got so flustered; I hadn't been asked out on a date since Frankie Goes to Hollywood were at number one. I mumbled and panicked: 'I'm old and married and my mum's ill in hospital.'

'Firstly, you're not old, and are you not allowed to listen to music if you're married, then?' He stared at me and I could see his one eyebrow rise sarcastically.

'Well, technically my marriage is in bits, and things . . .' I floundered, trying to step back and start again. 'I mean, I do listen to music and thanks for the invite, it's just I think I might just need to see how Mum is . . .' I blushed right up my face and my scalp prickled with embarrassment.

'That's a big riddy you've got there,' he said, smiling at me.

I laughed and took a deep breath. 'Might be my menopause arriving in time to remind me to start wearing big pants, give up underwired bras and take up bingo,' I replied.

He just grinned and said, 'Well, if you change your mind . . . ' He winked and passed me an illicit cooked scone. As I turned to leave, he said, 'Are you sure you don't want to come? It might do you good to take your mind off things and do something for yourself for once?'

I thought again of Mum and her diary. I could hear her voice – I should take this chance, and I knew she would agree with me.

I took a deep breath once more. 'OK. Thank you – if Mum's OK at the weekend, I would love to come.'

Clyde gave me a big daft smile and we swapped numbers, and I felt a flutter of excitement that I hadn't experienced in a long time. I rushed out the door before I changed my mind, like a gawky teenager at a school disco, and nearly knocked over Archie with the bunnet who was stepping in.

It had been eleven days since Mum had been admitted to intensive care. It seemed the cancer was taking its time, or she was holding it off. Part of me wanted her to go quickly and be free from pain, but the other part of me was grateful for this extra time with her.

She needed to hold on to see Janet and John, and her pals, and I thought she knew that. It was such a tangled mess of emotions. I was getting stressed at how long it was taking Janet and John to get here. I knew it was hard to drop everything and run, but I just didn't want them to miss her. Time was of the essence.

As if she could hear my silent plea, Janet called me. They had had a casting issue that she couldn't get out of, she explained, but she was heading home soon, and John had organised a flight for early next week. I couldn't wait to see them. We were all laughing and crying on the phone in the way you do when you're facing a death in the family and you're too far apart to hug.

I gave her an update on Mum and the diary. 'When I read about that trip to London in 1977, I couldn't stop laughing thinking about that tiny wee bedroom in that East End flat we stayed in – remember that? You went through the bookshelf saying, "Shite, shite and more shite," as you threw them all on the floor. And our John was trying on the slingback shoes and dancing about the bedroom.'

Janet said, 'Fuck, yes, I recall that; you were such a goody two shoes, tidying up behind us!'

'It was disrespectful, going through her stuff, Janet,' I said.

'We found that big electric Pifco "neck massager" and John was rubbing the cat with it. I still can't get that cat's face out of my head!' Janet giggled.

We hung up and I had a warm feeling right under my ribcage. It caught my breath and, for the first time in ages, I felt as though I belonged somewhere.

As soon as I put the phone down, it rang again.

'Sharon, it's your aunty Isa here,' boomed a familiar voice. 'Just to say, I've rearranged some prior commitments and I will be back home in the next week and I will come and see your mammy.'

We chatted details about accommodation and travel, then I plunged in with the big question that had been on my mind.

'Do you know if anyone has managed to get a number for Sandra? I just can't seem to find anyone who knows where she is.'

Isa went quiet and then muttered, 'Oh, aye, I think Bunty knows all about that, she'll have got a hold of her.'

I was startled. 'Really? That's—' I was about to inform her that Bunty had basically denied knowing her.

Isa interrupted quickly. 'What?'

'Um – that's great news. Can't wait to see you,' I finished. I didn't want to alert her that I had stumbled on their wee web of denial and lies; best not to give her advance ammunition.

I finished the call and stared down at the floral carpet. Something just wasn't ringing true. One minute nobody remembered

Sandra, the next they're all pally-wally. What the fuck were these women hiding?

I pulled out Mum's big red book, balanced it on my knee, flicked to the end and stared at where the ripped-out pages would be. What was missing from this story?

1977
October

House is freezing, wee John has mumps, Janet got sent home from school for shouting at the teacher and Sharon has period pains. This is when you hate being a single parent, when you have to deal with all the issues yourself. Not that Billy would have been any good, but someone else to be a babysitter when you're running to schools and doctors and trying to hold down a job would be fucking helpful. Sharon, despite being buckled by womb cramps, went up to Mrs Bradshaw's and did my cleaning shift – she's a great wee worker. She is worried about missing school as she wants to take exams and go to college. I want this for her too, and she knows I wouldn't ask unless I was desperate. Janet stayed in by herself. She is old enough to be in alone but I worry that someone will say I am neglecting the kids.

Went down to the post office to cash my benefit book, bought some bread and cold meat in Eusebi's. Laddie was in the butcher's again, trying to haul a carcass off the meat hooks. That's me barred for the third time. I'll need to go to the new supermarket, Kingco, for my butcher meat until Mr Cross forgives me and my stupid dog.

Saw the newspapers and some toffee-nosed politician called Jeremy Thorpe has been linked to the murder of a male model. What a scandal! I thought shit like that only happened in Glasgow. Talking about sex scandals, I heard from Bunty that Sandra's man Jim has got a bit on the side. We went down to see her in her new house, and Bunty asked her about it to her face. Sandra said she doesn't believe it and Jim loves her.

It was the first time we'd seen her in ages. Her new house is so tidy, not a thing out of place. The kitchen is top-of-the-range Formica and everything is bright yellow. She opened the back door and we sat in the garden so we didn't make a mess inside. She carries a damp cloth in her apron pocket for quick wiping down, like a fifties housewife. I don't think she'd told Jim we were coming, we're still banned from any contact with her. She kept nervously listening when she heard a car door shutting out in the front street.

Isa, Bunty and I all went to the bingo in the social club last night. Bunty is looking better, she always bounces back, but I can't believe her own family had a go at her. What bastards they are. 'Family is family,' she said.

Philomena had to work. Sharon kept an eye on the weans and studied her history books. She's fell out with her boyfriend and told me she doesn't need a man in her life. She said, 'All the men I know let women down, women don't need men.' She says she's a feminist now and keeps telling me that men are the downfall of working-class women. She could well be right. I am certainly tired of being treated like shit.

We saw Billy at the social club with Dirty Donna. He's looking fatter and that Rod Stewart feathered haircut doesn't suit a man whose hair is falling out at the top. He never mentioned the divorce letter but Donna was practically dry-humping him at the table and he looked utterly affronted. Billy hates public kissing. Jack the barman took me aside and told me that he was showing anyone that would give him the time of day the legal letter and playing the victim. What an arsehole – has he suddenly forgotten it was him that walked out on me because he couldn't put up with kids and get a fucking job?

Donna was wearing a big white Laura Ashley floaty frock like a second-hand bride. Remembering what my Sharon had said, I decided to take control. I walked over to them both and said, 'Make sure you sign my letter, Billy, or I'll be coming after you for child maintenance as well. Enough is enough.' I took my cigarette and stamped it out in their ashtray. I could feel their eyes drilling into the back of my head as I walked away. Fuck them.

Isa is bringing her American sailor to my house next week. I can't wait to meet him. I bet he sounds like Steve McQueen. She says I haven't to get too excited, she's still not sure he's being faithful to her.

She gave me a loan of her new LP by Meatloaf, 'Bat Out of Hell' – it's like nothing I have ever heard before, like opera and rock all at the same time. I can't wait to see if Legs & Co dance to that on *Top of the Pops*. My Sharon is right into her music as well, she loves much the same stuff as me, which is great. I draw the line at listening to her punk stuff, though, brings on my migraine.

Watched *Crossroads*, Miss Diane has a new boyfriend and Meg Mortimer is off to the lawyers, again. So many board meetings and takeover bids for a wee hotel off a roundabout.

November

Woke up late and put the oven on to heat up the kitchen for the kids going to school, the gas has run out and I can't pay it until my turn of the menage. We are really skint this week. I hate being poor. Sharon gave me her wages from the fruit shop to buy food. I am saving all my money for the kids' Christmas presents and pawned my wedding ring. My mum is giving me her Co-op stamps to help out again.

Mrs Bradshaw gave me a big frozen steak pie from her deep freeze as we were cleaning it out, but it stank when we defrosted it. I think it's been in there since Princess Margaret got married. She's a good woman, though, and her cleaning job gives me cash on the side, but it's a big house with a lot of work. It really exhausts me and the travelling can be a pain in the arse during the winter. I get the bus from St Enoch's up to Hillhead on the Byres Road and the place is full of middle-class students. A few times I have seen some famous faces off the telly as the BBC studios are near Mrs Bradshaw's place. I once walked past Dorothy Paul from *Garnock Way* outside the library and spotted John Cairney, the actor, coming out of Curlers pub. I felt really nervous and wanted to ask him for his autograph but I was too shy. I like the Byres Road, they have a delicatessen that sells beautiful cakes and lots of wee fancy shops that sell very modern ornaments and china plates. Sometimes, when I finish cleaning, I wander down there and mix with the hoi polloi as mammy calls them and look at all the clothes and wee jewellery shops. Folk speak right posh up there and have poodles or wee shaky dogs that have ribbons in their hair. Laddie would look out of place in the West End, they don't even have dog shit on the pavements.

I like to walk past the big fancy houses, gaze into their big windows and imagine me and the kids in there. Me at the big wooden kitchen table, dinner in the old Aga cooker, velvet curtains at the windows, the kids all sitting round reading books or playing with jigsaws, waiting for me to serve up a big roast. Then I come back to earth with a heavy bump. I know I am skint and I was married to a guy called Billy who wouldn't work and thinks he should be Rod Stewart with a pot belly. Now getting divorced, with three kids, and I know I will never find a decent man who will make me feel young and safe. I fucked up my life, didn't I? I hate this feeling. Never mind, maybe I will have a wee win at the bingo this week.

I popped up to see Janine too. She unbolted her door very slowly and checked it was me before opening it properly. It seems Alan is still acting really strange. I wouldn't be surprised if it was him leaving notes and climbing up the veranda. She says he's sitting outside the building in his van at all hours. Things can't go on like this.

CHAPTER 18

2019
Day twelve
Sharon

What a woman my mum was. Cleaning other people's houses, cleaning our house, catching buses, watching kids, scraping every penny, wishing for a decent man and dreaming about velvet curtains. But everyone we knew lived like that, robbing Peter to pay Paul as my mum used to say. She was a good mum to us, and my heart flooded with love when I thought about how open-hearted and affectionate she was. But, clearly, she had been lonely. She never did find another man as far as I was aware; she'd lived alone since Janet and John and I had left home. Her life dedicated to her wee house, working part-time in the local community centre and looking forward to our visits which, looking back, never had been frequent enough. She'd deserved better.

Bunty called as I sat in Mum's bedroom last night.

'Hi, hen, how are you?'

I updated her on Mum's diagnosis. Bunty took a breath, waited for me to stop speaking and launched into her own health problems, which she detailed in a lengthy, well-rehearsed monologue. Diabetes, scoliosis, arthritis and some I couldn't make out but you don't interrupt Glasgow women when they are telling you their ailments. After she'd explained what treatment and tablets she was on, I told her about the memories flooding back with the big red book.

'It's like you're all there in front of me, Bunty, it's full of stories and drama. My mum has a bloody good eye for detail, I can tell you.'

'Sharon, you must be heart-roasted with it all. I can't wait to see her and hear all about the diary. Oh, the old days, when we all had a waistline and tits that you couldn't tuck into your pants.' She laughed down the line.

'Er, yeah, those days, Bunty,' I said, laughing too. 'Listen, Philomena has been up to see Mum. Senga knows Isa is on her way as well. She'll be so made up to see you all. We could even start up another menage,' I joked.

'God, I've not heard that word in years, Sharon,' she said. Then added, 'That's good, hen, we can all talk, I cannae wait.'

'I'm going to try to speak to Janine soon – I have her care home details from Isa. Listen, Bunty, do you have a number for Sandra?' I asked. 'She's the only one I can't find.'

'Sandra? No, hen, you asked me that before. I cannae recall her.'

'Yes, you can, Bunty, I'm asking about your friend called Sandra. You said you weren't close the other day, but Isa says you were.' I was getting irritated now; they were definitely giving me the runa-round. 'Maybe you've forgotten her? She had blonde hair and was married to a guy called Jim. Does that not ring any bells? Isa was very clear that you would know about her.'

I was not going to give her the space or time to brush me off again.

'Oh, aye, if that's what Isa says . . . I think I do remember a Sandra?' She let out a forced laugh. 'Now if it's the same lassie I am thinking of, her brother's wife Helen has a cousin, Dougie, who married my niece Lisa; they got divorced the same year Charles and Diana got split up and she runs a hairdresser's in Paisley. I'll ask them,' she said in typical Glasgow style, where an entire family tree and surplus information can be shoved like an unwanted side salad into a word kebab.

'Thanks, Bunty, that sounds like something. Is Sandra still with Jim, do you know?' I asked.

Bunty went quiet. The line crackled and I thought she had been disconnected. I looked at my phone to check and then I heard her say, 'No, hen.'

And then she hung up.

1977
December

Got up early, ate some toast and got the kids out the door for school. Janet has lost her new anorak and is wearing three layers of my mammy's hand-knitted 'fancy cardigans' to keep her warm.

There's a rash of the scabies going round again. Philomena said the doctor is giving out big bottles of lotion that you paint on your skin and apparently you have to burn all your bedding and mattress to get rid of them. I don't know anyone other than Margo Leadbetter from *The Good Life* who could afford to do that. The rest of us just head to the steamie, hot-boil all our bedding and spray chemicals on our mattress and floors.

I am heading down to the Barras market this weekend to pick up some cheap curtains and a big bag of second-hand books. All I do is read when the kids are in their beds. I can lose myself in a good book. I like to read about women, spies, murder and sexy locations. Not love stories so much these days. Nobody in a Mills and Boon book has scabies, fights off a violent man over a pot of mince or has to give the provy man a quick grope at her boobs to pay off some debt. It's all too much sweetness and sometimes, when life is kicking you in the fanny, you can do without that, so I avoid them. I have been feeling down lately. Am exhausted cleaning houses, living in debt, worrying about Sandra and Janine and Bunty and dealing with the kids. That bastard Billy is swanning about like a drunk lord while my hands are raw with bleach. This isn't how I saw my life. I can only hope for a better council house to see me through to my forties. You never read about eyes burning with bleach in a Mills and Boon book, do you?

The school tortoise has gone missing and we think Janet has hidden it somewhere but she refuses to be drawn on the subject. I can do without this shite this week. I think I'll drop her off at Dirty Donna's house and tell her father to sort it out. I won't . . . but I am thinking about it.

Got a visit from Sandra, Bunty and Isa this evening. So, Isa is single again as her Dunoon Yankee Boy apparently did have a wife the whole time and another girlfriend from Dundee. She lost it when she found out. I heard she got the ferry down there with a wee can of paint-thinner and threw it all over his fancy car. Hell hath no fury like a Glasgow woman with a tin of Nitromors in her handbag. The security guys threw her off the base, not before she gave them a mouthful.

She was in my flat in bits, drinking a few cans. Bunty sang some good, sad, angry songs, Sandra held her tight and my Sharon emptied the ashtrays and gave us all a big speech about feminism and how men are the patriarchy and rule our lives. Janet came in dressed as Gary Glitter covered in tin foil and John tap-danced on the linoleum – it fair cheered us all up.

Laddie tried to hump Sandra's new leather handbag and the kids screamed the house down.

The Queen became a granny as Princess Anne has had a wee boy and called him Peter. Anne's husband Mark is really handsome and you can tell he loves her. 'Mull of Kintyre' is number one in the charts, and on *Crossroads* Sandy has a new girlfriend.

CHAPTER 19

2019
Day thirteen
Sharon

Janet had finally come home for the night and she looked fabulous. It was just her on her own; her husband stayed behind with her stepson as he had school to go to. Janet had never been a pretty child but she'd grown into her very striking looks. After a fleeting flirtation with speed and some other hard drugs in the late eighties, she'd found her own place in the world. She was shorter than me, with blonde cropped hair that made her huge eyes look less Boris Karloff. The play she'd been directing had had brilliant advance reviews ('dark, disturbing and compelling' – sounded about right for Janet) and was about to be opened to the public. She looked every inch the Soho artist with her Afghan coat, leather hat and wooden clogs that clattered about the floor and faintly reminded me of Mum's Scholl's from the seventies.

'So, the old bird is hanging on, good for her. I thought I'd never get here, Sharon – I'm so sorry, things kept happening. I would never have forgiven myself if I had missed her,' she said as she sipped water in the foyer of the city hotel near the hospital. She didn't want to stay overnight at Mum's and there was no second bedroom anyway. John had said he would be happy to take the sofa at Mum's when he finally arrived, hopefully soon.

I watched her closely and picked my moment.

'Remember that big red book I mentioned? It's very revealing,' I told her.

'Ha! I bet it is!' Her eyes lit up excitedly.

'You were a creepy child who choked people with a skipping rope and stole the school tortoise.' I laughed.

'I simply set it free.' Janet smiled broadly. 'Can I see the diary?'

'Sure, it's in the car. I'm trying to make sense of it all myself. Mum hasn't really spoken much since she told me to read it. Honestly, Janet, it's funny, scary, and really bloody sad. What a hard, fucked-up life she had,' I replied.

'Yeah, I was there Sharon. You left just before she started to get really depressed and moody,' she replied. A shadow of something I couldn't quite make out passed over her face.

That shook me. Guilt sat in my stomach like a bad dinner. I'd been so caught up in my own life, in getting away. I should have come home more often from university; I shouldn't have left Janet and John to shoulder that burden alone. What had happened to Mum?

Janet told me how she'd seemed to cut herself off, not going out as she used to, and her pals hadn't come around as much. She'd stopped singing to *Top of the Pops*, stopped laughing as loud, and had become old really quickly. It was no surprise that we'd all left the tenements and created new lives for ourselves. We were all running away from something, but I'd never thought Mum might have been too.

I sat quietly, trying to recall what Senga had looked like on my visits back home in the eighties. I clearly hadn't been paying enough attention.

We left the hotel and got into my car. We set off up through the Clydeside expressway to the hospital and Janet flicked through the diary as I drove. 'There are pages missing,' she said.

'I know. I don't know why, or where they are. I haven't got to the end yet,' I replied.

'You haven't read the whole thing yet? Why not?' she asked, staring at me.

'I'm just processing it all as I go,' I said.

I parked and climbed the stairs, walking through the big sliding doors to the hospital with the weary confidence of someone who had been there too many times. Janet followed on behind, her clogs drumming a beat on the Victorian concrete stairs.

When we reached Mum's ward, I said hello to Shirley at the nurses' reception station. Janet was right behind me, holding my hand.

Janet looked visibly shocked to see how frail Mum was. I heard her gasp and she let out a wee sob, her hand now at her mouth. I had forgotten how disturbing it was seeing Senga like this. She was asleep, propped up between all the wires and machines. Janet and I sat on either side of her bed and took turns holding her hand as she slept. Janet stroked her face and we sat for a good while in silence. Then the doctor came in to give us an update: an upping of medication; more blood tests.

'I'm sorry I didn't come back sooner, Mum,' Janet said quietly after he'd gone. Her face was drained of colour and she looked like a wee girl sitting there in the plastic chair.

I left her with Mum and went off to get us some coffees, just to give her some alone time to gather herself.

When I came back, we drank the weak, tinny-tasting, lukewarm coffee and laughed as I told Janet and Mum about Steven and how he's now into wild swimming and wearing cargo pants with crocs. Janet sighed dramatically, throwing her hands up as she rolled her eyes. 'He's a wanker. He always thought he was too good for you. You should shag someone else soon and enjoy your life.'

I giggled. 'Shh, Janet, Mum will hear you.'

Senga moved under the covers, squeezed our hands and opened her eyes. 'You're here,' she said with a smile to Janet. 'Good to see you, my wee lassie.' Her voice once more sounded dry and husky.

'Yes, I'm here, Mammy. It's so good to see your face,' Janet said. She bent and kissed Mum's head. 'I was just giving our Sharon some advice about that idiot she married. I think she should sell the house, take the cash and go travelling; it's all she ever wanted. She's still young. She needs to make sure she takes lots of selfies and puts them up on Instagram,' she added as she whipped out her vape and huffed out a cloud of blueberry-scented steam. 'And she needs to write a diary, like you did.'

Senga laughed quietly and nodded.

'Stop that now,' said a passing nurse as she popped her head into Mum's room and pointed at the vapour.

Janet slipped her vape between her knees. 'I'm bringing my skipping rope back with me next time,' she said to us after the nurse had gone.

Janet was quiet as we walked towards the hospital café for lunch. Then she turned to me and I could see she was crying.

'She said hello to me, Sharon,' Janet wept as she fumbled for her vape machine. 'The specialist said that sometimes cancer patients get stronger and . . . '

I passed her a tissue from my bag and she wiped under both eyes.

'Janet, I know, and I hear you, but it's like they get better before they get worse,' I said to her gently. 'I don't want you getting your hopes up. Mum is not coming out of here to resume her bingo nights with Maggie and wee Betty. She's comfortable, and that's the best we can hope for.'

Janet nodded silently and we hugged. The emotional strain of watching Mum waiting to die, never quite making it out of the murky depths of her medication fog to have a decent chat or say goodbye, was exhausting and terrifying. How did you make up for lost time? How did people do this?

I left after lunch and Janet stayed with Mum for a few more hours. I had things to do.

1977
December

Got up at eight in the morning, let Laddie out. Then I heated up the soup from yesterday, put the oven on to heat the kitchen and felt all the clothes on the pulley. They were still damp. This house is freezing.

I tried to give wee John a lie-in. He's been getting bullied at school again. I swear to fucking God, if anyone calls him a sissy once more I am going round to knock them out with the dog's leash. Lots of boys are good at tap dancing.

John keeps asking to see his dad. I came home from the shops one teatime last week and Billy was there, decked out in his platform shoes and Rod Stewart T-shirt playing Action Man on my hall car-pet. I hadn't the heart to throw him out, wee John looked so happy. I just wish Billy was more consistent with his parenting – my heart is roasted with him. And who let him in? I want to know when he is going to turn up, not have him sneak in when my back is turned.

My Janet tried again to 'accidentally' strangle one of Bunty's twins with her skipping rope, but got caught by the school mon-itor. That's another lecture for me about Janet and her 'macabre sense of self'.

The lassies met again last night and there's a lot going on.

Sandra got a loan of my Leichner make-up to cover another new/ old black eye. Jim doesn't like her wearing make-up but she needs to go to the housing corporation about the complaints she got with her screaming at all hours and them fighting. They might get evicted – her neighbours are churchgoing old people who weren't prepared for the hell that Jim unleashes on a regular basis. He's been dragged out by the cops twice for selling stolen goods but his mum keeps bailing him out and he escapes jail every time it goes to court. Am hoping he serves a long sentence soon to give Sandra a break, as he's convinced she has something wrong with her womb. If he finds out she's using my birth control pills I'm sure he will be up here in a flash, kicking me about the street as well. Sandra is like a deranged hostage – one minute she's showing us the lovely necklace Jim bought her, the next she's hiding the purple bruises on her body.

She said he got her a Goblin Teasmade, it's like an alarm clock with a kettle and cups that pours your tea two minutes before you wake up. That's all she needs, boiling hot water right beside her pillow. A walk to the kitchen would at least give her a five-minute break from him.

Isa has a new boyfriend, Andrew, who works beside Davie Dunsmore on the coal vans. She doesn't hang around with a broken heart for long. She's much more resilient than I am, I think. She likes them tall, dark and handsome but when he's scrubbed clean he's the shiniest, blondest, bluest-eyed young man you ever saw. My mammy says he looks like one of the Hitler Youth, and all that's missing is *Lederhosen* and a yodelling voice. Andrew plays the accordion, so that'll cheer all the neighbours up when he whips that out for the party. It's good to see Isa happy. That Tallahassee cowboy still doesn't know it was her who went crazy on the base with paint thinners.

But the biggest news came from Bunty.

First, she got a letter from the twins' dad, big Jackie MacNamara, in Spain. She says he owns a pub there and he wants to see his boys. Bunty said, 'Eleven years it's taken the bastard to want to see his sons, so he can run up my hump.'

We all agreed that she should tell the twins and let them see their daddy. There's enough weans round here without a father in their life and he wasn't a bad guy, just a big idiot who was good at singing Shirley Bassey songs. So hopefully in the New Year he'll see the boys. Sharon told Bunty not to come across as a man-hater. She said she's been reading all about an American feminist called Gloria Steinem and explained that women's anger can frighten men. I jokingly told her to have a word with Sandra, but Sandra didn't find that funny. Sharon said Jim is terrified of strong women and wants to 'uphold the patriarchy', whatever that means. She said he's nothing but a wife-beater.

I can't believe my Sharon used those words – 'wife-beater'. You think you can protect your kids from all that is happening, but it must be obvious to everyone that Jim is going to be the death of Sandra. Sandra looked shocked as well. 'Is that what you all think?' she asked.

'We're worried to death about you,' I said, truthfully.

Sharon is so grown-up, she will be applying to university one day, she says. I can't imagine anyone in my family could make it to university, but she is bright enough. I hope she does leave here and gets to see the world. There must be more out there for the next generation. My heart is fit to burst with pride.

Bunty is also in big trouble. The Devlins have sussed that she's been helping herself to her cousins' loot and selling it on. She's been stealing from the thieves and that's a bold move for a wee woman, but they've also now beaten up her cousins as well. To be honest, I don't care about her shitty cousins but it's getting dangerous now. She's worried it will escalate and they'll end up at her door again, this time with weapons, and you don't want the kids seeing that. What a fucking mess. A trip to see Jackie might be good to get her away.

I heard on the radio that another woman has been attacked in Leeds. So I switched the station over and had a dance to some Abba to try and take my mind off it.

CHAPTER 20

2019
Day thirteen
Sharon

After leaving Janet at the ward with Mum, I headed back to the flat to have a quick read of the diary, do some emails and find Janine's care home.

God, Mum was talking about the Yorkshire Ripper! I remembered the day they finally caught him; we sat and watched it on the TV. I was seventeen, it was the year before I left to go to uni, and in the year or so before that, when Janet and I were starting to grow up, it had felt as though Mum became paranoid about our every move. Now, with a girl of my own, I know she must have been beside herself. Even after they caught him, she still seemed on edge, scared for us to go anywhere alone.

There had been a documentary about it all on the telly earlier in the year, I remembered watching it with Steven – or rather, I watched, while he sat and looked at his phone. Apparently, the police had questioned Sutcliffe nine times over five years, and they'd let him go each time. Whenever Mum's diary mentioned the abuse Sandra suffered at the hands of her prick of a husband, I was in disbelief that he wasn't locked up. But if they couldn't put away that bloody psychopath it was no wonder Jim got away with what he did to Sandra. It felt as though we women lived our lives being dismissed, not listened to, ignored – even ones as loud and brash as my wee mum.

Janet would be packing up to fly back to London on the red eye tomorrow morning from Glasgow airport. She was coming back

147

up again in a couple of days, and hopefully John will have his new passport by then and be on his way too.

Time to go see Janine. The home she was living in was about twenty minutes from Mum's flat.

The nurse on duty looked surprised to see me. Apparently, Janine didn't get many visitors now. When I explained about Senga, her face changed. 'Oh, yes, Senga did come to visit Janine, but she hasn't been for a while. I'm sorry to hear she's poorly,' she replied.

I was led down a corridor to a large lounge, and I spotted a woman with long white hair and a fantastic bone structure who must be Janine.

'Janine, hen,' said the nurse, 'this is Sharon, she's Senga's daughter. Remember Senga?'

Janine looked up slowly.

'She's not so good at remembering things now,' said the nurse. 'Don't worry if she doesn't know who you are.'

'Where's Senga?' Janine asked. 'You're not her but you look like her.'

'I'm Sharon, her daughter. Mum isn't very well, she's in the Infirmary,' I said, sitting down next to her. 'She's given me her diary to read and she mentions you,' I added. 'Do you remember her friends?'

Janine looked confused.

'She's written that she came up to visit you in Easterhouse a few times?'

Janine smiled suddenly. 'Aye, she did. We sat on the veranda. She was a good friend, your mammy. She used to call it Ipanema; we pretended we were on the beach.' She let out a quiet chuckle.

'Do you remember Bunty and Isa and Sandra?' I asked carefully.

Her face clouded again. 'No, hen.'

I showed her the pictures I'd found in the diary. She looked confused. 'I don't know who they are. Where is Senga?' she asked, looking worried.

'I think you should probably leave her be now,' said the nurse.

I got up again. 'Senga sends you her love,' I said sadly, and I hugged her gently.

I sat in the car outside and cried for what felt like the hundredth time since I got back to Glasgow, and it was a proper release. Then I opened the pages of the diary to hear Mum's voice again, from when her life was all still ahead of her.

1978
New Year's Day

Got up early yesterday, gutted the house out, washed the windows, smoked a few fags and got the steak pie started. It was New Year's Eve!

Bunty, Philomena and Isa came round first, and we had a huge carry-out: wine, vodka and some cream soda off the Alpine van. We'd invited Sandra but Jim wouldn't let her out and she has a sprained wrist in a plaster, said she fell on the ice. Bunty's cousin says she saw Jim in La Trattoria, the fancy Italian restaurant near George Square, with a dark-haired older woman on a date. He was all over her like a dirty tom cat, and poor Sandra lying in bed as that bastard is out on the town. Her nice neighbour, Mrs Foy, said she would keep an eye on her.

The house looked smart, we had Donna Summer blasting on my stereo, windows wide open and we could hear people cheering down our street as the bells rang out across Glasgow to let us know 1978 was here. The telly is rubbish at Hogmanay – lots of old Scottish people in tartan dancing about as a guy sings about Loch Lomond. I have never seen a man in a kilt in real life but if you watch anything about Scotland on the TV you would be forgiven for thinking we all live in thatched cottages or dress in Highland formalwear to take the dog for a walk, while eating shortbread.

The kids were up dancing – my Sharon was all dolled up for her first big night getting to stay up late at New Year. When I was her age, I was with Billy, had a full-time job as a hairdresser and was trying hard to keep my man happy, letting him have sex with me just to make sure he never went with another lassie. I want more for Sharon. She is so smart, she will be the first in our family to go to college and get a degree. Imagine!

We had all the neighbours round to mine, people from across the back that we hardly knew. Davie Dunsmore brought up his cat (it doesn't like being alone) and it had a fight with Laddie in the hallway. There were babies lying in prams, and old folk sat in the big chairs as we sang songs and passed round whisky. There was dancing and partying till six a.m. All the kids ended up in one room, lying in beds covered in coats and full of shortbread and Irn-Bru as the adults conked out on chairs. A tangled mess of limbs, smelly feet and discarded clothes.

I know that Sharon got up like a silent safety officer, picking her way through the drunken, sleepy bodies to make sure all the cigarettes were put out and the fire guard was placed in front of the grate. Then she could finally sleep in peace.

This new year, 1978, holds so much hope for me. I am trying to get out of debt. I have even managed to pay for Christmas without too much begging and borrowing.

CHAPTER 21

2019
Day fourteen
Sharon

Janine's dementia had brought it home to me how cruel time could be. As soon as I could get Mum's pals around her, I would feel I had done something worthwhile. What a horrible, debilitating heartbreaking disease. It made me yearn for the past when these women were full of life and vitality. That New Year diary entry reminded me of times when they really did live large.

Mum's New Year parties were legendary. Even as a student in the eighties, I never saw people who could party like Senga and her pals. Mum loved doing her full Kate Bush rendition as we moved big lamps and small footstools like tiny stage-hands, so she could snake and move through the whole room as she belted out 'Wuthering Heights'. We would do backing vocals and Laddie would bark at all the noise and shenanigans. I could still see it all now, as though I were sitting right there watching it all again. The faded living room carpet that never quite reached the skirting boards; the pulley in the kitchen to dry clothes as a steaming hot soup pot bubbled away; the bedroom shared with siblings who had no concept of privacy. The shame of scabies, of free school meals and the mammies who cried to Tammy Wynette on the radio. These images replayed over and over again. My head and heart was full of Mum's diary.

Then there was me, sitting in the coffee shop staring at my laptop, wondering how the hell did I sort my life out? Senga had wanted so much for me and what had I done? Got an education, married a boring arsehole, had one daughter and bought a big house in Bristol, then played life safe until it had all fallen apart. Fuck, I was dull. My mum had more guts, determination and ambition in one finger than I had in my whole body. The more I read, the more I admired her spirit. I had been so keen to get away from her and the threadbare carpet, and cheap, faded bath towels. Now I couldn't tell her enough how much I loved and admired her.

I called my daughter, Louise, on FaceTime; I needed to speak to her. I needed to feel anchored to someone who loved me and made me feel human, someone who had never seen me as a failure. I was so grateful we had a close relationship.

She picked up immediately. 'Hey, Mum, how are you? How is Granny?'

'She's holding on, Louise, but she's weak. I don't know how long she has left.' I paused. 'I've told her all about you and my beautiful granddaughter. How are you? How is Poppy?' I asked. 'Can I see her? I really miss her.'

She held the phone over my beautiful sleeping granddaughter. 'She's great, Mum, she's sleeping more. I saw Dad, as you know. What the hell is going on with you two?' she asked with an exasperated sigh in her voice. During her pregnancy, Steven had been less doting father and more absent parent. To be honest, Louise had seen the signs of my marriage folding before I did. 'He's travelling and clearly moving on. Mum, don't let him walk all over you. Honestly, you're worth so much more than the way he treats you,' she said.

She'd said the same once before as we'd been sitting in her sunny garden, Louise rubbing her huge tummy. I had been doing what most middle-aged women did when their husband started wearing Joop aftershave, shaving their back and moisturising their eyelids: I'd ignored it and waited for him to buy a motorbike or come out as a drag artist. Louise had been able to see that I was upset and on edge, watching for signs of an affair.

Our daughter deserved honesty.

'Oh, Louise, you know what: he's a complete dick. He's started his life over, apparently, the mad fucker.' I laughed.

Louise sounded shocked: 'Mum, I can tell you're back in Glasgow – the swearing is in full force.'

'Yes, well, sometimes I need a bit of Senga in me to cope. I miss her, Louise.' I started to gulp tears.

'Mum, you're going to be fine. You and Dad have outgrown each other – it happens to lots of people. It might be the best thing to happen to you. Please stay strong for Granny. I love you, Mum,' she replied.

I thought about her words as I ended our phone call. It was true, I didn't think there was anything left that would make me sort things out with Steven. I'd never said this to Louise, yet she had just said it to me, and I needed to process it. Coming back home and putting distance between us, and reading about how my mum had coped with all life threw at her, had given me the strength to see there was no coming back from this. I needed to seek out things that made me happy, and Steven wasn't one of them.

Louise and I had always had a great bond; she was my priority when she was growing up. Steven liked to show her off when it suited him but, looking back, he really wasn't into singsongs or games or nappies. It didn't escape my notice that . . . fuck, I might have married a richer, duller, more annoying version of my dad. I was such a twat.

The coffee shop was busy, the work emails distracting. I decided to take the first step and email a lawyer about a divorce. I had my date with Clyde to look forward to as well. He hasn't heard of hot yoga, which is a positive thing. When I boldly explained that my husband had run away with a hot yoga teacher he'd just laughed and said, 'Bet you she's flexible and fucking annoying.' I liked Clyde; he didn't look as if he was living a life half empty.

1978
January

Woke up and the whole world is frozen. I can look all the way up to Barlinnie prison and the snow has etched a black and white landscape as far as the eye can see. The trees in the front gardens of the houses across the road look like frigid white statues and the ice has made patterns on the insides of the windows. This house is stone cold and damp.

The kids were chittering in their beds so last night I brought them into my room, filled up some glass Irn-Bru bottles with hot water and put them under my blankets and warned them not to kick them about in case they smashed and slashed our legs to bits. We all huddled up together and listened to Radio Luxembourg with the lights out and ate biscuits in bed. Janet wanted to tell ghost stories, but wee John begged her not to. I love having them in beside me, reminds me of when they were babies.

What will 1978 bring us? More money problems? Men giving me grief? I think I worry too much. Sometimes I lie in bed and feel as though a huge wave of worry is going to engulf me. Like it would swallow me up and leave me no way to get back out. I know my mum's generation had it harder with the war and stuff, but sometimes thinking about bringing up three kids alone and trying hard to dodge the debt men, keep a roof over our head and make money on the side can bring on a wee panic in my chest. Like someone is drumming my heart with a pot and spoon. Sometimes I get so frightened I can hear the blood rush in my ears. That's not normal, is it?

Bunty and Isa came and helped me clear up after the Hogmanay party. I had to go around the houses giving back borrowed tables, a soup pot, tumblers and chairs. Everyone round the closes looked so exhausted and worn out, probably hangovers and dealing with all the domestic issues family get-togethers can cause.

Bunty says they haven't seen Sandra in a few weeks, so we are going to check up on her this afternoon. Her neighbour, Mrs Foy, called the police again, as my mammy said Jim dragged Sandra out onto the street and threw her on the road. All her neighbours were talking about it, 'He's a fucking monster,' my mammy said, and I've never heard her swear like that. He never got kept in the police station, because apparently a drunken domestic isn't actually a crime.

I know it must be hard to leave, her being a Catholic and all. The new priest, Father Crawley, has been giving her marriage guidance. She told us the Father said she had to be patient as 'sometimes men hit women because women argue too much'. I was so angry at this. Jesus must be horrified these men excuse violence to his wee flock.

I met that Father Crawley in the Co-op waiting in the queue for chopped pork. I leaned over and told him he will be organising Sandra's funeral soon if Jim doesn't stop kicking her head in. He just looked shocked at me, told me to mind my own business and walked out without his shopping. Old Theresa behind the counter told me that I should be respectful to a man of the cloth. I laughed and said, 'The last priest ran away with your niece.' So that's me barred from the Co-op. I need to get my chopped pork from the butcher again. I hope they have forgiven Laddie for peeing in their doorway and dragging out a cow carcass from the meat hooks.

Sandra won't have a word said against Jim, she's like one of those Stepford wives from that movie, walking about thin as a broom, doped up on Valium and painkillers, making well-presented hot dinners and keeping the house clean. She actually showed me how to clean venetian blinds with a special hand sock, as Jim checks the slats for dust. What fucking man has time to check window blinds for dust? She said he hates anything being out of place, but he doesn't mind that her nose is slightly bent from being punched over the years and that her pinky finger can't bend properly from being broken backwards when he's in a bad mood.

We need to do something but I don't know what; we are all caught up in our own lives and business. Wee John has a dance showcase this week, Sharon has a huge school project about 'cooking with gas' and I said I would help her, and Janet has stuck chewing gum into Rhona Darroch's hair and the teacher wants to speak to me AGAIN. I have my cleaning jobs and, as if that's not enough, Janine has her nephew coming out of jail and she's throwing a party and wants me to do her hair. Davie Dunsmore gave me a run up in his coal van. I arrived in style and dust.

Bunty and Isa were already there when I arrived. Bunty already had her hair up and looked lovely, like a very sophisticated but sweary woman in a nice frock. I was in the middle of doing Janine's hair when Alan the Alpine man arrived uninvited, carrying a case of cola. Someone let him in.

Janine was mortified as she didn't want him in her house. He's been really creepy as fuck and pushy, calling on her at all hours and following her. 'Enough of this shit,' I said, leaving Janine's hair in rollers as Isa, Bunty and I took him down the close and sent him packing.

'She doesn't want you in her house, mate. Just leave her alone for fuck's sake, Alan,' Isa hissed at him. 'We've all clocked what you're doing.'

'We've warned you before – now we'll start reporting you,' I added, for good measure.

He was pretending to be offended and tried to make out he was pals with her but her nephew, fresh from the jail, shouted over the veranda at him, 'You come back here and I will do time for you, ya wanker. You just try me.'

So I think that's Alan told. He won't be bothering us again.

CHAPTER 22

2019
Day fourteen
Sharon

I slammed down the book after reading about poor Sandra. I was so fucking angry. It was good to see Mum kicking creepy Alan into touch though – don't mess with these women!

I got into the car, grabbed my bag and headed up to see Senga. I was missing Janet already; I would have spent a good few hours with her over a bottle of wine bitching the hell out of that diary entry. Having someone who shared our past life had been such a support. But it was back to just me and Mum again.

It was the weekend, so the hospital was that bit quieter. Her room was very warm. The familiar smell of boiled food and antiseptic was starting to become normal to me. Mum looked so peaceful, there yet not there. I brushed her hair and wiped her face with a flannel.

I told her that Clyde and I were going on our date. I had to tell someone. She smiled at me but said nothing. I couldn't quite believe it was happening, I was GOING ON A DATE! Wee Betty next door was coming back up to see Mum, so I knew someone would be with her for a bit this evening. I hated her not having a night visit and just because I was having fun that didn't mean she should suffer.

What the hell was I doing? My confidence was crashing. Here I was, nearly divorced, fifty-six years old and living in my mum's floral flat in Govan. How the hell had this all happened? What was I thinking?

I didn't have my own hairdryer with me – it had never made it into the suitcase when I'd fled Bristol in the rush to get home. Mum's hairdryer was like an asthmatic donkey blowing my head; it looked like the same one she used when she styled hair in the seventies. I decided to go with natural waves and the basic make-up I had in my bag. I checked myself in the hall mirror and I did look OK; I'd lost weight since being in Glasgow, which suited me. My eyes were surprisingly bright and my jeans fitted fabulously over my bum and, luckily, I did have decent underwear.

Fuck, what was I thinking? I hadn't been with another man in over thirty years.

The bar was in Glasgow's West End, up a wee cobbled lane with fairy-lights and whitewashed, renovated stables, and it was so gorgeous. I would never have found it myself. Tables outside with overhead heaters, lots of couples chattering and enjoying the atmosphere with waiters rushing about. It was busy and Clyde was there waiting, smiling at me, arms outstretched.

'Welcome to the posh bit of Glasgow,' he said, and reached out for my hand and led me in. He didn't look as young now that he wasn't standing behind the coffee counter. In the midst of so many students and young adults talking loudly, he looked more mature in his white shirt and navy coat.

'Drink?' he asked.

'Wine, I guess?'

'Guess again – the wine here is shit.'

We laughed and I finally relaxed. He put his arm around my waist as we walked to our table.

'Oh, please, not the waist, take my wrist, it's the firmest part of me,' I said, and laughed, holding up my arm.

'Stop that shit, Sharon,' he said playfully as he grabbed me tighter, before pulling out a chair for me to sit down. We sat in the candlelight and talked, and I felt as though I was being listened to for the first time in years. I told him bits about my life, we swapped stories and heartbreaks (his more than mine), music tastes and travel stories – well, a few holidays in the Maldives for me, and a world music tour for him, until he'd come home to bury his father and put down some roots.

'Let's go,' he simply said an hour or so later, and we headed to the concert. I found myself watching him as he talked easily to people and introduced me to friends. This was his world and he was in his element. He took my hand as we danced, and when he kissed me, it felt good.

'Shall we go somewhere else?' he asked, and I nodded, feeling a genuine flood of desire. Within twenty minutes we were in his flat overlooking the river, I was pulling his sweater over his head and he was taking off my good bra and pulling me down to his bed. The sex was surprisingly energetic and Clyde asked me what I wanted him to do. Steven's moves had become so predictable and our sex almost silent; this felt so new and exciting. Clyde's watch did get caught in my hair and he got cramp in his calf, so it was nothing like in the movies. But it was good and much needed – who knew going on top was such fun? I was exhausted but happy.

Rod Stewart was playing on his sound system, and he told me he was a big fan and once had a haircut like him. I told him, 'So did my dad.' It was the first time I had laughed that loudly in ages.

I will have to call Elaine and tell her about this tomorrow. And maybe Janet too. They'll be delighted! What a hoot.

1978
January, Thursday

Woke up to more snow. The kids are back at school but I am feeling so low, I don't even want to get out of bed. I don't know what's wrong with me. I suppose writing it down helps me understand what I'm going through – maybe I will look back at this book one day and think, Senga, you gloomy old cow, stop moaning about your life, some people have it worse. I have the new *Saturday Night Fever* LP but not even music can lift me out of this mood.

I don't want to go to the doctor's as I don't want tablets. The last time I went in to see him and tried to explain how I felt, he just stared at me like I was taking up his time. I just want someone to listen to me. I don't like feeling sorry for myself but there are days when I can't face lifting my head off the pillow.

Wee John needs a new winter coat and Sharon wants to go to France for the school trip and to be honest I think she'll need to walk there because I don't have the spare money. I hear there are cash-in-hand shifts at the seafood factory near my mammy's house, but the smell of all those clams and fish makes me sick and its freezing in there at this time of year.

Bunty said she would swap me the menage week to pay for Sharon's trip. It's so kind but I am just so fed up borrowing to get by.

The only thing that cheered me up today was seeing Billy Connolly back on the *Parkinson* TV show. I made sure I kept enough coins to slot into the meter to watch. I wish I could afford a television of my own like Mrs Bradshaw. But they cost so much.

I was up at the mansion yesterday doing the cleaning and the family are off to Portugal next week to buy a holiday home. Imagine being so rich you could fly to the Algarve in January to buy another house! I can't imagine having that much money. It must be like winning Spot the Ball and going crazy with cash. I am looking forward to it, though, as the whole house will be empty and Mrs Bradshaw's asked me to keep an eye on it. I can lie on her couch, feed the dogs and watch as much telly as I want. I might even wear her fluffy slippers, eat her good biscuits and treat myself to a wee half of vodka.

Met Billy at the post office yesterday. He actually wished me a Happy New Year. Donna was raging, she was standing there in a rabbit-fur coat, trying to sound posh buying stamps. Billy's eyes were red raw as he's allergic to rabbits but he probably hasn't mentioned that in case he seems 'weak', daft arsehole. He looked like he had got that myxomatosis, which is ironic. He looked older and fatter. I honestly look at him now and cannae imagine why I thought he was sexy or interesting. I must have been off my head at sixteen years old. What was I thinking? He used to slag me off for reading books and being interested in history.

I will be watching the telly tonight, that always cheers me up. *All Creatures Great and Small* is on. I might get some tips about animal welfare, for if I ever pick up another pig.

Sunday

Am feeling better today. I picked up a few *Reader's Digests* from Mrs Bradshaw (I love them) and read about a woman in Texas who used 'writing her feelings down' as a therapy for her mental breakdown, so I think this is a good thing to do, just keep pouring it all out. She did eventually get it published as a book about 'self-help' and became really rich and now counsels famous people in America. I cannae see that happening for me, can you imagine?

Sandra finally came over, along with the other girls. She told us Jim is being really nice to her and helping her do up the back bedroom. I always think something bad has happened when she sits there praising him, it's like she's 'overcompensating' (one of the words in the self-help article) and wants to convince herself that her life isn't constantly in danger.

I am exhausted with her, but we all love Sandra and we are all she has got. Jim has managed to stop her family from visiting and her wee mammy is worried sick, she's only allowed to see her at chapel. The only reason she gets to see us is that he knows if she disappears we will all be at his door. He hates us but he is playing it safe, letting her out when she is not showing any bruises.

Good news – I have scraped enough money to send my Sharon to France on the school trip. I might have to work a few extra shifts cleaning the pubs but at least we got there. My lassie will see the Eiffel Tower.

CHAPTER 23

2019
Day fifteen
Sharon

There were days when Mum's diary lifted me up with hope and days when I realised not much had changed, especially where mental health is concerned.

Women in my mum's day weren't allowed to have a mental illness. I recalled Senga saying, 'I don't have time for depression, I have two jobs and three weans.' What a fucked-up outlook. I was so glad she'd written things down. She was left to deal with her own problems and I think the diary did help.

Today was the day John finally got home to Glasgow. I couldn't wait to see him, so I parked at the airport and stood at the international arrivals to see him come through the gate.

So many people were pouring through the gate looking travel-weary and then . . . there he was. Tall and tan and lovely, our John, if not so young any more. Dressed in a fitted blue suit and pale pink shirt with a dark caramel overcoat, carrying his very chic luggage and not a hair out of place. He was definitely Senga's son; he had her cheekbones, and those brilliant blue eyes. We hugged so tight and I could smell that familiar old-fashioned scent that he wore, like grapefruit and woodsmoke. He dropped his luggage and cried in my arms. 'I've missed you,' he whispered.

'Come on, Sunshine Boy, dry your eyes, we're going to see your mammy,' I said.

The drive was pretty quick from Glasgow Airport to the Royal Infirmary. John waited for me to lock the car and, yet again, my feet found the familiar route up the circular staircase and along the pale pastel corridors till we reached Mum's ward.

Shirley was on duty. 'Is this our John we've all heard so much about?' she said as we passed her.

'Yes, this is our John.' I pointed at him and then quickly took him to the side. 'Look, prepare yourself, she does look very frail.'

'I just want to see her, Sharon,' he said, pushing open her door.

His face fell when he saw Mum in that bed, just as Janet's had. He took a big gulping breath, leaned over, kissed Mum's head and took her hand. 'I'm here,' he said, and I swear, even in her sleep she smiled.

She had called him her 'sunshine boy' when he was growing up. John had come out in his teens, which was tough in Glasgow in the eighties, and Mum never really spoke about it. But there was no holding our 'John Boy' back. She'd just got on with it, as had he. I could see why he'd left the city quite young; he'd been on the gay scene in the middle of the AIDS pandemic that had dominated the media at the time, but John had just been determined never to let fear get in the way of his life. He'd charmed the soul of everyone he'd met and worked his way up and through the restaurant business in Glasgow. He'd been the best front-of-house manager in every place he'd ever worked, eventually moving to Monaco. Then he'd gone back to his first love of dancing, and now had his own dance school in Madrid. I was so proud of him.

He took off his coat and jacket, draped them over the plastic chair and knelt beside her, wrapping her head and shoulders in long arms. 'She looks so frail,' he said as he gulped down tears. 'I've been away too long.'

And Senga opened her eyes.

My heart leapt in my chest: two sets of blue eyes staring back at each other, just like reflections on an azure pool.

'Mum, oh, Mum,' I cried out as I rushed to sit beside her.

John took the other side of the bed. We stared at her as if she were a new baby that had just been born. She looked at us both in turn. 'My weans,' she croaked. Then she closed her eyes again.

The young doctor came in and checked her notes and turned to us.

'Your mum is still taking water, but we need to discuss her care plan going forward,' he explained, clicking his pen incessantly. 'She signed a DNR form when she arrived and, when the time arrives for her to go, we will stay with that instruction,' the doctor added. 'I just want you all to be prepared.'

'We know, it's OK,' I said.

'Can we discuss this later?' John said. 'I've only just got here.'

'Sorry,' the doctor said, as he continued clicking his pen.

'You need to stop that clicking, though, it's making me want to scream.'

Senga's voice came from nowhere, stunning us into silence. Then the doctor laughed, we all laughed, and then John cried. As though a river had finally burst its banks, he let it all go as I held him. Watching someone you love die had you crying and laughing and screaming in regular cycles. Today was a crying day.

We spent a few hours with Mum, just chatting. John told her all his news, though she was very sleepy. Eventually Nurse Shirley came in and said, 'Right, you two, let Senga get her rest – away home.' We reluctantly packed up our bags and coats and left the Infirmary.

The drive back to the flat saw a beautiful sunset over the West End of Glasgow, with orange and purple streaks slashing the sky. John was staying with me at Mum's, on the sofa in the living room. We called Janet via WhatsApp when we finally got in and had unpacked John's bags.

'I hear sleeping on the sofa wasn't for you,' John said drily as Janet appeared on the screen in front of us. 'Are you too grand now?'

'Ah, fuck off, John!' she retorted. 'I'm too old for the backache and the flowers give me a migraine. You're looking good on the Spanish sunshine. How is Mum? I'll be back very shortly; the play is up and running and they don't need me any more.'

We gave her an update. John told her how shocked he had been, seeing Senga in the intensive care ward.

'I know how you feel. My heart dropped to my boots when I walked in,' Janet added. We nattered on for a wee bit, then Janet asked how my date had been. 'You've got a glow about you,' she said, peering at me on screen. 'You've definitely had good sex at last!'

We all roared with laughter. Once again Senga's weans were together, and nothing could come between us. 'He's texted me and asked if I want to meet up again,' I confessed. 'I think I might.'

I took the red diary out of my bag and handed it to John. 'You should read some of this before you see Mum again,' I said.

1978
February

We are all so excited to see the film *Saturday Night Fever*. It's set in New York and my God, how handsome is John Travolta? Mrs Bradshaw gave me a wee bit extra for my birthday and I have put it by for the cinema.

I hear there is trouble in paradise *again* with Donna and Billy. It was Bunty, of course, who gave me all the gossip. Apparently, Donna and Billy had a big fight in the street and her mum dragged them both back into the bungalow. Donna's mum can't stand the scandal – well, she'd better get used to it. Billy is a walking fucking scandal.

Took Sharon down to Reeta's Fashion in the Gallowgate to get her some nice clothes for her trip to France. She picked out some lovely checked dungarees and a gypsy top. She is so excited and she deserves this holiday. The passport came through last week and I had a wee pang of jealousy. I wish I had a passport and the chance to travel the world. But then who would clean the pub and Mrs Bradshaw's big house if I wasn't there?

Bunty took the twins to Spain on the bus to see their daddy, Jackie MacNamara. She said the bus was longer than labour pains and twice as painful but she can't afford to fly. The kids loved the beach and she told me, 'To be honest, I had a good time – he's trying to make up for all the shite he left me with.' She brought me back a big bottle of red wine and by fuck it was rough, it would have taken the paint off Davie Dunsmore's coal van. I peed red for days afterwards.

Made crispy pancakes and beans for the kids and started my new book, *Scruples* by Judith Krantz. It's about a woman called Wilhelmina Hunnewell Winthrop who's really fat, then goes to France and gets really thin, and ends up owning a boutique in Beverly Hills. It's brilliant.

CHAPTER 24

2019
Day fifteen
Sharon

I sat in silence as John went through Mum's book and her photos.

He had changed into some very neat skinny jeans and a mulberry-coloured sweater. We had made a big pot of tea in Mum's favourite rose-painted pot, with her matching china cups, and both of us were sitting on matching floral sofas.

I watched his face and reactions. It was as if we were doing Pass the Parcel with Mum's memories and taking turns to comment and reflect on pieces of her life.

'She was a good writer. I feel as though I'm actually in there with her. Why do you think she put it all down, Sharon?' John asked me as he wiped away tears. I didn't know if they were from sadness or laughter.

'I think she just wanted to validate her feelings and to have some "self-care", to quote some millennial-speak,' I answered. 'What a shitty time she had. I wish I could go back and give her money and the chance to have sex with Phil Lynott.'

John laughed and poured some tea, and said, 'When you left for Bristol, Mum kind of went quiet. We never saw much of Sandra and her pals; they drifted off,' he said. 'She quit the cleaning and started working at the insurance offices in town and things changed. She still saw a bit of Philomena and Janine for a while, I think, but after she moved house to here in Govan she spent a lot of her time with Betty and Maggie,' he replied.

'We all left her,' I said. 'I feel shitty about that now.'

'We all had to, Sharon, there was fuck all for us here, remember? She wanted us to do well, she encouraged us all to get far away,' John said, and I nodded. He was right, but it didn't take away the niggling seed of guilt in my stomach.

John asked me what I'd found out about the rest of Mum's gang. I gave him all the info and theories I had gathered so far.

'All that's missing is one of those crime scene boards with photos and bits of string linking everyone up,' he said.

'Trust me, I thought about doing that,' I said.

We decided we definitely had to find Sandra. Mum needed her wee gang of women around her before she went. John said he would do another social media search for Sandra and her extended family. I wolfed down some biscuits, drank more tea and texted Bunty to ask if she's heard anything more. We even talked about Davie Dunsmore – could he still be alive, and would he know where Sandra was?

1978
February, Tuesday

Woke up to the radio blaring somewhere in the house. The Bee Gees were singing 'Staying Alive' while we were nearly dying because Janet was cooking. I had to run quick into the kitchen and, sure as fuck, the place was billowing with smoke. Sharon was off to school early and wee John was making a pot of tea. I am not worried about him, he's careful. It's Janet I fear, as she doesn't pay full attention to a hot frying pan.

Managed to clear up the mess, get them out the door, get Laddie out for a pee and set off for work. Mrs Bradshaw has friends round tonight and she wants all her Doulton dishes cleaned and set out for the dinner party.

Sandra was round last night. She told me she thinks Jim might have been selling stolen cars as the cops were round asking questions and she was terrified of saying the wrong thing. Jim is giving her a bit more freedom now he is more preoccupied with the Devlins and whatever he's doing on the side. That's been good for Sandra and me as we can meet up more. She's still taking my pills.

Isa brought up a suitcase for Sharon's trip to France. It's a good one with a wee lock. Sharon is off this Thursday and I am so excited for her, she has a camera and a new purse with her French money in it. She has been up every night this week counting it out and picking all her clothes and sorting them over and over again. Mrs Bradshaw gave me a pair of soft leather sandals, a French dictionary and a pair of sunglasses for Sharon that belonged to her daughter, Stella; we are lucky to have nice people around us. It's taken a monumental effort to get that kid on this trip but I want her to travel and see the world.

Thursday

I took Sharon and her new suitcase to the school gates today and waved her off. My heart leapt watching her with all her pals, piling on the bus. She looked so happy. It will take at least a day to get to France by bus from Glasgow so God help those teachers with all those teenagers on that trip. Rather them than me – a full crowd of raging hormones, picnic bags and vomiting kids is my idea of hell. But what an experience for them all! Sharon has her camera and promised to take lots of photos.

Got the electricity meter reader man coming round; Bunty spotted him on his rounds and shouted up to my window to let me know, so I have the meter all prepared (took the X-ray paper out and made sure the wheel is turning fine). One day I am going to be able to afford electricity, a colour telly and a big fuck-off fridge. I wish I could go on that TV show *The Generation Game* and walk off with all the big prizes. Knowing my luck, all I would remember is 'a cuddly toy'.

Frank downstairs said he has a mate who is selling a new twin tub washing machine really cheap and he can bring it up for me. So, I am hoping I can get it this week as that old one I have is on its last legs and as much as I like it, the steamie is so hard to get to in winter. Mrs Bradshaw has a front-loading washing machine and tumble dryer in her utility room, it's the absolute height of luxury. Sandra has a twin tub too.

Spent all day wondering how Sharon is getting on with her big trip to France.

CHAPTER 25

2019
Day fifteen
Sharon

We stopped reading at the bit about the trip to France, which was brilliant. I remembered I felt so sophisticated as I walked about Paris in my new sandals and sunglasses. What an amazing trip I had.

John told me he cried for a day when I was away.

'You did not,' I said.

'I did, I was so jealous of you going to Paris, and Janet was rubbish at looking after me when you were away. I was traumatised.' He faked a big sad face.

John shut the book and I stowed it in my bag. We grabbed our coats and headed out of Mum's flat as quietly as possible so Maggie and Betty couldn't pop over for a Q&A. They would have held John hostage until they'd got his entire life and back story if we'd met them on the path.

We headed into the coffee shop, and Clyde was there, all smiles and geniality. We'd been texting today and he'd asked me out again, to dinner, whenever I was ready. I introduced him to John as we waited for our coffees. I blushed, of course, and gave the whole game away.

'So, he's the big ride,' John said as he pulled off his coat and folded it neatly over the arm of a tan sofa.

Flushed with embarrassment, I pushed him into his seat. 'Shut up, John,' I hissed.

'Have you enjoyed floating down the Clyde on his big boat?' he added with a smirk and a nudge.

'We're just pals,' I insisted, hoping Clyde was out of earshot.

'I don't give a fuck what friendship status this is; I'm just glad you've managed to have decent sex with someone who doesn't gargle mouthwash after he goes down on you,' John said as he sipped on his coffee.

'How do you know that?' I gasped shocked.

'Did you forget, you told me years ago? That chinless arsehole you married is currently posing on Instagram with Bendy Brenda or whatever she's called,' he said. 'I've been going through his social media. He's going bald and no amount of hair dye and DeSigual fashionwear is going to graft a personality onto that haunted pudding. So, enjoy the sex with someone new!' John and I laughed. 'And he wears crocs. For fuck's sake, Sharon – that's serial killer material,' John added.

I could see Clyde at the counter, watching me and smiling as he steamed the milk, giving me a sly wink. I blushed again. What the hell was wrong with me?

Clyde came over when the counter was quiet. 'How's your mum, have you seen her?' he asked John.

'Yeah, we saw her when I arrived and we're going back up now. By the way, Clyde, thanks for looking after our Sharon. She tells me you've been a good neighbour and friend to her.'

I stared at him, willing him to shut up. My God, this was embarrassing.

'No worries, she's been worried sick missing you guys. And please give your mum this for me.' Clyde handed John a wee bag with a scone in it.

'Thanks, Clyde, that's a lovely thought. I don't think she can eat this, but it won't go to waste: Sharon loves a big hot scone,' John said as we both got up and walked to the door. I shook my head as Clyde gave us a mock salute as we passed him.

In the car, John said, 'He's hot and he gives out baked goods; he's already better than that fanny you married.'

Mum was asleep when we arrived at the ward but we sat with her, quietly chatting. John rubbed some fancy skin cream on her hands and then we shared the hot buttered scone. The staff nurse came in and told us that Mum had had a comfortable day, and asked us if we knew that Philomena had been to visit again; she told us that Senga had briefly spoken to her.

John and I shared a look, then stared at Mum. But she was asleep, so we couldn't ask what they'd talked about.

1978
March

Sharon gets her photos from her trip to France today and is so excited. She had a great time there, am so happy for her. Her dad met her in the street yesterday and told her he has split up from Donna and he's now living with his cousin up the high flats in Dennistoun. She wouldn't give me much more than that, she says she's not a double agent and if I want to know what he's up to I should speak to him. He hasn't signed the divorce papers yet and I am worried.

I hope I don't run into him. I don't want him pleading to come back. The divorce papers cost enough as it is, without him trying to wheedle his way back into my life.

Bunty, Isa and Sandra are coming to meet me after my cleaning job as I have been invited to Mrs Bradshaw's daughter Stella's wedding and they are going to help me find a nice frock. I have a Provident cheque for £15 and I can get something nice from town. It's been ages since I bought myself anything new and I'm due a wee treat, surely? I have lost a bit of weight over the winter so I can get a good dress and that will see me right through the summer.

The town was quiet because it was a midweek morning, so I made my way along to Buchanan Street and into the big Fraser's store. Wandering round the make-up and perfume counters, I pretended I was a woman with cash to spare. I walked about with a determined pace, as if I often shopped at Fraser's on a Tuesday morning for perfume and make-up.

The ladies who worked on the cosmetic stand looked frightening and hostile to me. It was as if they knew I had a bit of lino in my shoe to stop the rain soaking my tights. I kept moving, sliding between the counters and avoiding eye contact with the ladies. They wore tight uniforms, big hair, bright blue eyeshadow and ruby-red lips as they chatted to the rich, bored women in beige, belted trenchcoats who carried leather handbags. I slipped between the counters and then on a big fancy display I spotted the perfume Tweed, which I had always wanted to smell. I saw the advert on telly and it looked so expensive and chic.

The perfume woman spotted me looking at her display. I tried to duck away before she came near me but she moved in front of me and blocked the way. She had a big blonde bouffant hairdo, and a pink blouse that was tied at the neck in a huge pussycat bow. I shrank under her stare.

'Would you like to try?' She leaned out to me, smiling and holding up the fancy bottle of perfume between long, red, talon-like nails.

My confidence left me. 'I cannae buy it,' I told her and started to walk away, feeling ashamed.

'That's OK,' she said. 'Here, let me spray you and you can try it out.' Her smile was kind. She was probably just another working woman like me, trying to make a living.

'Thanks,' I said, and offered up a wrist.

'No, this is how you use scent,' she said as she stood back.

She told me that when she sprayed the scent I was to 'walk into the mist' and I felt like a million dollars. I wasn't the woman with a hole in her shoe, I was Farrah Fawcett Majors heading to a film première, I was Princess Anne getting ready for a dinner party. I did what she said and walked into the spray and could feel it tingle on my face and the smell was just heavenly. I love Tweed perfume. If I ever get enough cash this Christmas, I am going to buy myself a bottle of that scent.

'Lovely, isn't it?' she said with bright eyes and a huge smile that changed her whole face.

'Gorgeous, very chic,' I said.

She opened a drawer beneath her glass counter and slipped me a tiny sample sachet and said, 'Enjoy.' I almost cried at her kindness. What a lovely woman, to do that for me. I walked past the big shop windows, looking at myself, smiling and flicking my hair like the woman in the Tweed advert on the telly, occasionally sniffing my scarf and inhaling the beautiful scent.

I met up with the girls and we all had a great day and had a fish tea at the café near Glasgow Cross.

I told them that I'm saving to get a new TV and Philomena is going to let me help her sell some football cards.

Bunty was telling me Janine has got a phone fitted in her house. A veranda *and* a phone? we all joked. She's going up in the world indeed – we'll start calling her Joan Collins soon. We knew it's because she's still scared after Alan, though, and we don't blame her. Maybe Sandra should get one too? We have a phone box at the end of our street and I use to it call the six people I know who have a phone. I can remember all their numbers off by heart, but if more of my pals get phones, I am going to have to get a wee book and start writing down numbers.

CHAPTER 26

2019
Day sixteen
Sharon

John and I got up early. He went for a run around the park and then jumped in a cab to go up and see Mum and spend some time with her. I had some business to deal with and a meeting with Bunty.

The café was buzzing this morning and Clyde didn't serve me, so I could only wave at him as I arrived. He looked really pleased to see me, which was nice – it had been a while since I'd had that sort of reaction from anyone. I found I was spending more time in the coffee shop than ever before, as an excuse to see him. I had been on the laptop since eight a.m., dealing with work and some Skype meetings with new clients, but my head wasn't in the game.

I was waiting for Bunty to arrive. She'd called me yesterday to tell me she wanted to come and see Mum, and I'd arranged to meet her here. She had to get two buses, and insisted on telling me the whole route, including all the big shops she passed; it was a job getting her off the phone.

The door pinged and I saw a wee woman in a blue puffa jacket with short grey hair push her way past the crowd at the counter. She was searching the café; her body language was that of a woman who was happy to bob and weave and make herself known to anyone who wanted to look at her. I knew that face.

'Bunty, over here,' I shouted, and pointed to the seat opposite me. I grabbed my laptop bag off it to make room for her.

She stopped and stared at me. Her head tilted to the side and a smile spread over her face as she got closer.

'I hear your man has left you, Sharon, what a prick.'

The exquisite bluntness of a Glasgow woman – nothing beats it.

'Nice to see you, Bunty – glad to hear you still know everything about everyone.' I hugged her close. She was small and wiry and smelled of a perfume that I couldn't quite recall.

'Isa told me. You look great, hen,' she said affectionately.

She put her big brown handbag down between her feet and told me to get her a cup of tea. 'Oh, and maybe a wee cake,' she added.

'They only do raw cakes here,' I shouted back as I made my way to the counter.

'Why's that? Can't they cook?' Bunty replied.

Clyde nodded his head to me, indicating to come around the counter and join him. 'Give her that,' he said and held out a plate.

I laughed, and took her the warm scone and butter with a big mug of tea.

She picked up the scone, split it in two with the accuracy of a sushi chef and lathered butter into the middle, took a big bite, gulped some tea and smiled at me. Once settled, she launched right into it.

'How's Senga? I haven't seen her in a few years, am up near the Campsies now, but we kept in touch on the phone and that,' she told me as she mopped melted butter off her chin. 'Fuck, these are good – who makes these?' She held up the remains of the scone. 'The big fella?'

'They are good, aren't they?' I replied.

'You've had his scones as well?' she said with a twinkle.

'Yes, I have.'

'Aye, so your mammy, how is she? So much has happened in all these years, people move away and move on,' she added.

'She's not got long, Bunty. I just wanted you all to see her together. As you know, I'm trying to get Isa up, and Philomena has already visited a couple of times. You were such a huge part of our childhood. I saw Janine too but she's too frail to visit and

I think it would be upsetting for her. John is here, he's with Mum just now at the hospital,' I said between sips of coffee. 'And Janet's coming back tomorrow.'

'Aye, we were right close – remember my twins were raised with you lot. Your mammy was a rock to me,' she said through a watery smile. She wiped her hands on a napkin and leaned in closer, fiddling with the rings on her fingers.

I smiled and said, 'Her book . . . you, Isa, Philomena, Janine and Sandra are all in there. I think that's why she told me about it and where to find it. She wants to see you all again. Do you recall her ever speaking about her diary?'

A cloud passed across Bunty's face, something I couldn't quite make sense of.

'I remember her big red book,' she said, looking away. 'What's it about? Does she say much about me?' she asked, peering over her glasses, her eyebrows down.

'Well, it's mostly from about 1976 and I think it stops about 1978. It jumps about a bit and I'm not entirely sure where it ends – there are some photos, and some pages missing,' I explained.

Bunty looked up sharply. 'Missing?'

'Yes. I haven't got to that bit yet, so I don't know why.'

'So, you've all had a look at it, then?' Bunty looked agitated. 'Janet and John too?'

'Well, sort of – we're just processing everything, Bunty, it's a lot to take in.'

The silence stretched as Bunty drank her tea.

'Can you help me contact Sandra?' I asked. 'Last time we spoke, you were going to ask around for her details. John's also been trying to track her down.'

Bunty shook her head. She stared at the ceiling, deep in thought, then looked straight at me. 'We lost touch. I cannae tell you any more than that.'

'That's weird. You thought you knew someone who might know where she is, the last time we spoke, remember? Your cousin the hairdresser or something?' I pressed.

Bunty looked away. 'I don't know, hen. No one knows where she is.' She stood up abruptly. 'Right, let's go and see Senga.'

So that was case closed: the brown bag was lifted, the puffa jacket pulled on as she shook off crumbs.

Bunty didn't speak a word in the car, just stared ahead quietly. It was unsettling. At the hospital I led her up the stairs and along the corridor, as I had done so many times with various people recently.

'Will John still be here?' she asked. She seemed very nervous.

'No, he'll have just left, he's away back to Govan,' I replied.

I could see her brace herself, wrapping her jacket around herself as though in preparation for battle. We opened the door to Mum's room.

She was the same as yesterday, quietly lying there.

Bunty clutched at her chest and shuddered when she saw Senga. Walking over to the bed, she took Mum's hand. 'Senga, Senga, it's me, Bunty,' she whispered. 'I'm so sorry, hen, we haven't been here for you.' She wiped away tears and laid her head on the bed.

Mum shifted slightly and put her hand on Bunty's head and gave it a gentle pat.

'You're here now,' she said.

Isa
Stow-on-the-Wold.

I was halfway through the rails of cashmere jumpers on the top floor of the big John Lewis in town when I heard my phone buzz from inside my handbag. My niece set it extra loud for me so I'd be able to hear, thinking it was funny, and now I can't switch it back from the earth-shattering racket.

'Hello, Bunty, how are you? I'm just in the shops at the minute so I can't hear you very well – what was that? What do you mean there's pages missing? No, you daft cow, I don't have them . . . Right, say nothing. Speak to Philomena and see what Senga said to her. I'll call you later, and I'll come up the road so we can be together. I hadn't realised how ill she was.'

Fuck's sake. This is it. Can't put it off any longer.

1978
March

The cooker has broken, so that's breakfast fucked. Honest to God, this is the last thing I need. The weans went to school with no breakfast and I gave them the last of my cash to buy something at the tuck shop.

Frank downstairs has got me a new one but it smells funny and I am absolutely convinced something is burning in it. I have now become paranoid and have spent the night cleaning every single element and inch of the oven.

Sandra came up with Isa, Bunty and Philomena and we went to the pub, but not for long. For various reasons, everyone is busy. Isa has been looking after her granny, Nora, who lives up Drum-chapel. Philomena has been selling loads of her football cards at the factory and is making a tidy profit.

Bunty told me she got a load of denims off her cousin – she is selling them cheap and gave me a cracking pair of Levi's that fit like a glove. She's not learned from her last beating or the Devlins' threats, but I won't say anything if anyone asks. I want to get a colour TV so I am going to help her sell them. Sandra is scared Jim is in too deep with the Devlins too. I don't want another row with Billy so I am keeping out of his way: I just want him to sign the divorce papers and let me be free.

Got a new book from the library – *The Thorn Birds,* about for-bidden love with a priest in Australia – it's very racy. How come all the priests round here are like wee eighty-year-old prawns? I've yet to see one that doesn't make me think Jesus is having a laugh. My eyes are sore from reading it so fast.

CHAPTER 27

2019
Day seventeen
Sharon

John and I had breakfast together this morning, before we left for the hospital. Janet was flying back today and we were going to meet her at our old home in Shettleston. Maybe seeing the old place and walking around our old streets would give us some perspective about the past. Who knew? It just felt right to do it. Maybe Davie Dunsmore was living in a parallel time, still sitting in the local pub talking about his night out with Elvis. If he was, we could ask him where the hell Sandra was.

John had already been on Skype for an hour to Carlos, who was dealing with a burst pipe at the dance studio. 'There's always a drama when I leave,' John huffed, and then he got on with shouting in Spanish to a plumber as the internet on the dongle kept wavering.

The road to the hospital was busy; it was peak traffic time. I lost my patience about six times and swore loudly at a van that veered into my lane near the Clyde Tunnel. 'Fuck you, arsehole,' I shouted at the man as we drew level.

'You can take the lassie out of Glasgow,' John laughed as I swerved and righted the car, avoiding disaster.

Mum was stable and comfortable, according to the doctor. I was getting sick of the word 'stable', as if she were a wobbly bike that they'd managed to put wheels on and guide along in a straight line. John sat with her and I headed back to the café.

I wanted to see Clyde today, when I knew the coffee shop would be quiet and we could talk. We'd been texting a lot but I still felt a bit out of my depth and unsure – technically, I was still married, still trying to find Sandra and always worried about Mum, so I was not the best person to be in 'the present' at the moment.

'Hello, stranger,' he said as I waited for him to finish serving some of the mummies who'd come in with babies wrapped around their torsos in elaborately confusing knots.

'Hi, sorry, I know I've been a bit quiet,' I said.

'That's OK, how are you?' he asked as he expertly poured foaming oat milk into a latte.

'A swirl of emotions, to be honest, like a giant trifle layered with guilt, fear and worry,' I said.

'That sounds like the worst trifle in the world: angry jelly topped with terrified sprinkles,' he said with a smile.

'That's exactly it,' I replied. 'I'm still married, and I'm about to go back to my childhood home, which has stirred up all sorts of new emotions. I can't think straight. Fuck, I am a bore, sorry. Please give me a takeaway coffee?'

'Just call me when you can,' Clyde said easily. 'I really enjoyed being with you and I'd very much like to see you again some time. But there's no rush. Tell me when you're ready. I can wait.'

He passed me a coffee and gave me a wink. Amid the rush of emotions, I felt my stomach flip.

Janet had flown back to Glasgow, dropped off her bag at the hotel and taken a cab to meet us in Shettleston. John and Janet hugged tightly as she got out of the car.

'Is this where the milk bottle factory used to be?' she asked as we all stood outside Mum's old house, pointing to a row of very modern six-to-a-block flats with double-glazed windows and blue pipes sectioning off the front gardens.

Our old street looked so different. We hardly recognised the place. 'It looks so small,' Janet said as she stood in our old close. The tenements were no longer as imposing as we remembered them – now blasted to a rosy pink, with security doors and buzzers for each tenant.

We used to run through these streets and all through the back courts, plastic sandals skidding on the Victorian flagstone, and we would jump over puddles and hide in the outside shared toilets that some tenements still had. There were derelict wash-houses out in the back courts in those days too, where women in the olden days boiled water to do their laundry. Quite a few wash-houses fell down with age and some kids died in the rubble. We were always warned to stay away from them, but of course the dark, dank wee buildings were such a draw to kids. We played houses in them and built fires where the boilers had been.

That was all long gone. The back courts were now smooth concrete and lit by tall, fancy lamps, with smart-looking bin shelters and a range of multi-coloured wheelie bins. No kids were out there playing now – there was a sign that said 'No Ball Games'.

The ghosts of our childhood were all around us but we never saw anyone we knew. The pub was gone; the butcher's, fruit shop and social club long gone too.

We took a photo of the three of us with the tenements behind us to show Mum when we got up to the hospital.

I shut my eyes and thought of the diary.

I could still see my mum, Isa, Bunty and Philomena leaving the pub and letting the door slam behind them as Laddie waited to walk them up the road. Sandra always went in the opposite direction. Vibrant young women with a scraggy dog barking as they clutched handbags and each other's arms, singing 'Blanket on the Ground' as we hung from the bedroom window watching them, the occasional flare of a cigarette marking out their journey as they came up the street.

Memories.

We had found everyone but Sandra. Where was she, and why wasn't anyone in touch with her any more? Maybe people didn't like remembering what happened to their pals back then. As my mum would say, a little knowledge was a dangerous thing.

Sandra had been swimming in dangerous waters; had she survived?

1978
April

Sandra stayed over at mine last night – that bastard Jim has punched her legs black and blue. She ran through the streets in her housecoat and slippers and made it to mine after midnight, Laddie barking in hysteria as she fell through my door. The whole close near got woke up. Frank came up to see if we were all right. He was in his vest and looked like he'd just pulled on his trousers.

'Has that bully bastard battered that lassie again?' he asked me as I was trying to get Laddie back into the house.

It seems the whole world knows Jim beats Sandra, but nobody can do anything about it.

'Let me get the polis,' Frank said.

'No! No . . . please don't,' Sandra pleaded. 'He'll kill me if I bring the police to his door – please, Frank, don't.'

The old man stood his ground. 'I will listen at my door downstairs, hen, and if he comes round here to look for you I'll take a hammer to him,' he said, puffing out his bony chest. The sight of him in his vest and old trousers, trying hard to look after a young woman who was beaten down, was heart-wrenching.

But Jim never came near.

'The drinking has got worse and the money isn't coming in – I think he's upset the Devlins as well, so he takes it out on me.' Sandra sat there rubbing her skinny legs.

'Sandra, you need to get away from him, he'll end up killing you, pal,' I sobbed as I gave her a cold, damp cloth to soothe the bruises.

She came into bed with me, her frail body curled up in the foetal position like a small animal trying to make itself tiny to hide from prey. We lay there in the night, watching the orange streetlights make patterns on the ceiling. Listening to Radio Luxembourg on low playing Steely Dan and ELO, her breathing slowed down and she finally fell asleep. Poor wee soul. Sandra married for worse, but she still has the wedding photos up on her walls, like a constant reminder of how happy they should be.

Bunty, Philomena, Isa and I need to have a sit-down and figure out how to sort this. Word on the street is that things aren't working for Jim because he tried to take a sneaky cut out of a deal. Old Tam Devlin is a violent bastard and he won't take anyone messing him about. I'll ask them to come round in the morning so we can talk to Sandra together. We need a plan.

CHAPTER 28

2019
Day eighteen
Sharon

John was sleeping soundly when I woke up, so I crept around the flat quietly. I got dressed with a notion to head to the coffee shop, but as I opened the door I got captured by Betty and Maggie.

'How's your mammy?' Betty enquired as they stood like guards blocking me: immovable, unshakeable and waiting for answers. Handbags over their forearms like sturdy weapons, and head-scarves tied tight under their chins in big bows.

'She's still hanging on, ladies, how are you two?' I replied, trying to deflect the onslaught.

'I have diabetes, and she's got new tablets for her stomach,' Betty said, pointing at Maggie without blinking through her owl-like glasses.

'Has your husband been in contact? Jessie in the community centre tells me you're having a fine time with the big laddie that runs the queer hawk café,' Maggie butted in.

'The queer hawk café?' I said, annoyed at their snipe at Clyde's coffee shop.

'Aye, that café that sells cakes made of carrots and watery tea – the big fella who has all the hair.' Betty mimed a long ponytail, which Clyde didn't have. Maggie watched me like an aggressive, nosy stoat, waiting for a reply, lips pursed in anticipation.

I took a deep breath and stared them down.

'Well, Mum is still with us, my soon-to-be-ex-husband is still away shagging a yoga teacher, me and Clyde have had sex in his flat and I think I might shag him again. Tell that to Jessie, who-ever the hell she is. Anything else, ladies?' I said this all with my head held high, deliberately trying to shock them.

Their faces broke into big smiles. Handbags were humped up their arms and they made to move off. 'Good for you, hen, tell yer mammy we were asking for her,' Betty said, and they set off out of the communal door.

I rang Elaine on the way to the café and she laughed out loud when I told her what I'd said. 'Sounds like you've made your decision about Steven,' she said. 'Good on you. Change is afoot, for sure.'

1978
May

The weather was so good so I flung all the big windows open and did a spring clean. The whole place got gutted out, I mopped under all the beds and got the cupboards cleaned. Mrs Bradshaw is off to her house in Portugal, so I have a week off. Though I am still doing extra shifts cleaning the local pub, as the TV man is coming round and I am finally getting a new colour TV. It's taken lots of saving, selling football cards in the social club with Philomena, and selling jeans for Bunty, but I've finally made the deposit and convinced the Radio Rentals man that I can afford the HP payments. Philomena, who has the most regular job, put her name down as guarantor in case I failed to make the weekly instalments.

I am so excited and this time it won't have a meter on the back and the kids are so bloody happy. They can watch cartoons in colour, see the Banana Splits in all their glory, and *Coronation Street* is going to look like real life. The whole world is orange and brown with swirly bright carpets.

We are having a party to celebrate 'The Telly' arriving. Philomena, Janine and Bunty are coming over – we have sausage rolls and some vodka for a wee night in. *Top of the Pops* is on and that's going to look amazing in full colour. Can you imagine? I feel like a proper toff. Next I will be getting a phone and running about like her from *The Good Life*, making prawn vol-au-vents and sherry for my guests!

Things are looking up, except Billy turned up like a bad penny this morning as I was beating the carpets out the back. He looked terrible, but that's not my problem. Luckily the kids were at school as he stood there in dirty flared jeans, smelling of drink too early in the day.

'What do you want, Billy?' I asked him as I slammed the beater into the dusty carpet. Mrs Wilson was at her window, watching us like a hawk behind her net curtains.

The dust and dirt billowed around us and the sweat ran into my eyes with the physical exertion of attacking the thick pile with the flat beater. I don't think it escaped his attention that I was thinking of battering him as I was going at it.

'Do you need a hand?' he asked. Standing there, his hands in his pockets, looking like a small boy waiting on a beating.

I stopped and really looked at him, and he shrank under my full glare. I heard he was out of work again; at least he'd stopped hanging around with the Devlins.

Where was that vibrant young man who'd held my sixteen-year-old pregnant belly and sung Beatles songs to me under the summer sun? What happened to him? I genuinely felt sorry for him. I loved him once, and he is the father of my babies.

'I don't need your help, Billy. Go and look after yourself, you're a mess,' I said. 'Be a better man for Donna and sign those divorce papers for me.'

'I'm sorry, Senga,' he said and just walked away. I watched him go through the close and stared until he disappeared into the shadows. Tears were flooding down my face.

I wept buckets battering those rugs, I don't know what came over me. Must've been my hormones but there was just something so final and sad seeing him looking so broken. But I can't go back to having him in the kids' lives. He will tear their wee hearts apart with his stupid behaviour. You don't get this shite in a love song, do you?

Mrs Wilson came out the back close. She had a headscarf wrapped around her rollers and her wee pinny tied round her stout body. She was carrying a glass of water and as she put it in my hand and gave me a hanky for my face she took the carpet-beater out of my fist and had a go at the rug. I forgot how much she liked battering carpets.

She's a good wee woman.

'You did the right thing, hen, you're just getting on your feet, you don't need that man back in your life,' she said breathlessly as she whacked the carpet. Two women getting all their sadness and anger out on a patterned rug. You don't get that kind of therapy with a hoover.

Can't wait to see my pals tonight. I wish Sandra was coming but she's back home with Jim and there's nothing we can say about that now. I just hope she won't forget about the plan we've made.

CHAPTER 29

2019
Day nineteen
Sharon

Senga and her carpet-beater. I could still see it hanging behind the coal bunker door. There was a girl in my class who used to get beaten with one and we saw the red ring marks on her back when we went swimming. Senga, thank God, never really battered us – she threatened the Scholl's to the legs often but rarely followed through on the threat. Her angry voice was enough to make us shudder with fear.

That felt like the end of Mum and Dad's relationship too, finally. I knew I had reached the same point with Steven. There had to come a point when you just accepted you couldn't see a way back.

And what was Sandra's plan? I was desperate to read on.

Senga was looking the same today as she had yesterday, drifting in and out of consciousness. Bunty had been up each day since she arrived, sometimes with Philomena too, sitting with Mum, chatting away to her as if they were having a full-on conversation. So far, it was just Bunty's wee animated head bobbing about, nattering away as Senga lay there with her eyes shut, far away in her own wee place. I sometimes thought (and hoped) that Mum's mind was somewhere nice, somewhere she'd never been, like Hollywood or a tropical beach or a holiday that never involved rain, wind or a bingo stall. Still no sign of Isa; we were all just waiting for the old gang to be reunited.

'I did another search for Sandra on Facebook yesterday,' I said to Bunty today as she was leaving. She looked startled and hoisted her bag on her shoulder immediately, walking out into the corridor. I followed her out.

'Have you now?' she asked, turning to me.

'Mum's mentioned a plan in her diary, you know,' I added. 'Know anything about that plan, Bunty?'

She shook her head and started searching her pockets and making a fuss about looking for something. Classic distraction tactics. Then she said, 'See you later, Senga,' over my shoulder and headed off down the corridor, her wee feet moving fast as she pressed the lift button repeatedly. She would not turn around to see me standing there outside Mum's room, watching her go.

Janet and John have been poring over the diary all week, but they haven't read as much as me. 'Did Davie Dunsmore really meet Elvis?' John said – he was absolutely fixated on him.

'I think Davie might have been lying,' Janet replied. 'He talked a load of shit. But we should look him up as well, while we're here.'

Clyde texted me and suggested we go to his place for supper. I debated whether I should go. John was ironing his clean shirts and said, 'If you don't go, I will.'

'Oh, for fuck's sake, Sharon, go,' said Janet. 'It's not like you have a line of young men asking you to drop your fancy pants. If Mum's diary has taught us anything at all, it's to grab life. I'll go and sit with Mum. Have a night out. We'll be fine, won't we, John?'

'Wear something nice and shave your moustache,' John added, laughing, shaking smart shirts and hooking them round Mum's wooden coat-hangers.

I knew they were right. Clyde was a wonderful distraction and I did enjoy his company. But my own life was complicated enough without trying to figure out my feelings towards a new man. I didn't even know if there were any feelings. I think I was just flattered. Louise would be horrified if she knew her middle-class, middle-aged mum was shagging a younger guy she'd met in a Glasgow café whilst she was meant to be looking after her dying mother. But life seemed so bizarre just now. And afterwards, I could say with certainty that a fit young man throwing me about his bed was good therapy when I was grieving and in mental turmoil.

1978
May

Got up early and organised the ironing, let Laddie out for his pee and broke open a packet of Club Orange biscuits for the kids' breakfast. Sharon is taking wee John out on her paper round to shown him the ropes. He wants a job when he gets older so this is a good way for him to start. Janet is taking a giant rocket model she made from *Blue Peter* to school for her science project and am worried it will fall apart the minute she lifts it. She went round all the doors for empty washing-up liquid bottles and the thing is fucking huge and covered in sticky glue. If she doesn't win the school prize, she might actually fire the rocket at the class.

I am loving my colour telly – my eyes are square watching it now I don't have to worry about putting coins in the back. *World in Action* was on last night about the poor men who came back from Vietnam and how the Americans turned their backs on them, then I watched an old film with Bette Davis in. Am getting too old for *Top of the Pops* now, full of kids bopping about to shite, and that weirdo Jimmy Savile staring at wee lassies gives me the creeps. I have switched over to *The Old Grey Whistle Test* and a British group called The Police and an American one called Blondie. I ended up watching until the wee black dot dissolved and they played the National Anthem.

I told my cousin Monica some more about this diary in my latest letter but I don't think I want anyone else to see my personal thoughts and feelings and, to be honest, I can't remember if I've been shitty about people so they all might go mad if they see it.

I was watching the news and they said another young woman has been found dead in the North of England and it looks like there might be a serial killer on the loose. What the fuck is wrong with men that they have to go out and hunt down women and kill them? Someone is hiding that man, and until people speak out he'll never get caught. The cops don't really take violence against women seriously until they start turning up dead in numbers. I hate the world sometimes.

Sandra has been round at mine a few times this week. She's looking OK. She told me Jim has been away working on the cars again and the Devlins have let him back in on their deals, so fuck knows what trouble he will be in this time. Hope he gets the jail and gives us all peace this summer. She mentioned she's started saving some money again and has found a brilliant hiding place. Philomena has taken Isa's suitcase, the one Sharon borrowed for her trip, over to her place to fill with clothes and bits – just in case.

Went to the pub with the girls; Philomena and Bunty have started a club for a bus run to Saltcoats and it's £2 a week. I love the bus runs. It's for adults only – we went to Ayr last year and ended up drunk at the mini bingo on the seafront and Bunty got into a fight with a woman who said she was eyeing up her man. We know that was a lie because Bunty is rubbish at bingo and can't look at two things at the same time. We won a giant stuffed toy panda – it was the size of a two-man tent and we could hardly find room for it on the bus home. Frightened the weans and Laddie half to death when they saw it and we ended up giving it to the church for the raffle.

CHAPTER 30

2019
Day twenty
Sharon

One of the saddest things was reading about how little Mum got
to travel and see the world. Even after we left, she never went anywhere really exotic – all her holidays were in Scotland to her pal's
caravan or down to Troon beach for the day on the bus. She never
had any of the big adventures that she often spoke about. She
lived vicariously through her Jilly Cooper and Jackie Collins sexy
fantasy books, but in reality she played life really safe. She had
never had a day when she could go carefree to a beach – child-free,
without worrying over money – and just wiggle her toes in the
sand. Her young life had been a succession of worries, fears, and
grabbing tiny bits of happiness when she could.

At the hospital it was much of the same, a well-worn routine:
climb the stairs, feel the last-minute heart-thump before you
opened the door, then sit and hope for change. But there was no
change with Senga, no better and no worse, and hoping she would
get better was innately futile.

I had been here almost three weeks and so much had happened.
Last night with Clyde had been unexpectedly amazing. He had
opened some nice wine and we'd sat at his place in the dark,
watching the cityscape through his big windows, listening to
some music. He'd showed me some photos of his family and his
past adventures and I'd let him see the photos of Senga when she
was young. 'She was banging hot,' he said, and I punched his arm.

'That's my mum, you!'

The diary and Mum's pals had engulfed my entire life, so it was good to get mildly drunk, kick off my shoes and laugh for a night.

But now, over my morning coffee, I was still unable to locate Sandra. It wasn't for lack of trying. There was no online footprint for a woman of Sandra's name or age or past history that I could find on Facebook or anywhere else.

Given the events in the diary, I had to face the fact that she might not be alive. No one would give me any definite information on her. She was like a shadow, a misty intangible ghost.

I wasn't going to give up, though. Next stop was going to be the records office in Glasgow where they registered births and deaths. If Davie Dunsmore was alive, he would know everything. He would be in his nineties by now, by my estimation, and he might still have the ability to chat to us.

Janet had gone to Glasgow Airport earlier to collect her husband Anthony and stepson Josh, who'd flown up this morning. It seemed everyone was getting on with their lives and I was either stuck in the past or stuck in the present, chasing ghosts on the internet. How could I move on?

After a visit to Mum at teatime, we all went for dinner in Glasgow's West End. The hospital had my mobile number and my phone sat on the table through all the courses, as we tried to enjoy a family get-together. The place was buzzing and the Italian food was exceptional. The owner was Giovanna, the granddaughter of Edmondo who used to run Eusebi's café in Shettleston where we'd grown up. We remembered her grandad, he'd been pals with Senga, and it was lovely to see her. The weans of Shettleston meeting decades later over good wine and home-made lasagne.

A few bottles of wine later, we staggered back to our respective abodes. Maggie was at her window watching as John and I sneaked into Mum's flat like guilty teens at eleven p.m.

I got a call from the hospital after midnight. Senga had deteriorated suddenly but had then rallied again. She was awake and wanted to see us.

1978
June, Saturday

Me and the girls went round to Isa's to try out some new heated rollers she said her brother got her. Someone had burgled the Littlewood's store last week and there was quite a haul of fancy goods going round the scheme.

We were all sitting in Isa's front room listening to her Meatloaf LP when the doorbell rang out and Isa got up to answer it. Sandra's tiny wee body peeped round the door. Turned out the Devlins had Jim away on a job down south for the whole weekend. It was so good to see her.

We all got up to hug her but as she smiled at us we saw another fresh bruise right across her cheek.

'Fuck's sake, Sandra, one for the road, was it?' Isa blurted out. Me and Bunty stared at her, giving her the 'shut up' eyes.

'What? I'm sick of no one talking about it,' she said.

Sandra didn't know what to do. She wouldn't look anyone in the eye. Bunty got Isa to go and make her a drink to get her out the room, and then told Sandra that if we did her hair all big it would make her bruise less noticeable.

I went to talk to Isa in the kitchen. She was raging, banging cups and glasses about. 'We need to do something about this, Senga,' she hissed.

I said, 'I know, Isa, and we will help her. But she's got to want to do it, we can't force her. You know what she's like if we try to talk about it – she shuts down.'

It was such a nice warm night so all of us with our big hair and fluffy slippers sat out on Isa's front close on her new lawn chairs – I don't know what lawn she was planning to put them on, but we used the front kerb outside the tenement. We took Bunty's portable radio out with us and as 'Summer Nights' finished playing for the nine-hundredth time this week, there was a news broadcast about the first woman to sail around the world by herself. Imagine that – a woman alone on a boat. Probably some posh fancy woman with a lovely life already – if anyone deserves a year's peace sailing around by themselves it's women like us. So, there we were, sitting with our vodka and orange squash, pretending we're sailing off on some super-yacht to the Bahamas. Isa lifted her glass, pretending to be ship's captain, and said, 'Ladies, starboard you can see the Hawaiian islands and portside are the lush lands of Tahiti. Now where do you want to get off?'

We all laughed loudly, as the only view we had was Laddie trying to mount a wee black mongrel who was having a shit outside the social club front door.

We spent the rest of the night talking about our imaginary holidays and where we would go if we could, watching the sun set to a fiery blush over the chimney tops of Glasgow as we wiggled our bare feet on the warm concrete pavement.

Sandra said, 'My mum's cousin, Charlotte, you know her that used to work in the old folk's home in Newlands? She's moved to Spain with a man she met on holiday. She's sent me pictures and it looks really nice.'

We all looked at each other. This was it.

Wednesday

Philomena had another Pippa Dee party, and the clothes for the kids were brilliant, she's really organised. She's actually a gaffer in the factory now and if she put her mind to it she could run the country a whole lot better than the Labour Party right now. Philomena is one of those women who can get up at six a.m., get the kids out to school, wash the windows, take her turn at the steamie and do a full shift at work and come home to an immaculately clean house, and none of her kids have ever had nits. She's still Wonder Woman.

'Senga, I've managed to sell four football cards and skim some money off the Pippa Dee – how much is Sandra's flight to Spain?' she asked me.

I told her I checked in the travel agent's and it's about £30 all in, plus she'll need some spending money. I have the secret stash of all the money we are hiding, for Sandra to escape, in a plastic Tupperware dish inside the base of my twin tub washing machine. It's the perfect place – nobody would ever rip that apart looking for hidden treasure.

Sandra turned up to the party with cheese and pineapple sticks and Isa brought her famous clootie dumpling. We had some Bacardi and lovely Mateus rosé wine that Bunty had bought for our wee night in.

Philomena has a lovely house. She lives in the ancient bungalow behind the steamie and it has its own back garden – some of these wee old houses go back to Victorian days and there's even a stable to the side of the house that she uses for chickens. They frighten the absolute fuck out of my Sharon and the noise off them would make you piss your tights, but she has a constant supply of eggs.

She decorated it herself and of course she can paint and wallpaper like a professional – she can do everything except keep a man, she says! Tony, her man, went to Australia to pave the way for them to emigrate but Philomena said, 'When he left, I just realised I didn't want to go and the house was better without him,' so he's still in Brisbane and she's still behind the steamie with her chickens and two daughters.

We told Sandra about the 'escape money kitty' and she burst into tears. Jim's desperate to get her pregnant and he's saying they should get her womb checked out to see why she's 'sterile'. If only he knew she was still on my pills. I really hate that bastard, he won't leave her alone. She confided in me that he's making her have sex all times of the day and he's getting rough with it too.

We need to buy her a one-way ticket to Spain. Jim will have absolutely no idea where she has gone and that's the way we need to keep it.

I got myself a nice nightdress and a casserole dish at the Pippa Dee, left Philomena's with a tray of eggs and headed home. It was a good night.

CHAPTER 31

2019
Day twenty-one
Sharon

I frantically called Janet at the hotel and we jumped in a cab to pick her up. The shock and fear had sobered us all up.

We got the taxi up to the Royal Infirmary after midnight. Janet, John and I watched the city flash past, the ancient Glasgow high street with its historic buildings looking ominous in the bright moonlight. We ran up the stairs, quickly pushing through the double doors and finally reaching the hushed ward. A nurse was waiting at the door, and she ushered us in and quietly walked back out.

We reached Senga's bed and she was lying there with her eyes open, the curtains wide apart. She was staring out over the view of the motorway with some high flats in the distance that looked as though they were draped in fairy-lights, twinkling against the dense Glasgow sky.

'Mum,' Janet whispered as she sat on a hard orange, plastic seat and took Senga's hand. I took the seat on the other side, with John next to me, desperate to speak but yet not wanting to overwhelm her and break this magical moment of seeing her periwinkle-blue eyes looking out to the moon.

She turned her head and smiled. 'My weans.'

Tears brimmed from my eyes and ran down my cheeks, and my heart felt as if a huge balloon was swelling inside me and threatening to escape through my throat.

'Mum, we're all here,' John said.

'I know, I see you,' she whispered, and held on to our hands. 'I felt like I was on my way, but I haven't seen Isa yet. I can't go anywhere until they're all here with you.'

She lay still and opened her mouth to speak, then closed it again, as if she was thinking about what to say. Then she took a deep breath and spoke.

'Bunty was here, she never shuts up, but she had a good chat about the old days. You know, I used to wear hot pants,' Senga rasped with a smile that caught me off guard.

'Oh, Mum,' I leaned over and stroked her face and laughed.

Mum took a sip of water, then lay back down, and we did what all Glasgow people do when faced with impending silence or death – we started to laugh and tell funny stories. Reminiscing, sharing wee memories, taking turns to get her attention, just as we'd done when we were kids. Mum smiled as we chatted away. This might be the last time we would share a moment like this and we were grabbing at it like greedy babies on the breast, holding her hand and trying to draw the last bit of love from her flesh.

Finally we went quiet and Senga stared at all of us.

'I'm so glad you're here. You need to look after each other, my weans,' she said. She smiled at us; her face bracketed with deep wrinkles on papery skin, her hair so thin we could see her scalp and the full shape of her skull. She looked as if she was somehow unfinished, not a whole human being, solid and present. I tried not to cry again.

'We're reading your book, Mum,' I blurted out to fill the silence.

'I know; Bunty and Philomena won't stop talking about it,' she said, and she whipped her head round and gave me a very focused stare. 'Have you got to the end yet?' It was quite a surprise to see her look so alert.

'No, not yet, but nearly,' Janet said as she glanced at me, quizzically, with an eyebrow arched.

'Good. Now let me sleep. Next time you come, bring my floral document folder with you, the one with my important bits in it.

I'm looking forward to seeing Isa again. Tell her to come soon.' And she simply shut her eyes and went back to sleep.

We sat there till six a.m. and watched her breathe steadily and quietly through the night. Nurse Shirley came in with some mugs of tea for us on a tray, held them out and said, 'She's not ready to let go. You get home and get some sleep. We'll call you if there's any change.'

1978
July

Woke up early and stuck my heated rollers in. I went to Mrs Bradshaw's daughter Stella's wedding. Not the church bit but the massive party in their big garden up beside the BBC in the West End. She had a huge marquee out the back and lots of fairy-lights everywhere. Every tree was lit up and all the tables had fancy candles on them.

I can't tell you how magical it looked, and Stella looked beautiful. They are such a good family to invite me and not once was I introduced as the 'cleaner', I was there as a proper guest. I got them a bread bin set out of the catalogue and Stella was really nice about it, even though it looked cheap and not something she would really have in her house I suppose. I am lucky to have nice people to work for.

There was me wearing a new flouncy gypsy style frock from C&A and a pair of glittery sandals I got from the charity shop. I looked gorgeous. My hair looked bouncy and full of curls with half a can of BelAir hairspray on it and two big side combs. I felt posh.

They had amazing food – a whole Black Forest gâteau, a sherry trifle, individual prawn cocktails, dried toast and pâté spread and trays and trays of wee scallops in shells. And huge jugs of Pimm's! I kept forgetting that the sweet-tasting drink was actually alcohol and had to slow myself down from gulping it. Didn't want to get pished drunk and show myself up.

I admit I was a bit nervous but all the people there were so relaxed and they included me in conversations and even asked me about my life. Of course, I never told any of them I was a cleaner and I have X-ray paper in my electric meter and I owe the provy man forty pounds, I just said I worked in admin and I lived near the city centre, which is technically correct, give or take four miles.

The live band was just amazing and I was totally starstruck. I recognised a few people off the Scottish telly as Mr Bradshaw works in television – he's a producer or something. I was hoping Billy Connolly would be there but it was mostly people I vaguely recognised and I practised not staring at them while trying to figure out who they were.

Stella's man Edward had a lovely family as well. His mum was an actual judge and she was fascinating to chat to. She was telling me that women need to take greater strides to enter the judicial system and make the 'playing field' more acceptable to societal needs. I agreed with everything she said. Some of it went over my head but I kind of got what she was talking about. It was the kind of thing my Sharon says a lot.

People just left their handbags and shoes on the grass and it took me ages to stop worrying about my stuff being stolen. I kept forgetting I was in a private garden party and not down the social club where you couldn't really leave your bag alone for too long or someone would have a rake through it.

As the music played and the afternoon turned to night, I was having such a ball. I sat back and looked at all these well-dressed people, and thought how amazing it must feel not to worry about money or bills and just buy what you want and give your kids anything they need without stressing about how to pay for it.

Stella got changed into an amazing Biba dress and let her hair down and danced round the whole wooden dance floor that was laid at the back of the garden. She got the best man to ask me up to dance and soon the whole place was mobbed, people doing their own version of *Saturday Night Fever* moves. It was a great night. I haven't had such a good time in ages.

As it got really late Mrs Bradshaw got her nephew to drive me home in his dark green E-type Jaguar. I felt like a Bond girl in such a flashy car, I lay back in the seat and watched the city lights through a haze of Pimm's. I had a box of cake for the kids on my knee courtesy of Stella, so that broke the Bond girl spell. You never see some sexy woman called Velour Valentine sitting with a bag of doughnuts on her lap, do you?

Still, it was lovely.

As we hit the East End, I pretended I lived in the nice houses up at Sandyhills, like Sandra's, and got him to drop me off near her house. I didn't want him seeing our scabby old tenements with Frank downstairs sitting in his vest playing the spoons on his knee, drunk and shouting at the moon.

I walked home in the dusky warm night, the sound of disco ringing in my ears and dogs barking as I neared my own flat.

Janet was waiting up and demanded I tell her every single thing that happened. Then she told me my false eyelash was stuck to my cheek.

Let Laddie out for a pee and made myself a cup of tea for bed.

CHAPTER 32

2019
Day twenty-one
Sharon

I couldn't sleep so I spent the morning dusting Mum's ornaments, just as I used to when I was a kid. Her wee flat was so tidy and I thought my burst suitcase and clothes on the floor made the place look so shoddy. I didn't want to take her stuff out of the wardrobe and move her bedroom about to suit me, though – that would feel too final.

I felt a huge wash of guilt, as though she might walk back in at any moment and say, 'What a bloody mess, the place looks like Annacker's midden,' which was her favourite saying back in the day, though I still don't know who 'Annacker' was or why he had a midden. So, I cleaned the house and organised the living room, moving John's bedding to the side while I hoovered.

John was out for a run and Anthony and Josh had gone out sightseeing. We were all going to stay close together till Senga decided it was time to let go.

I walked through the grey rain of Govan and headed to Clyde's café.

He was occupied dealing with customers, and the place was heaving – school-run mums congregating near the front, big fancy pushchairs blocking the entrance, with a clutch of screaming toddlers wandering about, sucking on pouches of mushed stuff (organic, no doubt). It was nice to be able to see him, though.

The yummy mummies finally left, but before I could speak to Clyde an elderly woman came in, put down her handbag with a thud, took off her coat, unravelled her scarf from around her neck and sat close to me. She had thick, curly, white hair. I caught a whiff of perfume and I recognised it. Tweed by Lenthéric, my mum's favourite scent.

I burst into tears. Clyde started to walk over, but I waved him away and mouthed, 'It's OK'.

I could feel arms around me and hands lift up my face.

It was Isa.

'You OK, hen?' she whispered, offering me a soft cotton hanky.

She sounded so different from the Isa on the phone, her accent was softer. Her face was round and smiling, her steely eyes were behind designer glasses, and she looked every inch the suburban wife in tasteful jewel-coloured linen top and white pencil-tailored trousers with leather loafers. She looked like a Glaswegian Gloria Hunniford. Just seeing her was bringing back so many memories.

'Sharon, sorry I went off the radar, hen, I was just tying everything up back home and making plans to come. I hadn't properly realised how little time Senga has. Bunty said you were spending lots of time here so I thought I might find you.'

'I'm so glad you came. Mum really will be so happy that you've made the journey. I've been reading all about you in the diary she wrote. Bunty and Philomena will be bursting with happiness as well: all the girls back together. And Janet and John will be over the moon to see their favourite sweary auntie.'

She leaned over and mimed, 'Tea,' to Clyde, who was standing at the counter watching us. 'Who's the big fella at the counter? He's not taken his eyes off you since I came in – and have you heard from your man yet? How's your wee granddaughter? You must be missing her,' she said.

They all wrong-footed me every time, asking personal questions and throwing me off track; it was like sparring with a top-flight lawyer. I felt as though I was sixteen again and having to explain my life to her.

'My "man" has bolted with a young woman who does yoga and the baby is doing great. I really do miss her,' I said, wiping under each eye with the hanky.

'Well, we all thought you and him would never last; he was always a big streak of piss,' she mused.

'I didn't know you knew about him?' I stammered. 'I haven't seen you since I left Glasgow to go to uni.'

'Oh, aye, your mammy and I kept contact for years – she sent me some of the wedding photos. She never liked him either.'

Clyde brought her a cup of tea over and she delicately added her own sweetener.

He raised his eyebrows at me. 'Are you OK?'

'She's fine,' Isa said, and drank some tea, appraising Clyde as he walked away.

I never knew my mum even discussed my life. I thought she hardly spoke to anyone when she moved to Govan. But of course she still had contact with her pals. Seems I didn't know much.

'So, tell me what happened with you and your man – are you getting it sorted?' she pressed as she broke a biscuit in two and nibbled it.

'Isa, that's all in the past. I don't really want to go over that just now,' I said.

'But you love the past, Sharon. You're never done asking questions about it, from what I hear,' she said, folding her arms and staring at me.

My guard flew up, and I sidestepped. 'Listen, Mum woke up for a wee while last night and mentioned you.'

Isa looked at me steadily. 'Did she?'

'Yes, she did,' I replied. 'She really wants to see you, quite urgently.'

Isa dabbed her mouth with a napkin and kept eye contact. I decided to approach the Sandra issue again; maybe this time she would tell me something.

'What happened to Sandra, Isa? I know she was in trouble. Did she leave Jim?'

Isa fiddled with her handbag, pulled out another big white hanky and blew her nose, almost covering her whole face.

I reached into my purse and pulled out the brown envelope, slipped out a photo of Sandra, Senga and Bunty sitting outside my mum's close in the sunshine in their slippers, and other photos of the gang too. I slid them across the table and let Isa push up her spectacles and have a good look.

'God, look at us all back then. Look at your mammy,' she said with a catch in her voice, then a watery smile.

I pointed to Sandra and said, 'That's Sandra – remember her?'

Isa squinted more closely at the photo, her arm comically going back and forward to focus in a huge attempt to recognise a woman she spent years being friends with but was now somehow trying to convince me was a vague stranger. 'Oh, aye, I remember her, she was a lovely lassie.' She sighed and looked again at the picture, then put down her cup and picked up her coat and handbag. 'I've arranged to see Bunty and Philomena later today and we can all talk then. I don't want to say any more until we're all together. I am going up to see your mammy now – will you give me a lift?' She got up and put on her coat. I had no choice but to follow. 'She would be so proud of you, you know.'

My heart lurched at the past tense. People were already getting used to her going and, although it was inevitable, I was not ready. I had spent this short period of time watching her slowly fade and now somehow this gathering of her pals was making it all feel so final. I was not ready to say goodbye to my mum.

1978
September

The house is bloody freezing and the country is going to the dogs, according to newspapers. There are strikes and industrial action up and down the length of Britain and the prime minister, James Callaghan, has that look on his face that I have when the provy man, the debt man and the electricity board are at my door demanding money that I don't have.

It seems the unions have the government by the balls and the leader of the Tory party, Mrs Thatcher, says the country is in crisis. She resembles an old headmistress that I had in primary school, all tweed jackets, flat sensible shoes, blonde hair sprayed rigid and a voice like a drill sergeant.

The news on the telly and on the radio is full of doom and gloom and 'we are facing the worst winter ever' is repeated often. Obviously these folks have never had to do without a decent meal or cope with debt, or they wouldn't be so worried. I'm an old hand at this game. Getting the electricity cut off and facing eviction is just a regular Tuesday to me and my neighbours.

The bin men are planning a strike and the thought of the bags out the back piling up is worrying me, though. These old tenements are already rife with rats and mice; all we need is a bin mountain and we will all die with the plague.

As if things aren't bad enough, Bunty came up last night and told me one of her cousins has been found dead, his body discovered by some kids in a derelict house.

'He lay there alone, battered to death, and we couldn't find him anywhere.' She almost broke her heart crying. 'I blame the Devlins but I can't prove it. That's me done with the dodgy stuff. I have kids to look after.'

Sharon took the weans in the bedroom and left us. Isa and Sandra came up with two fish suppers and we sat all night with Bunty. That's what pals do.

It will be the second funeral in two weeks. Janine's aunty Marcella died a fortnight ago with the breast cancer. They had her funeral at St Timothy's chapel and then the wake at Grassbank Bowling Club up in High Carntyne. My mum's aunty Nancy was a neighbour – nice people, she always said. Marcella had left Glasgow after the war and was rumoured to have married an Italian gangster in New York but came back a single woman with a few quid to spend. She was the only woman I knew who drove a fancy open-top convertible in Glasgow. I always thought she looked like a film star with her pink chiffon scarf wrapped round her head and sporting fancy sunglasses. My mammy called her 'the Jackie Kennedy of Carntyne'.

It was a huge event. I went to the mass in the chapel, it was so stuffy and hot and I spent the whole time up and down on my knees and feet – there are so many instructions in the Catholic service, you would need a wee booklet to explain it all. You could tell all the Protestants in the place as they mumbled through all the prayers and couldn't keep up with all the responses and catechisms. Myself included.

Being of Irish descent, Marcella's wake was like a community street party. Me, Isa, Bunty, Sandra and my mammy all went along. The purvey was unbelievable – I had never seen a whole side of salmon on a buffet and they had a band playing as well. I had been to worse weddings than that funeral.

As usual, there was a drama. Jackie's family, the MacNamaras, were there, and they started a full-on verbal bun-fight, with Jackie's sister Caitlin calling Bunty a 'bad mother'. Bunty reminded Caitlin that Jackie now dresses as a woman and sings songs for lonely sailors in Spain. And she didn't just say it to Caitlin's face, she took the microphone off the singer and shouted it over the top of the fiddler playing a lament. Caitlin got dragged out for trying to throw a tumbler at Bunty and then the music just started back up like nothing had happened. Fiddles and dancing and laughter took over the screaming and anger.

After the buffet, I heard shouting through the bar and yes, of course that fucking idiot ex-man of mine, Billy, had turned up.

Him and Jim were going at it – apparently Billy called Jim a 'tight-fisted Fenian' and what a mistake that was at an Irish Catholic funeral. I think it was funny for most of the crowd to watch a man try to bare-knuckle box in a pair of tartan trousers and five-inch platforms. Billy ended up being ragdolled by the women in Marcella's family – they are a fucking feisty bunch. They left him flat out in the car park.

Catholics and Protestants fighting over religion has no place at a funeral but neither Billy nor Jim have ever had any sense of respect. The awful thing was, Jim ended up taking out his rage on Sandra and made her leave the wake and go home with him. She had to grab her bag and run as he pulled her by the arm right off the table. Davie Dunsmore said she was crying outside and Jim was screaming into her face. For the first time in my life, I wished Billy had been better with his fists and punched that fucker out.

The crowd started singing 'Danny Boy' and the place regained a sense of peace again. I will need to check on Sandra tomorrow.

Isa and I were sat outside at the bowling green and had some time away from the music and fighting. The sun was going down and it was so peaceful and warm, we took off our tights and slipped our shoes off and sat there like we were at the beach.

Isa was telling me she was behind on the rent again and she'd heard the Devlins lend money out without any questions. I reminded her about Bunty's cousin, and that the interest charges those bastards put on a loan was not worth the worry – she didn't want to get herself involved with that lot. 'We can club together, Isa, and get you through a couple of weeks till you're back on your feet. Stay away from those robbing bastards,' I said.

The doors banged open and we could hear the band play loud for a moment, and there was my mammy staggering out from the crowded party – two sherries and she's steaming drunk. Isa and I stared at her. She couldn't see us and didn't think anyone was watching. She walked to the side of the club, kicked off her slingback sandals, pulled off her cardigan, sat down her wee handbag and lay down on the bowling green lawn as if she had just gone to her bed.

'Time to go, then?' Isa said as we fell about laughing.

My mammy was mortified when I told her. She told me she woke up the next day with a slice of salmon and four sausage rolls in her handbag.

CHAPTER 33

2019
Day twenty-one
Sharon

I dropped off Isa at the hospital. I felt she and Mum needed some time together alone. John was heading up later, so Mum would always have someone with her.

Clyde came around to Mum's flat, I managed to smuggle him in without Betty and Maggie standing sentinel and quizzing him about his life. He looked so big in Mum's floral living room, he took up all the space. He brought wine and I told him about my search for Sandra.

'Maybe these women just don't want to talk about her?' he said, filling up my glass and trying to settle on Mum's two-seater sofa that was chock-full of rosy cushions.

'They're not telling me the truth – something isn't right.'

'And you can't find anything about her anywhere?' he asked.

'No, believe me I've tried, but when they're all back together with Mum maybe they will tell me more. If Sandra doesn't want to be found, then that's that. It's just a mystery, is all,' I said.

Lying in his arms in my mum's flat felt so delicious – it was such a good distraction, two people spilling out all their dreams and desires. It was weird to think that I had shared more with Clyde than I had with a man I had been married to for more than three decades. Clyde told me about his travel plans and asked me to come with him.

My head was in a spin, what was happening to me? This wasn't in my life plan – get divorced, sell my house, go travelling with a man I met in a café?

'We'll see,' I replied.

'Sure, but please do think about it,' he said.

I told him about a job ad I'd seen for a local PR firm – I had the application form to fill in.

Clyde got a cab home later that evening and I swear I saw Maggie at her window, watching and clocking the whole thing. She was the Govan sentinel. I will have to give her a debriefing tomorrow.

John spent most of the night in the Royal Infirmary with Mum. She repaid his dedication with a smile and a hand-squeeze; I think that was the most she could do. We felt as though she was just waiting for the moment we were all together at last. The nurses were looking after her with such care and attention. I think she had become their favourite patient; their faces were becoming so familiar to us now that I could literally have told you the shift rota if anyone needed to know.

The diary was preoccupying me. I was going through page after page, poring over every word trying to figure out why everyone was being so evasive. I flicked to the end, skipping a few pages, and saw it finished abruptly in late 1978. The last page and a bit was ripped out, leaving a strip of uneven paper at the top saying *1978: November. This is the worst thing to happen.*

The rest was missing and time was running out.

1978
November

Well, as the newspapers predicted, the country has gone to shit. Dead bodies can't get buried, the bins are piled up on the streets, rats are running wild through the back courts, the council has called a state of emergency, the country is full of strikes and it seems the government is as about as fucked as that time Davie Dunsmore looked after the pub for a night.

Mrs Bradshaw said the only way to save the country is to vote Tory in the election next year, then we'll have a female Prime Minister. Maybe a woman will sort this mess out?

I don't know much about politics, but even I can see the state of Glasgow. This winter is set to be one of the coldest ever and I am worried sick about the bills. I will get the meter wired to the street supply if needs be.

Isa, Bunty and I are having a night in, playing some music and eating Isa's home baking. Isa says the winter of 1978 is going to be like World War Two, when everyone will need to gather round and help the nation by saving food and baking our own bread. Well, that's me fucked.

I don't understand how people can't run a country. If I can run a house on a budget and make sure everyone does their bit, then surely the men in suits can do it too?

Sharon and Janet have been climbing over the school fence and sneaking back wee bags of coal, as the old school down our street has a huge mountain of it and it has spilled right into the playground. The whole street has been helping themselves to it, and the police are thin on the ground as they have enough to deal with, supervising the striking workforce up and down the country. It's not really stealing – if it's just lying there unused. Well, that's what I am telling myself.

Time to go. Isa is at my door. It's snowing heavily outside so I grab my big fake fur coat. We are going to the pub, but I am going to see Billy first to get him to sign the divorce papers. I will write later.

CHAPTER 34

2019
Day twenty-two
Sharon

That was the last entry in Mum's book. I went back to her cabinet and took out her floral folder, the one that held all her important documents. I remembered it from our childhood. She'd asked me to bring it, though I didn't want to look in it as it would mean things were final. Then I called Louise to tell her what was happening, we had a tearful chat, and I promised I would say goodbye for her.

I left Steven a message to say I was ready to talk about divorce.

Janet, John and I were on our way to the hospital to see Mum. Bunty, Isa and Philomena were there already. I hoped Senga would open her eyes and see all of us were there with her. It felt like a weighty moment of reckoning.

CHAPTER 35

2019
Day twenty-two
Sharon

As the three of us walked into the hospital room I could see Isa sitting with Senga, tears falling down her cheeks as she grasped her old friend's hand and watched her take rasping, shallow breaths. Isa's thick silver hair was as wild and curly as it always had been, clipped up in colourful combs.

The bright blue jumper with a fancy brooch and a face with full make-up was the Isa in full colour that I remembered from the diary. The elegant façade she had presented in the café was gone; here was the loud, sweary, smoky and ballsy-as-a-boxer woman from my youth, but now crushed, looking at her old pal.

The room was suddenly crowded, with us all gathered around Senga's bedside. Bunty was standing at the end of the bed, rearranging the flowers she'd brought for her. Philomena was looking out of the window. Janet and John were either side of Senga's head.

'Isa, it's so good to have you here with us,' I whispered over Mum's tiny frame in the bed.

'It's hard to see her like this, but she must be proud of how you've all turned out,' Isa said. She looked at John. 'How are you, John? You married now, son?'

'Yes, to a lovely man, Isa, and I live in Spain,' he said, smiling.

'Oh, that's grand, son,' Isa said as she stroked Senga's hand. 'We all knew you were gay, even way back then.'

Janet said, 'I didn't.'

229

We all laughed and enjoyed a moment of warm silence in the room. 'Still as direct as ever,' Isa said to Janet. 'Good on you.'

Janet smiled.

Senga seemed to be disappearing into her bed, a mere sliver of a human being. I lifted up the red book and Isa gasped as her eyes locked on to it.

'Listen, I just wanted to ask you all some questions about this.' I waved Senga's diary. 'You said you would talk about it when you were all back together. My God, the stuff you all got up to has been hysterical to read about. I couldn't put it down.' I laughed.

Mum stirred in the bed, shifted her head round to me.

'My dad used to dress as Rod Stewart and was riding a woman called Dirty Donna,' Janet said.

Bunty looked at Isa and Philomena.

Isa sat quietly.

'Mum asked me to read this before she went downhill, but there's a bit missing at the back, save for the top which only has a few pretty strange lines: *1978: November. This is the worst thing to happen.* So, I think you all need to tell us what happened in November 1978.'

Isa looked uncomfortable. 'Yes, well . . . I've been thinking about it a lot since you first told me about the diary on the phone. And listen, hen. I know you think your mammy wanted you to know things, but it's really not for her to decide. Not while she's like this. You can give the book to me if you want.'

'But Isa—' I began, confused.

'Sharon, I just wanted to come here and sit with your mammy. I don't want to get into business from many years ago that you're best staying out of. And I really don't think she needs that either.' Isa was girding herself and Bunty looked shifty.

'Thanks for your concern, Isa, but I think I know what my own mum wants.'

Senga's heart monitor began to quicken, each beep faster than the next, hanging in the air between the women.

'Look, hen, you're upsetting your mammy. I really don't think she meant for you to be going through old memories and rehashing things.' Philomena sounded anxious.

As the monitor continued to beep loudly, Isa stood and held out her hand to me. 'Why don't you just give me that and I'll take care of it for you? We'll put it away somewhere safe.'

'What? No. Mum wanted us to read it, I know it, she asked me specifically to find it. Why are you being like this? I don't understand.'

John placed a hand on my shoulder and tried to calm me, but I shrugged him off. Bunty tried to interject, but no one was listening to her. Her hands clutched her handbag tighter, her knuckles turning white as she wrung the handles together.

Philomena had her head bowed.

Isa stared at me. 'Listen, hen, I'll not ask you again. I need to see what she wrote. I need to see it now.'

'But what's it to do with you?' I asked.

'Because you're not supposed to know! No one is supposed to know!' Isa raised her voice.

Janet interjected, much more calmly than me. 'Know what, Isa?'

'Know what she – what happened to – UGH!' She threw her head back in exasperation and stared at the ceiling for a breath. 'For fuck's *sake*. That bastard is still playing havoc with us from whatever part of hell he's rotting in.'

I clutched the book to my chest as a small child would a teddy bear.

Janet addressed Isa now. 'Who? What do you mean? Who are you talking about? What the *fuck* is going on?'

'ENOUGH!'

Everyone turned to Bunty, from whom this demand had erupted. I stared wide-eyed at the little old woman in the cardigan. John looked incredulous, searching the faces of the others for some indication of what was going on. Isa had stood up at Bunty's outburst and was breathing heavily.

'Bunty . . .'

'No, Isa. I'm sick of this. I'm not having him cause any more trouble between us, not now.' She exhaled and sat herself down on one of the empty hospital chairs. 'It's been long enough. It's time they knew. Senga obviously thought so.'

The room went silent. Senga's heart machine beeped and a nurse came in. Nobody said anything. Everyone was frozen like a tableau of statues. Senga's eyes were open and she was watching us.

As the nurse left again, Isa slowly sat herself back down beside Senga. Silently, she grabbed Senga's hand.

Mum let out a cough.

'Open my folder, Sharon,' Mum whispered. 'Go right to the bottom and you'll find my will. Look there for the missing page.'

I held my breath for a moment; I hadn't wanted to go anywhere near this until I had to. But I did what she asked and spotted scrawled blue biro on a torn page.

Bunty cleared her throat. 'Read it out loud, Sharon.'

I can't think straight. My mind's racing, I can barely stop my hand shaking long enough to smoke. I shouldn't even be writing this down, but I need to get it out of my head and I can't fucking tell anyone. The whole night is such a blur now. One minute I'm outside the social club, in the middle of telling that pathetic idiot Billy to fuck off and leave me alone for good, and the next I'm being dragged up the street by Philomena out in the snow in her good wedges, shouting that we have to go to Sandra's NOW.

When we got there that bastard Jim had his hands on her, and we all just went for him. It was chaos. I just remember thinking he was going to kill her, right there in front of us on that fancy lino he let her buy. So, without really thinking, I grabbed the big cast-iron pan on the counter and whacked him round the head. I was just trying to get him off her. He fell and there was blood everywhere. We ran out. I think I might've fucking killed him.

'Jesus CHRIST!' Janet exclaimed.

I stared at my wee mum, lying there in her hospital bed, and let the paper slowly fall to the floor as I slumped back on a chair, speechless.

Mum lay there staring at the ceiling.

Isa cleared her throat. 'Yes. your mammy killed him,' she said quietly.

Disregarding the red signs on the walls, she got up and opened the window a crack, lighting one of her famous hand-rolled cigarettes. No one batted an eyelid.

Bunty looked between Isa, Philomena and Senga. She nodded. 'That's right. And as much as we've tried to forget it, we can't. It's haunted your mammy for forty years.'

Isa blurted, 'It's haunted us all.'

Philomena pointed to the missing page and said, 'He was going to kill our Sandra, and maybe us too, who the fuck knows? He'd found her with the money, knew she was leaving him. It was self-defence. He just dropped to the floor like a sack of potatoes and never moved. Senga saved us all and we've never really thanked her. She's kept this secret to the end. She's the brave one.'

I saw tears in Mum's eyes and a sad smile on her face as Isa put her head down into Mum's hand and kissed her.

'What did you do?' John asked, his voice shaking. 'Call the police?'

'Did we fuck,' said Isa as she stroked Mum's hand. 'The cops were never away from Sandra's and they did nothing to help her when he was kicking her all over the street. We just left him on the floor and we all ran out.'

Senga nodded her head quietly.

Janet whipped out her vape, had a puff and asked, 'What happened to Sandra?'

'She went to the funeral and wept at his grave like a good grieving widow. She was good at crying, was Sandra, plenty years of practice. And then she took all the money we had saved up for her and fled to her cousin in Tenerife. She's still there, as far as we know,' Bunty said, fiddling with her handbag, looking for a paper hanky.

The room sat in heavy silence until Senga coughed and made a strange throaty noise. 'Listen,' she whispered.

It was barely audible. Everyone leaned forward to hear what she was saying.

'Don't think badly of me, but I didn't want to leave here without telling you all the truth,' she said in a sandpaper voice.

Janet leaned over, gently grasped at Mum's shoulders and said through tear-filled eyes, 'Mum, we don't ever, ever think badly of you; please don't do this to yourself.'

'Oh, I don't regret killing the bastard, I just didn't want the secret dying with me. I'd do it again in a heartbeat,' Senga replied, her voice stronger, sounding like the mammy who could shout your name from three streets away on a summer's night.

Isa laughed and said, 'That's oor Senga right there.'

Mum closed her eyes and the nurse came in and broke the spell. 'Right, everyone out the room, put that fag out and get rid of that vape, we need to see how Senga is.' She clapped her hands to get us moving.

We stumbled out into the corridor in a daze.

'Well, that was fucking unexpected, killing a man with a pot? I didn't have that on my "Mum's bedside death bingo" card,' Janet said as she pocketed her vape machine.

'Janet, please, a bit of respect,' Philomena hissed.

John was holding on to the wall with both hands in front him, doing his deep-breathing technique. 'You OK, John, son?' Isa hugged him from behind.

'Yeah, just . . . dear God, Isa, the shit the lot of you went through. You are all wee warrior women,' John said, standing up straight now and looking at the three women who were lined up against the pale hospital wall like criminals awaiting their mugshots.

Isa replied, 'Aye, I didn't know your mammy was writing it all down, but it's over now.'

'I just can't take it all in, I need to know everything that happened. Who found his body?' I hissed at Bunty, just as the nurse came out and told us to go back in but to be quiet as Senga was very weak now.

Bunty took my arm and led me back in to see Mum. 'Not now, hen. Let's say goodbye to your mammy and tell her we love her.'

Senga's brilliant blue eyes were open and she smiled at us in turn as we whispered our farewells. The late evening sun streamed through the big Victorian windows and lit up the room. Surrounded by her friends and family, she finally took that one last breath. At that very moment a flock of starlings shot off the hospital roof and swooped over the Glasgow skyline, dancing over the busy city as though to music only they could hear. Mum's eyes were closed.

'Goodbye, Senga.' Bunty waved at the wee birds through the window. 'Travel well, my good friend.'

CHAPTER 36

2019
Three days later
Sharon

The coffee shop's bell jangled repeatedly as we all filtered in. Clyde came around the counter and showed us all to the big oak table at the back, before putting the 'closed' sign on the door. He kissed me on the cheek and said, 'I'm so glad to see you,' as he squeezed me.

Isa winked at me, looked at Clyde and said loudly, 'Bet you he knows how to stuff a panini!' Clyde laughed and threw a tea towel over his shoulder. 'Right, coffees, everyone?' he asked. 'Tea for six,' Isa shouted. 'We don't want thon posh coffees that you young folk drink, like hot watery milk.'

Janet whispered to John, 'I want coffee – go and help Clyde.'

'Mr Blue Skies' by ELO was playing on the sound system. Mum loved that tune.

Bunty, with her eyes still twinkling, was dressed in a slightly shabby Chanel knock-off two-piece with perfect make-up and a huge handbag. She sat down first. Janet whipped out her vape, and the smell of blueberries floated over our heads like a theatrical smoke machine ready-made for the set of our small drama. Isa, silver curls still wild, jangling in elaborate chunky jewellery, dressed in a bright linen artisan smock and high-heeled sandals, turned to Janet.

'That fella will throw you out for that; you're not allowed them indoors,' she scolded, as though she hadn't smoked a roll-up cigarette out the hospital window three days ago.

Janet laughed. 'Sharon gets "special privileges",' she said, doing quotation fingers in the air.

Philomena was the last to arrive, apologising and throwing off her hat and coat before sitting down.

With tea, cups, milk jugs and coffees all placed on the table, Clyde disappeared into the back and turned down the sound system. We waited for the door to close behind him.

'Right, shall I start?' Bunty said, her hands clasped in front of her like a politician at the lectern. We all stared at her, waiting for someone to disagree or jump in. Nobody replied: it was obviously a rhetorical question, because Bunty looked as though she was about to launch into her maiden speech. 'So, are you ready? Well, it was the winter of 1978, it was snowing and bitterly cold and I had just recovered from a urine infection—' Bunty began.

'Fuck's sake, Bunty, don't haver.' Isa looked at her impatiently. She put down her teacup, adjusted her heaving breasts, fixed her bra strap then huffed a big breath and said, 'Look, here's what happened. So, it turned out Sandra's neighbour, that wee Mrs Foy, had heard her screaming, and she knew Jim was a wife-beating bastard. She phoned Bunty's mammy, who got hold of Bunty at the pub. We grabbed Senga, who was outside persuading your dad to sign the divorce papers – which he did.' She threw up her arms to signify drama. 'It was all fucking happening.'

Janet downed her coffee, eyes agog. 'This is better than some of the plays I've read.'

Bunty put down her teacup and, not wanting to miss out on a good story, cut in. 'As soon as your mammy spotted us, she knew something was wrong, and we bolted like the clappers all the way up Glenfadden Street. The snow was up to here,' she pointed at her shins. 'We were sliding everywhere in the ice and snow, my heart was pounding, we were sure we would be too late to get to Sandra. Philomena here fell over twice outside the Co-op'. She pointed at Philomena.

'I was wearing my good cork wedges; I could hardly walk, never mind run in them,' Philomena added.

'I remember them!' John said.

Isa rolled her eyes and continued. 'Your mammy, me, Philomena and Bunty got in the front door as Sandra was trying to get out of it, but Jim managed to get his arm around her throat and dragged her backwards, back up the hallway and into the kitchen. We ran up her hallway screaming and trying to free her, but the bastard had a kitchen knife.'

John looked at me aghast, hands at his mouth. 'It's like *The fucking Shining*, what a terrifying scene,' he said.

Janet butted in loudly. 'He had a KNIFE? Fucking monster.' She put her head into her hands.

Bunty, Isa and Philomena just stared at each other; it was as if they were bearing witness to this grave situation for the first time in forty years. I don't think they'd ever spoken the words out loud.

Philomena added, 'I was pulling his hair, trying to get him off; the lassies were just jumping in, screaming and punching at him. It was chaos.'

Isa continued. 'It all happened so quickly. We just couldn't get him to let her go and Sandra was going blue in the face, so your mammy picked up the cast-iron frying pan off the cooker and banged him on the head. You could have heard the clang all the way to Govan. He fell, straight to the floor.'

Philomena butted in and said, 'I was pacing the floor in shock. We all just stood there; we didn't know if he was dead or if he had just blacked out. All I could hear was a dog barking across the back, and there was so much blood seeping onto the floor. I remember that as clear as day: your mammy in her fake fur coat holding a frying pan, the bright yellow kitchen sticky with blood, the twin tub pulled out, and the snow blowing swirls through the back door.' She stared through the big glass window of the café, as if she were right there in the moment.

'We panicked,' Bunty said. 'We just took the knife out of his hand, wiped it on my sleeve and put it back in the drawer. We grabbed Sandra's bag and coat and ran down the hall. We got out into the street and belted it back up the road, stumbling about in the snow – it was surreal, like a bad dream. We all split up and headed home. Senga still had the skillet in her big bag and when we reached the main road she threw it like a shot-putter right over the fence into the deep snow at the back of the milk factory. It was full of timber and rubbish; nobody would find it until after the thaw.'

'I remember Sandra stopped to straighten her wedding photo down the hall as she left, fuck knows why – still keeping up appearances, I suppose,' Isa finished.

Janet said, 'Did he die there? Why didn't the police investigate it? You must have been shitting yourselves.'

Suddenly, Bunty broke down and started crying, big heaving sobs. It seemed her storytelling bravado had worn off. She wrung a small paper hanky through her fingers. Then she took a big breath, wiped her eyes, gathered herself and said, 'We just pretended it never happened. We wanted Sandra out of there, she was like a stuck record crying, 'Oh, God, oh, God, oh, God,' all the way up the road. She kept looking back and fell into the snow sobbing – me and your mammy had to practically drag her to her feet and get her out of that street before curtains started twitching. It was fucking horrible. He'd discovered her trying to leave him.'

Isa held her hand. 'Look, we were absolutely petrified. We waited to see what would happen; we were all on tenterhooks. Couldn't sleep a wink. Then the news came out that Jim had been found dead on the floor of his kitchen, stinking of booze. We read in the local paper that Mrs Foy, their neighbour, had said she'd seen some men enter the house late at night. She'd heard a fight breaking out and then, after a few minutes, they'd driven away in a dark car. She called the police when she couldn't get an answer at the door the next day. She said she was worried about Sandra, not him.'

'Good old Mrs Foy, the hero we never knew we needed,' Bunty added.

'The cops were told Sandra had left him the week before and had been living with Senga, so she was in the clear. It was the winter of 1978, the local services were on their knees, the bin men were on strike, and the mortuary had bodies piling up. They called it the Winter of Discontent, and at the end of the day a local wife-beating, half-baked gangster found dead in his house after a fight – case closed. Even Jim's mum didn't argue it. Bunty's right: God bless Mrs Foy, because I'm sure she saw us leaving that night – someone was definitely at her bedroom window – but she said nothing. We all got alibis in case anyone questioned us, but nobody did.' Isa shrugged her shoulders and put her arm around Bunty, who was openly sobbing into her own hands.

Janet, John and I were sitting quietly, taking in the enormity of what these women had been through. Who were we to judge them? Sandra would have been stabbed at the very least, and strangled to death at worst, if they hadn't stepped in. They had looked after each other through thick and thin; they had been closer than most marriages, and the protectors of each other's lives.

It now explained why Mum had become so nervy and anxious, and why the women had stopped seeing each other as much. They'd solved Sandra's problem but created their own devastating secret that seemed to have sapped them of their strength and unity. The thing that cleaved them together had split them apart.

'We didn't know Senga had written it all down. To be honest, I don't think she was ever the same after that night. None of us were if truth be told. But Sandra got free,' Bunty added through a face mottled with tears. 'I don't regret it. Jim was an evil bastard.'

They all sat quiet for a moment, taking in the story. The big clock ticked on the café wall and the slight buzz of the neon sign broke the silence.

'Does Sandra know about Mum? Where did she end up?' John asked.

Isa said, 'We know where she is; we've always known. We kept contact with her over the years. She got married again to a nice fella over in Spain. She's happy and settled, but it took her years to get over what happened and she always blamed herself for Jim's death. We didn't want you finding her, Sharon, and bringing all this up; we were just trying to protect her. I went over to see her a few years ago. She's doing great and runs a lovely wee hotel on the Costa Brava with her daughter Agnes.'

'That's Senga backwards!' John blurted out.

'We know,' Isa said with a smile.

Two days later we held the funeral for our mother, Senga Gray. We played some Elvis hits and 'You To Me Are Everything' by The Real Thing, one of the songs she used to sing to us as we lay in bed in the big tenement. The crematorium was full of all her old pals and neighbours. It was good to see my daughter, Louise, and Poppy and everyone made a fuss of the baby. John, her sunshine boy, and Carlos were there, dressed up to the nines and helping to carry the casket alongside Janet's husband and stepson. My pal Elaine brought her daughter Gabrielle and of course Clyde supported me at the service. It was such an outpouring of love for our mum, the amazing Senga.

Even wee Shirley, Mum's nurse, came along. It was such a lovely day and a great service. For a small woman, Senga had been a mighty presence. One floral tribute called her the Queen of Shettleston.

As the service ended, I spotted an elegant, slender woman in a fawn coat and boots, with her hair in a white chignon, put down a bouquet of bright marigolds at the front of the coffin. As she turned towards me, I recognised her beautiful face. She smiled and hugged me. 'Your mother was the most wonderful woman I've ever known. She saved my life, you know,' she said, tearfully.

We still had so much to talk about, so she decided to stay a while longer to catch up with all her pals from the menage. I got to meet her daughter, Agnes.

EPILOGUE

Life moves on slowly after you find out your mum was once a vengeful killer with a frying pan. Nothing can really top that.

John and Janet went back to their busy lives, but the family WhatsApp group remains alive with chat. I sold the Bristol house and split the money with Steven. I'm still living in Mum's flat, though it is a bit less floral, and I've caught up with more of her old pals. I tracked down Davie Dunsmore in his care home so he could come to the funeral, and he showed me a photo of him and Elvis – he told me he once kissed Lulu at the Dennistoun hall dance. Who knows? I've seen him several times since and the stories just get better and better.

Clyde and I are getting along just fine. Louise and her family have been to visit me a few times and they all muddle along well. I help out in the café when he's busy and I have a new PR job lined up in Glasgow. I'm planning on travelling a bit before I get too stuck in my ways again. Clyde says we should go to Spain to visit our friends and family there, and then head to Cuba. I'll go once I've signed my divorce papers.

I've got an Instagram account and put up pictures of Clyde and me lying in bed, eating carbs.

And I have started a diary; you can find it online.